THE DEATH OF LASZLO BREYER

MARC W SHAKO

This is a work of fiction. Names, characters, businesses, places, events and incidents are either the products of the author's imagination or used in a fictitious manner. Any resemblance to actual persons, living, dead, or undead, or actual events is purely coincidental.

This book is for Jojo, who motivates and inspires me to do more than I thought was possible, and who keeps me sane when it's all too much. Thank you. X

And for Mum and Dad, without whom I'd be nothing, in more ways than one. Thanks for always being there, and for being the reason I've never lost the argument "my mum/dad is better than your mum/dad".

#Undefeated

Special thanks to

My main man Armen, my best mucker Bren, and the super cool Forever Ewa. Your feedback and support kept me and this book in shape. You should thank them too, dear Reader, this book would be littered with typos and lazy writing if not for these beautiful people!

And last but by no means least... I firmly believe that the best friend a writer can have besides inspiration and a pencil is another writer. For me, Isabel Fuentes Guerra is that other writer. Your constant support and feedback is a massive help, which I would be lost without. I do miss our little chats!

THE DEATH OF LASZLO BREYER

Something had changed. Everything had changed. Was this what it felt like to be dead?

Bright light radiated red through his tired eyelids. Though he couldn't say where he was, there was the inescapable sense of another person in this place with him; somebody close, both in distance and in feeling. There was a warmth, finally a warmth, to offset the harsh, endless winter. Thoughts flashed of people past. Of Jenny. Of Tommy. And Bryan. A kindly young homeless man named Danny. Lucy – a beautiful artist. And Daniel Cross – the man who lived in a museum of the macabre. Whether in reality or just in this strange netherworld he found himself in, Jack Talbot smiled to himself. There was a connection to all of these people. A warmth, like that which emanated through his closed eyelids. Not complete though.

Something else was in this place. Something cold. Dark. Savage. He surveyed the desolate moorlands; a dark cloud hung in that blue sky. A black belligerent cloud which rolled. Rolled and swelled until it dominated the horizon. The warmth dissipated, and a chill descended.

More thoughts flashed. An old man. His cheeks wet as hot tears fell onto the limp, broken body of his daughter. Three angry young men, reeking of booze, souls poisoned by hatred. Ink drops darkened the pale blue sky, a smattering at first, then a deluge, till it was pale no more. The thick angry cloud now filled the sky, casting an unshakable sense of foreboding over that bleak and barren landscape.

The names of the others; of Jenny; Tommy; Cross; were still there, but now as distant as that black horizon. Voices echoed over the dark moorlands he found himself stranded upon. Cold winds whispered through the long grass as thunder growled; its deep rupture reverberating through the heavy atmosphere. Then, silence.

An icy spray of invisible droplets fell over his back and the hair on his arms reached to where the torn cloud parted revealing a huge, bright full moon. Then the silence was shattered by an ungodly noise. The baying of a creature from the beginning of time. Jack Talbot span, trying to locate the source of that deathly howl and as he turned, from the distance, a black mass bound towards him. With outlandish speed a huge dog-like creature gained upon him from the horizon. Gained with a terrifying inevitability. Faster and faster. And as it neared one name stood out above the white-noise static of all the others.

Breyer. Laszlo Breyer.

PRELUDE

David Ellis turned away from the illuminated window and buried his head in the pillow, 'Shut up, Fred, for fuck's sake.'

Mary groaned and rolled over, 'Maybe there's something wrong with him.'

Outside, the red eye of the security camera blinked through the dark. This one focussed on Freddy, an old Golden Labrador, as he whined and barked into the tall swaying conifer trees which lined the half acre of landscaped garden surrounding the plush detached property.

Inside the luxurious house, next to the master bedroom in the study, a monitor blinked between the view from this and the four other cameras that oversaw the lavish grounds. The view flickered from Freddy, to the driveway dusted lightly with snow as the shadows from the windswept trees waved across it, to the side entrance of the house. The rear aspect was next, then the front door flicked on for the five second time frame, before disappearing to reveal an unusually unnerved Freddy who danced excitedly in the thin layer of snow. Then, he stopped and snarled at someone, something, out of frame. The security light snapped on.

'There's fuck all wrong with him.'

'Maybe just go and check the camera,' Mary said, her tone making it clear it wasn't a request.

David kicked the quilt off and swung his legs from the bed straight into his waiting slippers as if on autopilot.

Inside the study the glowing monitor flicked back to the view of Freddy. He switched between a wild bark and a whining cower, torn between protecting the family and primal fear. From the bottom of the screen a long shadow grew. Freddy backed away baring his teeth.

David shuffled into the study tying the belt on his silk dressing gown. Rubbing his eyes he approached the monitor, which flicked to a wide shot of the driveway. The leather creaked in protest as he slumped into the chair and pulled it up to the large desk. From this part of the house, Freddy's growls were drowned by the bitter wind which whistled through the cold winter evening. David yawned as the monitor went through the motions.

Then, from outside, came a pained yelp.

David sat up. His heart pulsed in his ears. He leaned in towards the monitor, hoping the closer perspective would compensate for the bleariness of his vision. He'd heard Freddy bark and whine before, but he'd never heard anything close to that yelp. He span to face the window. To the area of garden where Freddy was kept. He swallowed hard, but his mouth was bone dry. Turning back to the screen, at the front door all was well.

'Come on. Change... change.'

He drummed his fingers on the desk before coming to his senses, remembering he could watch any of the cameras with the touch of a button. He reached down at the control panel and jabbed at the button marked "Camera 3" bringing Freddy's kennel to the centre of the screen. David squinted at the grainy black and white image for a second, and again rubbed his tired eyes. It was hard to make much of anything out with the blanket of snow camouflaging the scene; only the shadows gave away where the hard edges and boundaries were. One shadow was missing. The long, ominous shadow which had been creeping towards Freddy had vanished. Everything else seemed normal but for one detail; David rubbing at his eyes didn't change anything. Freddy was gone.

'Shit.'

David tramped downstairs re-tightening the belt on his dressing gown. In the kitchen he rifled through his drawer, ignored the ball of string and screwdrivers and WD-40 and assortment of light bulbs and grabbed the torch. Outside, the wind whipped up again. He looked down at the torch, unsure of the last time he'd used it and flicked it on, off, then on again. Gripping the cold barrel, he stood by the back door.

From upstairs came a click and warm, welcoming light cascaded from the landing.

'What's going on?'

David's grip released on the torch and fastened again just in time to stop it falling to the floor. He breathed deeply, 'He's gone... again.'

'What?'

David sighed, 'He's gone again. Your beloved Freddy.'

'Well go out and find him.'

'What do you think I'm doing?' he snapped. 'Go back to bed.'

He heard muttering as the light went off and then the only sound in the house was again the sound of that biting wind.

David stared longingly upstairs in the direction of his warm bed, then turned back to the door. He did the maths. It would take ten seconds, maybe fifteen, to get outside, round the corner and to the back of the property. Once there, he would check the rope which tied Freddy. If it was chewed through (again) it was nothing serious, just another escape attempt. He could come back inside, go back to the nice, warm bed upstairs, and start looking for him tomorrow. Thirty seconds. Max.

And if it wasn't an escape attempt?

He frowned. Deep down he sensed that this was different from the other times that Freddy had escaped; that the scene on the monitor was somehow wrong. He couldn't swear to it, but he thought he'd seen a shadow on screen as he entered the study. He drew another deep breath, turned the key in the door, and opened it.

Once outside, the bitter wind snatched at his dressing gown as he strode to the rear of the house. *Five seconds*. The silver torch beam twinkled on the snowy ground a few feet ahead of him. As he rounded the corner the harsh security light flooded his tired eyes. *Ten seconds*. He shielded them, before turning his attention to the kennel and rope. He kneeled to inspect the rope when, above the wind, came a sound from the trees. He span, half falling against the house, and trained the torchlight into the dense greenness of the conifers.

'Freddy?'

The wind died to a whisper. In the distance a car door slammed shut and he thought about calling out to the neighbour for help. But what would he say? That his dog was missing?

'Fred?'

He stood now and gingerly stepped towards the trees, bobbing and leaning to get a view through the branches, his heart racing.

Then he heard it.

A low growl.

The pounding heartbeat rose in his ears again as the torch settled on a pair of glowing eyes.

'Fred. Stop fucking about,' he shouted, unable to control the quiver in his voice.

As he stepped back, he noticed footprints leading into the trees. *Too big for Freddy's?* His mind was at the point of contemplating the patch where whatever it was stopped walking into the trees and started to be dragged

Please not Freddy

when, between the gusts of wind, the growl rose.

David dropped the torch. He turned and sprinted for the door. Behind him, he heard the trees part. His shadow shrank in the fallen torchlight only to be swallowed by something huge. He stumbled around the corner and leapt at the kitchen door expecting to feel the cold grip of death at any moment.

He threw it open and burst in, locking it behind him as he slumped against it onto the cold floor. His hands trembled as he

6

placed them over the part of his chest where he thought his heart might escape.

He waited for scratching on the door. Or Freddy's whimpering. Nothing came. It was a minute or two before he rose on unsteady legs and drew both bolts on the door for the first time since he could remember.

'Fucking stay out there then you stupid mutt.'

CHAPTER ONE

Low morning sun blazed through the flimsy curtains and cast an unwelcome light on Jack Talbot. He groaned and rolled over, a flailing arm knocking empty beer bottles from the cluttered bedside table. The sharp clatter drew a deep moan from under the covers. He peered over the edge of the bed at the disturbance. His blurry eyes focused first on the bottles rolling on the laminate flooring, and then to the framed photo among them. He reached down and grabbed the picture. His steel blue eyes beamed, his strong arm pulling his wife Jenny in close. A snapshot of happier times behind fractured glass. An involuntary whine escaped at the sight of the newly broken picture frame. He sat up and set the picture on the bedside among a glass-henge of bottles. He stayed there, head lowered between hunched shoulders for what could have been anything between two and ten minutes, before lurching to the bathroom.

The bathroom light burst into life and Jack entered shielding his eyes from its luminous glow. He about faced, turned off the light and shambled back in. In the cool darkness he checked his worn-out face in the water-marked mirror. He looked older than in the picture; much older than the five years which had passed since the photo was taken. Jack sighed at the sight of his sorry reflection before plopping down onto the cold toilet seat. He'd given up on standing to urinate at about the same time he'd changed beer for red wine.

He stared at the dust and dirt that had accumulated in the corner of the room. It was the little things like this that Jenny would never have allowed. The grime in the bath where pristine white once prevailed. The dirty mirror. The second, bone-dry toothbrush. Reminders that taunted his loneliness at every turn.

He groaned himself to his feet and flushed. He crossed the short space to the bathroom cabinet and flicked the mirrored door open. It too was a pitiful sight. A solitary brown bottle stared back at him. He struggled at the child-proof lid and shook one of the green and white capsules into his clammy hand.

He was tapering the use of Fluoxetine, the headaches were testament to that, and the fucking insomnia, but today he needed a serotonin kick. Or something. He placed the capsule onto his tongue, shut the bottle back in the cabinet and filled the grimy glass with cold water. He'd been taking the happy pills since Jenny left. *Was taken.* He paused before reopening the cabinet and staring at the half-full bottle. He grabbed it removed the lid and tipped a handful into his clammy palm. Maybe fifteen, maybe twenty. *Enough to do the job?* He stared into his own empty eyes in the mirror and thought of Jenny's disapproval at what he was contemplating.

But Jenny wasn't here.

He let out a sigh and raised the handful of green and white to his mouth. As his hand reached his mouth a loud banging came from downstairs. He jumped and the pills fell and bounced around in the empty sink. He sighed and swilled the pill in his mouth down. Another series of bangs came from downstairs.

Jack tottered downstairs and watched as a large wavy outline beat the frosted glass of his front door. Jack presumed the figure must have seen him coming but was banging just to be a pain in the arse.

'Alright, alright,' Jack muttered to himself as much as anyone, not wishing to raise the decibels any further than was absolutely necessary as the banging continued.

'Come on, Jack,' came the voice from outside.

Jack undid the bolt and latch before opening the door till the chain snapped tight. The flustered face of Bryan Dempsey peered through the gap. At 42 Bryan was two years Jack's senior, but his full head of jet-black hair and smooth features made him appear at least two years younger, especially since the bottle had had its way with whatever had remained of Jack's youthfulness.

'Let me in, Jack, it's urgent.'

It was way too early for this shit. Whatever particular brand of disturbance Bryan was peddling at this hour, Jack was not buying.

'Fuck off, Bryan.'

'This is official business, Jack. It's to do with Jenny.'

Jack turned to look at the living room, awash with empty bottles and fast food cartons. Somewhere under there was the Jennifer Talbot Remembrance Museum. The settee they'd argued about. The curtains. The coffee table. That fucking dreadful rug. All arguments Jack had lost which now served as a constant reminder of his past life.

Bryan pushed on the door, 'I don't want to have to...'

Jack was already sliding the chain lock off, 'Keep your hair on, nobhead.'

He stood holding the door for Bryan to come in and caught sight of Tommy Wainwright sitting bolt upright in the car outside. As per these days, he looked pissed off. Bryan gingerly stepped inside. Jack followed and opened the curtains exposing the full extent of the mess in the living room.

'Jesus, Jack.'

'Cleaner's a lazy bastard,' said Jack. He, of course, didn't have a cleaner.

Bryan knew this and half smiled. 'Seriously, are you doing alright?'

Jack opened his arms to present the living room in a what-does-it-look-like gesture. 'Take a seat,' said Jack, sweeping old pizza boxes and newspapers from the settee.

'You're alright, I'll stand,' replied Bryan. He cleared his throat, readying himself for the important announcement.

Jack sensed the hesitation. 'Go on.'

'Where were you last night?' Bryan spat the words from his mouth.

Jack saw the serious look on his face and decided not to fuck around with him, even though it gave him enormous pleasure. 'Here. Why?'

'All night?'

Jack paused for a moment. It was hard to keep track of the days since he'd befriended the bottle. Days had a nasty habit of rolling themselves together until they all felt the same. Had he been out yesterday? Or was that one of the days he slept through? Even if he had left the house, he wasn't about to help Bryan Dempsey out.

'Yeah. I haven't been out for a bit. What's...?'

Bryan cut Jack off mid-sentence, not wishing to prolong the agony, 'It's Laszlo Breyer.'

The ground seemed to heave beneath him.

Bryan reached out a steadying hand. 'Whoa. You OK?'

The mention of the name was a rock in the pit of Jack's stomach. He hadn't heard it since it was whispered at Jenny's funeral. He thought that when Breyer himself was committed to the ground nine months ago *Ten months ago? Whatever* that that would be the last time he would have to hear that cursed name. Bryan spun Jack round and sat him on the settee. Jack could feel the colour draining from his already pallid features. His lips tingled, it felt less and less like his face was his own.

'Sorry, Jack.'

Jack regathered his senses a little before looking up, 'What's going on, Bryan?'

'You won't believe me. I'll have to show you.'

Bryan helped Jack to his feet and he staggered upstairs and dressed in suitable clothing for the harsh winter that awaited him. He breathed in deep gulps of air, choking the sob that lurked in the back of his throat knowing that if it was released, it might be impossible to control. He couldn't bear to go back downstairs and look at the sympathetic gaze of Bryan. Fuck this mess. He drew in another deep breath. In through the nose; out through the mouth.

As he made his way back downstairs, he broke the promise he made to himself and looked up at Bryan. Bryan stared back with the words "I'm Sorry" practically tattooed on his handsome features. He was surprised that as he opened the door for Bryan to leave, the 'you-can-do-this' clap on the shoulder never arrived as he passed. They left the house and Bryan retraced his footsteps in the crisp layer of snow that had fallen the previous evening. Jack shuffled behind thinking that it had been nothing like this cold the last time he had ventured outside. He lifted his gaze from the snowy path and caught sight of Tommy, still seething, behind the wheel of their unmarked car. This journey should be fun.

'Shit, I've left my mobile.'

'We won't be long,' Bryan replied, stopping to see if Jack wanted to go back.

As it was, he didn't, and they went to the car.

The journey passed in silence. Jack decided early that he would only talk to Tommy if Tommy spoke first. As Jack climbed into the back seat Tommy's eyes burned at him in the rear-view mirror. Total silence. *Suits me. It wasn't my fault.* Every now and then Jack felt the burn of Tommy's glare in the mirror, but opted not to return the gesture. It wasn't Tommy's size that bothered Jack: Not at all. Never had, never would. Jack had fought and beaten bigger guys than Tommy before. This just wasn't the time or the place. Plus he was more interested in trying to figure out where they were going. In the back of his mind he already knew. And the one repeated word on the first three signposts confirmed it. Thankfully, the journey was to be a short one. From his place it was only a fifteen-minute drive to the cemetery.

2

A bored constable guarded the ornate stone cemetery entrance as Tommy led Bryan and Jack inside its walls. The expanse of snow shot a bright glare from the low winter sun into Jack's tired, bloodshot eyes. Shielding them, Jack remembered thinking that the cemetery was huge for a town of this size and wondered suddenly why he'd never bothered to find out. Probably because – in the grand scheme of things – it wasn't important. That and the thought had only dawned on him when he came to bury Jenny. The words still didn't make sense. How could she be gone?

It wasn't my fault.

They filed through the cemetery, but they weren't heading for Jenny's grave. *What is this?* Jack traipsed behind Bryan and Tommy, the crisp dusting of snow crunching underfoot as they marched towards the crime scene. Then Jack saw it. In the far corner near the railings, some two hundred yards ahead – an area guarded by another young constable, cordoned off with blue and white tape.

Police line. Do not cross. Do not pass go. Do not think about drinking.

He knew that part of the cemetery. The farthest corner from the entrance, which backed onto an expanse of woods. That was where the unmarked graves were. The unknown. Or undesirables. It was where they'd buried *him*. The glare made it difficult to see what lay beyond the familiar blue and white tape. That and Tommy's broad frame obscuring the view. Was it really what it looked like? Surely not. Jack zoned out for a moment transfixed by the clouds of breath that swirled around the back of Bryan's head. They were only a few yards from the crime scene when Jack's trance was obliterated by the sight before him.

Tommy flashed his badge at the waiting constable who nodded and lifted the tape for the men to duck under. The constable gave a nod of recognition to Jack. He nodded in return, though couldn't for the life of him recall the young officer's name. Not that it really mattered. Tommy and Bryan parted. Jack couldn't believe what he had glimpsed moments before, but now there could be no doubt.

'What the fuck is this?'

Tommy cast a glance at Bryan.

Bryan spoke, 'You've no idea?'

'I told you I haven't been outside,' he paused, incredulous.

Surely it was impossible. He'd have remembered this. There were things you didn't just forget. Not replying to a text message; plausible. He frisked himself for his phone. *It's at home. Never mind.* Forgetting to lock the front door; maybe. This? This was something he'd definitely remember. Wasn't it?

'Is this what it looks like?'

Bryan nodded, 'Body snatching.'

Jack stared into the ragged black hole juxtaposed against the surrounding snow. The earth didn't look as if it had been dug out. The scene resembled something more like an explosion: As if the ground had been forced out from within. As if whoever had done this had dragged the body out. The thought of somebody dragging a badly decomposed body through frozen earth sent Jack's stomach rolling again. But he had to see. He took a step closer. One of Tommy's ham fists grabbed his coat.

Jack turned and fixed eyes with Tommy, 'You don't honestly think I had anything to do with this?'

For the first time that morning Tommy spoke in a frozen cloud, 'He did kill your wife.'

Jack paused, 'She was your sister. Are you a suspect?'

'Alright boys,' Bryan interjected.

His voice raised, but the words held little conviction. He looked like a man who hoped he wasn't challenged. He was a big guy, but the thought of having to separate Jack and Tommy again was probably not appealing.

'Nobody's saying you're a suspect Jack, we just need to tick you off our list.'

Jack paused again, staring into the empty grave, 'Looks like it was taken from within. Rather than dug out.'

Tommy and Bryan exchanged a glance.

Bryan spoke, 'That's what we said. But the ground...'

'Almost frozen,' Jack interjected thoughtfully. 'If they've dragged him out through that...,' he broke off contemplating the idea as Tommy and Bryan had after their first arrival, 'there should be bits of him all over. What about prints?' Jack hadn't noticed before but in the bright glare of the sunlight there were prints at the other side of the grave.

Bryan said, 'We're just waiting for forensics to get down here.'

'Looks like two sets.'

'One is the groundskeeper,' Bryan replied. 'The other set is strange. Animal.'

Jack looked at the detectives, who seemed fully aware of the implications. The animal prints were huge, dog-like, just as he remembered. 'Where is the groundskeeper now?'

Tommy frowned, 'We're done here. We don't need your amateur opinion, Jack.'

In his hangover haze, Jack hadn't noticed the forensics team approaching. They crunched single file towards the scene. Jack probably knew each of the five-man team by name but couldn't recognize them through the glasses and face masks. The constable lifted the tape and they nodded in turn and ducked under. The first forensics officer spoke to Tommy. Tommy was probably telling him to get done as quickly as possible and get out before the press got wind.

Bryan took Jack to one side, 'We don't know what we're dealing with here. Would it be OK if we had you on hand, in case we've got any questions?'

Jack was only half listening, lost in some time-warp dream remembering the last time he was here. He wondered if there was a chance that this grave robbery would put him in some kind of danger.

Tommy stepped closer, before Jack could utter the "no" he had prepared in the back of his mind, 'I think you had something to do with this, Jack. You're coming to the station and when we're done with the groundsman, we're going to question you.'

Tommy was an imposing guy, but Jack put on his best poker face, 'Fair enough, Tom. I've got nothing to hide,' he said, unsure of whether or not it was the whole truth, 'but I'm not sure you're thinking clearly on this.'

Tommy and Bryan frowned.

Jack continued, 'There's clearly only one set of prints leading to the grave and two leading away. You already know that the groundsman is the owner of one set. Which means, if I understand you correctly, that you think I hovered into this cemetery, dug up the body of my ex-wife's killer, for Christ knows what reason, put on a pair of animal-foot shaped boots and ran off to wherever those prints lead. Where is that, by the way, *detective*?'

Tommy's face flushed red, 'Get him out of here, Bryan.'

3

Tommy had left Collins babysitting Talbot in reception and now circled around the back of Bryan, who was sitting in one of the uncomfortable moulded plastic chairs in Finchley station's cramped interrogation room. Tommy's hard-soled shoes clipped off the light green linoleum as Bryan went through the formalities: introducing the suspect and date-stamping the tape. From across the table the old groundskeeper looked up with pale blue eyes. His thin frame made him appear older than he really was. Tommy thought that the old boy might also be losing marbles. He noticed the old man's hands were shaking.

He leaned over the desk. 'In your own time, Mr Parks, tell us what happened.'

The groundsman nodded, 'I came to work and I was doing the rounds.'

'What time?' Tommy interrupted.

'Sorry?'

'What time was it?'

'Oh, I came to work at...' he paused and rubbed his stubble, before shifting his gaze and glancing at the green-grey wall.

Is this a lie?

Tommy didn't go for all of that body language 'looking up and to the left means a lie' bollocks. A lie is a lie. Different people show different signs. Somebody lies? He knows.

Parks continued. '...it would have been six, and I was doing the rounds. Making sure everything was tidy and so on. And I saw the mess there. I thought it was kids. The usual stuff. They mess about in there. There's a hole in the railings, so they get in through there. They come in and mess about. Usually it's just things like throwing flowers around. Other times it's worse. Graffiti-ing the headstones or tipping them over. Bloody kids these days.'

Tommy cleared his throat to lead the man back on track.

'Oh, and then I saw it. It stood out, because of the snow. The difference in colour. So I went up to have a look. As I got closer I could tell there was something serious. That corner is where they keep the undesirables. There's unmarked graves. Criminals and whatnot. Anyway, I get closer and look down, and the hole's empty. So that's when I called you lot.'

Tommy looked at Bryan. Bryan turned to Mr Parks. He was over sixty years old, and had a kindly face. Tommy had scrolled through Parks' criminal record before the interview. He wasn't unfamiliar with the inside of a police station, but the few things on his record were all for shoplifting. Just food, a few years ago, when he couldn't afford to buy it. Nothing in the line of body snatching. Then again, if a man is short enough of money to shoplift, he might be easily persuaded to do things he wouldn't normally. Like help somebody get into a locked cemetery.

Bryan smiled. 'Mr Parks, you said you were doing the rounds, then you saw this, so you called it in, is that right?'

Parks nodded, 'That's right, yes.'

'And you called this in right away?'

'Yes.'

'At eight-thirty.'

'Half-eight, yes, I remember because the news had just finished on the wireless.'

'So you were doing the rounds from six to let's say eight o'clock, found this, and called it in.'

'That sounds about right. Yes'

'It snowed a little last night, Mr Parks,' Bryan said. 'There were footprints in the cemetery. I noticed them when we walked in.' Parks' forehead had started to bead with a thin film of sweat.

'I just want to be clear; you say you had been doing the rounds for two hours, saw the crime scene, and immediately called it in.'

'That's right. Why?'

Tommy sat opposite the elderly suspect and pulled in his chair as close as possible. Parks leaned back a little.

'The thing is Mr Parks,' Tommy leaned in closer, 'there were hardly any footprints in the cemetery.'

Parks swallowed. He glanced at Bryan as if he could somehow help.

'You said you were doing the rounds,' Parks was looking back at Tommy now, 'but there were hardly any prints. It looked to me like you had almost gone straight to that grave and spent some time there. But if you were there for two hours, before calling this in...'

'I... I...' The old man stuttered, not sure of where they were going with their line of questioning.

'What were you doing for two hours at the grave?'

Mr Parks' hands were shaking. He glanced from Bryan to Tommy; good cop to bad cop.

'There were two sets of prints at the scene. Yours, and an animal's. Do you see what I'm getting at, Mr Parks? If it wasn't you, am I supposed to believe that this man came back from the dead?

Parks blurted, 'It wasn't me, I swear it.'

Tommy continued, 'Now, when I look at your record here, I see some minor blemishes, but nothing in the way of body snatching. So I ask myself: could it be that you were helping somebody?'

'I can explain,' Parks blurted. 'I wasn't at the grave for two hours. I wasn't at the cemetery for two hours.' He choked on the words. 'I was late for work. If anyone finds out that'll be it for me. If I lose this job, I can't afford food or heating. Please, don't tell anyone.' He rubbed his forehead.

The old man's eyes welled with tears. 'I've been having trouble sleeping lately, since Doris, my wife... I'm alone now. The state pension's hardly enough. That's why I have to work.'

Tommy glanced down at the man's record. Mr Edward Vincent Parks; Born 1944. Jesus. Poor old bugger is pushing seventy.

There came a gentle rapping on the door. Tommy nodded to Bryan, who reached for the tape recorder, 'Interview suspended at nine twenty-three.'

A head poked in the door. A round-faced, red-headed officer.

'Sorry to interrupt, Detective, but it's quite urgent.'

Tommy rose and looked at Bryan, 'Get Mr Parks some tea and biscuits, eh, detective.'

Bryan nodded and started to follow Tommy out of the room. Tommy heard Bryan asking Parks how he liked his tea as he stepped into the hall. He glanced along the dull grey corridor into reception and saw the sorry figure of Jack Talbot, dozing in a plastic chair. He shook his head and for a second wondered what it was like for Jack to be on the other side of the law. He quickly dismissed the thought.

'What is it?' Tommy asked turning to the overweight desk sergeant who had interrupted his interview.

'We've just had a call, from somebody in Carlton.'

Tommy shrugged. Carlton was the next village from Finchley. A tiny place, picturesque, full of large detached property and oozing middle class. Where the real big spenders lived. Not a lot going on but that's the way we like it thank you very much for asking old chap. Tommy frowned. Collins was clearly afraid of Tommy, and Tommy got quite a kick out of it.

'W...well, a dog was killed.'

'You interrupted my interview because some ponce in Carlton's pooch died? This had better be good, Collins.'

'B...but on the call, they mentioned something, I think there's a connection to the cemetery. Footprints.'

Tommy was all ears.

Bryan watched from the corner of his eye and saw his partner's body language shift. Tommy loved the chase, and the chase it seemed, was on.

Tommy turned, 'Bryan.'

Bryan looked up and came over.

Tommy took control, 'Collins, go and finish that cup of tea.'

'Milky, two sugars,' said Bryan.

'And give him the good biscuits. The ones that you eat,' added Tommy.

Collins just stood there.

'Go on,' Tommy urged.

Collins left and Tommy turned to Bryan, 'We're going to Carlton.'

'Carlton?'

Tommy nodded and strode back into the interview room. Parks had pulled himself together a little.

'A quick question, Mr Parks.'

The old-timer looked up, 'Yes?'

'We're you anywhere near Carlton last night?'

'Last night? Not likely. I was in bed at eight.'

'And have you seen anything suspicious the past few days? Anybody hanging around? Anything out of the ordinary at all?'

Parks was already shaking his head. Tommy walked over and offered a hand to Mr Parks. The old man stood and shook it.

'You've been a very good witness, Mr Parks. Very helpful.'

Parks smiled.

'Somebody's going to bring you a cup of tea and some biscuits. When you're done, tell somebody at the front desk and they'll take you back home, OK?'

Parks beamed from ear to ear. A frown fell over his genuine features, 'What about my being late?'

Tommy winked, 'No-one need know.'

Bryan shook the old man's hand and they left Mr Parks in the room.

'I don't like him for this,' Bryan said.

Tommy nodded, 'Yeah, there's no way,' he said.

They walked into reception and over to Jack Talbot. Slouched into one of the uncomfortable plastic chairs, snoring loudly.

'This one, though... he knows something.' Tommy kicked the bottom of Jack's shoe. Jack woke with a start. 'Come on.'

Jack looked up at Bryan and Tommy, 'Are we ready? You can drop me off at the Co-op, I need to get a few things...'

Beer, wine, cigarettes. Tommy wasn't impressed. 'Forget it. You're coming with us.'

Jack slowly raised himself to his feet, 'Great.'

Sarcasm always was one of his strong points.

4

Jack endured another silent car journey, before which he had tried to scrounge cigarettes from Bryan and Tommy. Bryan did the most British thing ever recorded and apologised for having quit a few weeks earlier. Tommy just shook his head disdainfully. Jack's mouth was sticky dry and the break in drinking was exacerbating the already monstrous headache that had settled at the base of his skull. Tommy watched Jack's eyes mournfully follow the passing "Booze Brothers" off-licence and shook his head.

'Where are we going?' Jack asked, more to take his mind off the beer than to get information.

'Carlton,' Bryan replied.

He continued, but Jack had already stopped listening. Something resonated within him, but he struggled to put his shaking, beer deprived finger on it.

The tiny village of Carlton was about ten miles north of the cemetery. It was difficult to describe Carlton as anything other than picturesque, with its reclaimed brick houses and explosion of flowers in the summer. The "river" meandered through it (the locals called it a river, though size-wise it was more of a stream). There was an excellent local butcher, a paper shop, and an antique shop (which was probably the only thing that wouldn't succumb to the massive new Tesco supermarket that had opened midway between here and Finchley). Even the local pub would struggle now that beer was available for less than fifty pence a can. Christ he was thirsty.

'Got anything to drink, Bryan?'

Tommy sighed and reached under his seat producing a large but half-empty bottle of water which had sat there for Christ-knows how long.

Gee. 'Thanks.'

After another few minutes of silence they turned into Carlton. There was little snow here, despite the forecast. What patches were left were fragile plates which sat gently atop the grass as if placed there by the lightest of hands. They drove past the Dog and Gun where the landlord seemed to be playing his own variation on chess outside, dragging empty crates and manoeuvring kegs around an invisible board. Not even opening time. They turned from Main Street into one of the few side streets. Jack didn't notice which. His mind was on opening time. The houses here were bigger than the cottages which lined Main Street and all had high privet hedges or fir trees lining the property. The car jerked to a halt outside one of the fir-bordered properties, causing Jack to spill water down his coat. He was certain Tommy had done it on purpose but lacked the energy to argue. Jack was about to offer to wait where he was when Tommy addressed him again.

'Come on.'

Jack didn't reply. He couldn't be bothered. That, plus his tongue felt like a well-worn carpet. Funny how the lukewarm, month-old water had done fuck all to quench his thirst. He exited the vehicle and joined the detectives at the high wrought-iron gate. Bryan pushed the intercom. A bleep quickly came from the other end, and before Bryan could say "police" a low buzz emanated from the intercom box. Tommy pushed the gate open. They crunched their way up the gravel drive and were greeted at the door by an ashen-faced man in his late-forties.

He extended his hand, 'David Ellis.'

First Tommy, then Bryan took Mr Ellis's handshake, Bryan handling introductions. He turned to Jack, who deliberately kept his trembling hands pocketed, 'And this is consultant Jack Talbot.'

Consultant? Tommy badly tried to control his wayward arching eyebrows at the introduction. Ellis didn't notice.

Once inside David Ellis retold the incident to the detectives, who stood opposite him, and the consultant, who sat (much to Tommy's poorly-masked chagrin) on the plush settee. David sank back in his armchair as they watched the long shadow grow from the bottom of the screen on the CCTV footage. Jack felt a prickle of cold as he watched, and judging by the way the air in the room changed, so did the others.

Creepy shadow aside, there wasn't much to see, and as creepy as it was, Jack guessed it must have been whatever he had seen outside that had shaken Ellis to his boots. David recounted everything, the barking and whining, the dog's fear, and disappearance.

Tommy spoke, 'So you went out to look?'

Ellis stared down at his feet, avoiding Tommy's gaze. *Shame.* 'I went but... I thought he was angry at me for going outside, so I left him. It was dark, and...'

Bryan cut him off this time, 'Can you take us to him?'

David stood up, 'It's between those two trees.'

His hand trembled as he pointed making Jack think about his own shakes. *I could murder a beer.*

Ellis continued, 'If it's all the same with you, I'll wait in here.'

'Of course,' Bryan smiled his sympathetic smile.

'Can I get anyone a drink?' Ellis asked.

'That won't be necessary, thank you.'

Tommy just shook his head as his face contorted into the best sympathetic smile he could muster. Then Jack felt the eyes of his former colleagues on him. Begging him not to ask for alcohol at ten-thirty in the morning.

'I could murder a cuppa,' he finally said.

Tommy and Bryan clearly weren't happy, but Ellis smiled wanly and disappeared into the kitchen.

Out in the yard Tommy crouched and fingered the frayed ends of the rope which, until last night, had held Freddy. The same wafer-thin plates of snow dotted the lawn, aside from one shaded patch near the trees which could have displayed the signs of struggle, or might just be the odd way the snow had thawed. Either way, something felt wrong. Bryan stalked towards the body as if he were expecting it to jump out and attack him. Jack loitered around the edge of the wall where the thaw from last night's snowfall had softened the ground. He gazed into the trees which almost certainly were part of the same wood that backed onto the cemetery they'd just left. He looked down and saw footprints. David Ellis's. Size nine. Slipper. He'd come around the corner in the morning to check on Freddy. Amongst the slipper prints was something else.

'Tommy, come and have a look at this.'

Tommy dropped the rope and made his way to the crouching figure of Jack. He instinctively edged around the area which could yield prints. Jack pointed. Tommy squinted at another print partly obscured by Ellis's slippers. It was longer. Deeper. Without a shoe.

'Animal?' Tommy offered.

'Yeah, but way too big for a family Labrador. Deeper too, from somebody taller, heavier.'

'Like at the cemetery,' Tommy added, almost in disbelief.

Bryan recoiled from the trees, 'Oh Christ,' suppressing a reflex gag he said, 'Guys.'

When Jack turned round, Bryan looked about the same colour as Ellis. Bryan pointed the two of them into the trees and they bookended the carnage. Dragged a few feet from the garden, the Labrador's carcass was strewn, gutted. The innards were spilled, chewed, from a gaping hole where the animal's belly had been. Parts where the flesh was stripped exposed bright white bone. His soft yellow fur was matted with thick red blood. It had only half clotted, so recent was the kill, so violent the injuries. The throat was torn out. The bottom jaw removed. Jack turned into the trees and vomited.

It felt like an age before Tommy spoke, and when he did, his voice was quieter. 'I'll call forensics, let them know what we've got here. Get someone to analyse the CCTV.'

He walked back over to the footprints while making the call as Jack emerged from the trees. Tommy glanced over. Jack knew what was on their minds. The violent death that befell the dog was the same MO as the murders which culminated in his wife's death. The violence. The animal prints.

The Breyer murders. They were looking at a copycat.

Tommy clicked his fingers as he spoke into his handset. Jack and Bryan turned as Tommy said with a raised voice, 'Tell me again what you have at the cemetery. Animal prints, yeah, we saw those and... And fur.'

Jack spat a mouthful of sour saliva onto the lawn in a failed attempt to suppress the involuntary swallow. The hair on the back of his neck on end. This couldn't be real. A copycat going to this much trouble would certainly know who Jack was. Which meant he could be next.

The footprints at the cemetery had suddenly become deeply troubling. It looked as if Breyer had come back from the dead. Either the copycat was lucky, and it was a coincidence that it appeared this way, or it was deliberate. The copycat had been biding his time, waiting for a perfect confluence of circumstance. He'd waited for the snow to start, then raided the grave so that when he left, there was one set of prints, leading away. All on a night when there was a full moon. Yes, it was either a coincidence, or he was dealing with somebody of incredible intelligence, and saintly patience. A very dangerous combination indeed.

As Tommy ended his phone conversation, Bryan called over, 'We'd better get back to the station. Jack you should come with us. It might not be safe at home.'

Before Jack could tell him there was no way he was not going home, and if he never set foot in the station again it would be too soon, Bryan's mobile vibrated awake. Bryan answered. His brow furrowed. Jack and Tommy turned to one another. Bryan ended the call without speaking. A moment passed before he locked eyes with Tommy.

'There's been another. In Bromley.'

5

As Tommy's car hummed along, heading for the small market town of Bromley, Mike Marsh awoke in one of its back streets. Bromley had a population just shy of forty thousand, rising to forty-eight if you included the surrounding villages which shared the same postcode. It was fifteen miles further north and a little less upmarket than Finchley. Testament to this was the High Street, one of many in Britain in its death throes (the others were already long dead); the struggling shops that couldn't afford the rent in the new shopping centre awaiting foreclosure here, and at any given time it was possible to count the number of shoppers ambling down the few side streets branching off from it. The area had once been home to workers at the local car factory, but when 2008 came and the credit crunch took its toll, the factory closed, and Bromley fell on harder times. The town had made a mini recovery when a cake producer had decided to move production there, but for a few this salvation came too late. Some lost their homes and had no family to help them out. One such man was Mike Marsh.

Mike had fallen foul of the credit crunch and spiralling debt saw him lose first his job, then his wife, and finally – unable to make the mortgage payments alone – his home. Being a proud man, one relatively new to the area with few friends, Mike felt there was nobody to turn to for help. Before he realised the speed with which his downward spiral had picked up, he was on the streets.

Always a bit of a loner, Mike only knew a handful of Bromley's homeless community. He liked a couple of them. Phil's situation was almost identical to his, and the guy known only as 'Brum' made everyone laugh (partly because of his thick Birmingham accent). The one man he disliked was Terry.

Terry was an old-time homeless guy. Like Brum, he was one of Britain's forgotten war veterans. Unlike Brum, Terry returned from Iraq with post-traumatic stress disorder and a drink problem. About ten years Mike's senior and thickset, Terry was argumentative and belligerent. Everyone in Bromley knew who he was, and he was no stranger to the police. Nobody knew where he had come from. The accent was a strange brew of Scottish, Yorkshire and something else, and difficult to tag. The long-term homeless guys said he'd just appeared one day and that was that. Terry had a problem with everyone, but his particular favourites were foreigners. Anyone who didn't appear Anglo-Saxon was a target for abuse. Mostly verbal. Sometimes physical. They arrived on these shores "like rats, deserting a sinking ship" and "stole all the jobs", according to Terry. The jobs Terry was talking about were mostly minimum wage. Mike had also heard Terry saying, "I wouldn't get out of bed for minimum wage".

Go figure.

This winter was Mike's third on the streets. The first couple were manageable. By no means a cakewalk, but the weather was relatively mild and never strayed below zero. This winter was the one he had been dreading. Never a fan of colder weather, this winter was harsh, and every night temperatures had dropped below freezing. Mike had found an alley behind a new office building on the outskirts of town barely wide enough to fit a car. There were wheelie bins and a recess in the wall which gave good shelter from the bitter wind. The location wasn't ideal (closer to the town centre was better), but at least here he'd be away from Terry.

That recess is where Mike was this morning, and faced with the unusual sight he was, his mind flashed back to something amazing which had happened a few weeks earlier.

The first fall of snow had come, and the temperatures had been flirting with zero for a few days. Mike had dug some cardboard boxes from the bins to lie on. The difference in temperature each layer offered was startling. But it wasn't the boxes, or the recess for that matter, which had brightened that particular freezing morning. He had awoken blurry eyed to the unmistakable crunch of footfall in snow. Although, awoken isn't really the correct word here: In really cold weather, on the streets, you were never really asleep. Your mind shuts off from consciousness when it can't stay awake any longer, but that respite never lasts long and certainly shouldn't be referred to as sleep. On this morning, through his blurry eyes, he made out a tall figure disappearing around the corner. But it wasn't the figure that was remarkable; it was what the figure had left. In his peripheral sight Mike could make out a large brown paper bag. He sat up and dragged it over. Reaching inside he pulled out the following: one inflatable pillow; a 1.5 litre bottle of water; one store-bought cheese and ham sandwich; and (these were the real lifesavers) a set of thermal underwear - one pair of long johns (white, medium) and a matching long-sleeved thermal vest. He never found out who had left the bag. (Brum and Phil had also received such bags, though none of them ever spoke about it. Being given relatively expensive gifts was not something to boast about. Having something worth taking was never good for the homeless. And, just for the record, Brum and Phil had no idea who had left the lucky bags either. Terry, as it happened, received nothing.) That was what Mike woke up to three weeks ago. What he had just woken up to on this morning was something less pleasant entirely.

When Mike's vision came into focus, he lurched back into the recess, unsure whether or not to trust his eyes. He had a feeling that the naked man in front of him wasn't the benevolent lifesaver. Mike was staring at a skinny, but toned, white male, mid-thirties. Just under six feet tall, the man's chest rose and fell quickly and plumes of hot breath rose into the chill morning air. His bare feet were planted firmly in the two inches of snow, but he did not shiver. His wild eyes stared from his chiselled Eastern European features. Eyes such a light shade of brown that they took on an amber, almost gold hue like dying autumn leaves in the bright morning sun. But it wasn't the fact that the man was stark naked that caused Mike to jerk back. It wasn't the eyes, nor the apparent imperviousness to cold. It wasn't the fact that he was covered in dirt. It was his hands and lower jaw. They were covered in thick, dried blood. It had dried in streaks down his throat and onto his chest.

Mike finally spoke, 'Are you OK?'

The man replied, 'Give me your clothes.' The voice was deep, and the accent was northern English with a hint of something from the Eastern Bloc.

Given the man's state of undress, the request seemed reasonable. Given the man's hellish appearance, arguing seemed idiotic. Mike slowly stood, hands raised, palms outward as if facing a gunman. He reluctantly removed his blue woollen jumper, grey tracksuit bottoms and one-size-too-big black trainers. He would have to raid the clothes bank in the supermarket car park again. He stood in his thermal underwear, the cardboard boxes protecting his feet from the floor, and started to remove his vest. This he wouldn't be able to replace at Tesco.

The man raised a hand. 'No,' the Eastern accent more pronounced, 'just the others.'

Mike nodded a "thank you" and passed the clothes over. The naked man snatched them and quickly dressed. Before Mike could say anything, the man shot a frightened glance back over Mike's shoulder. Mike's gaze naturally followed the amber eyes of the stranger. Two office workers appeared from around the corner clutching cigarettes. Mike spun back to look at the man. He was gone. His footprints the only evidence that he'd ever existed. Mike stood in his thermal underwear and breathed a cloud of relief.

Later he would hear that in the night, Terry had been murdered. He would hear this and know who had committed the heinous crime. Mike figured that Terry had finally said the wrong thing to the wrong person. The same person who had taken his clothes. A bullet dodged.

Anyone who saw the scene between Mike and the naked man that day would have thought two things. Firstly, that Mike was lucky to not meet the same fate that had befallen Terry. Secondly, anyone who knew him that had seen the stranger would have sworn they were looking at Laszlo Breyer.

6

They parked and headed for their destination. As Tommy, Bryan and Jack neared the scene, they spotted a small crowd around the police tape and made straight for it. It had always struck Jack as odd that the public couldn't sense the threat in the air like someone in his line of work could. Or worse, that they *could* sense it and didn't care. Turned on by the excitement of conflict and death. Tommy flashed his badge at the waiting officer and told him to move the boundary further back. There was nothing to see from here, but it wasn't in Tommy's nature to take chances. The three of them entered the cold, wet brickwork of the alleyway. Tommy Wainwright stood between Jack and Bryan and they stared at what was left of homeless Terry's body. It had been given the same treatment as Freddy the Labrador.

'Jesus,' Bryan whispered. 'We need to get forensics down here a.s.a.p. and get them out of here before the press get wind of this.'

Tommy nodded, shielding his mouth from the smell with the back of one of his ham fists. 'They'll have a fucking field-day if they see this poor bastard.'

'We need to see if anyone knows anything and ask them to keep schtum,' Bryan added.

Jack stared down at Terry's ravaged corpse and was amazed at his own reaction. Maybe he'd been desensitised by what he'd seen with Freddy, or maybe his hangover was on the mend, but this time he was able to cast his detective's eye over the crime scene without discomfort. The victim was a large man, early fifties, though possibly younger due to what looked like the all too familiar signs of alcohol abuse. A gentle steam rose from the open wound where the throat had been torn out. Worrying for a man of this size, not to be able to defend himself. Jack glanced at his arms. No defensive marks or wounds; the attack was a surprise, probably while the victim was asleep.

Suddenly, at the far end of the narrow passage, something caught Jack's eye. Movement.

Tommy followed Jack's gaze into the street at the end of the alleyway. From the moment they had arrived he'd noticed the homeless man peering down the alley at them. He stood out because he was wearing white, not a coat; most unusual considering the weather. Tommy turned his back to the coatless man and took out his notepad.

'You've seen him too,' Tommy said to Jack.

Bryan looked at Tommy. Tommy scribbled notes whilst talking to Bryan, 'Don't look now, but since we got here there has been a homeless guy at the end of the alley. Got no coat on. If we approach him, he runs, we lose him. So you wait here. I'll go around the block,' said Tommy.

Twenty minutes later the four men were awaiting breakfast in a local greasy spoon. Chipped laminate topped tables with moulded plastic chairs. The smell of grease was just enough that Jack could bear it. Today's hangover now manageable enough to stomach a fry-up; if he'd been hungry, which of course, he wasn't. Food was the last thing on his mind. For now at least, he'd have to make do with a cup of tea strong enough to reasonably make three cups, given enough milk.

'Do you think he'll come back?' Mike was wearing Jack's coat. His face screwed into a frown.

Tommy was about to answer, but Jack got there first. 'Honestly, I think if he'd wanted you dead, he would have done it already. He had the opportunity, didn't take it. I would say you've seen the last of this man.'

The creases in Mike's forehead relaxed. Tommy let Jack's interruption slide. He knew that Jack had an ability to put people at ease. Bryan, on the other hand, flushed a dark pink colour, clearly annoyed at Jack taking over the good cop role in the investigation.

Jack continued, 'If we got you a sketch artist would you be able to describe him do you think?'

'I'll never forget that face,' said Mike. 'Those eyes. Almost amber they were.'

Tommy and Bryan's eyes fell straight on Jack. They both knew the significance of that. Jack shrugged it off as if it were nothing, 'Good man. We'll get you down to the station. All the tea you can drink down there, Mike.' Jack offered with a wink.

Mike nodded and smiled a little. He looked down at himself, then asked, 'Can we stop by Tesco's first?'

With a fry-up a piece polished off, the detectives stood by the car with Jack. Without his coat, he shivered in the chill of the air, getting little warmth from the pale winter sun. Mike struggled to make out the conversation from the back seat of the car.

'Are you sure Breyer didn't have family? Apart from the wife.' Bryan frowned.

Jack nodded, understanding Bryan's reasoning. Amber eyes are unusual, and it would make a strange coincidence. Could it be Laszlo Breyer had a brother? A twin even. Or maybe it was simply that the copycat had coloured contact lenses. Not impossible. To this point the copycat had clearly done his homework. Jack's mind was racing as fast as the hangover would allow.

'Not as far as I know. I'd have to check the files again. See if we missed something first time round.'

Tommy stood forward staring down at Jack, 'Listen. There is no "we". *You* aren't a detective anymore. This is not your case anymore. And there's no way you're looking at those files. You had your chance. Remember?'

Bryan turned to Jack, 'Give us a minute, Jack.'

Jack walked away as Bryan carefully remonstrated with Tommy, 'Listen. You two have previous, I get that. But the fact is, nobody knows the Breyer case like Jack. He could be a massive help on this thing.'

Unlike Bryan, Tommy didn't try to control the volume of his voice. 'How come you're siding with him?'

'This isn't about sides. There's a killer out there. A dangerous one. It's pretty obvious now that the killer's not Jack. Not only that, you know fine well Breyer wanted him dead. However you feel about him, it stands to reason that this copycat would come after Jack. If he's with us, we've got a better chance of catching this maniac.'

Bryan was a better politician than he was a detective.

'Fine. But you can babysit the bastard. If he winds me up, I won't be held responsible.'

'Good. And is it too much to ask for you to be civil to him?'

Tommy just glared. Too much. Way too much. Bryan held up his hands.

Without another word, Tommy turned to the car. Bryan turned to tell Jack their decision.

'Tom?'

Tommy looked up, one foot in the car. Bryan's face was pale, his mouth a cartoonish letter o.

'Where is he?'

7

'Fuck him.'

Tommy and Bryan were heading for the first choice in their search for Jack - the taxi rank outside the shopping centre. With

Mike sitting in the back of the car in his coat, Jack's quickest, and therefore warmest, route out of town was by taxi.

Bryan turned to Mike in the back seat, 'If you see Jack, give us a shout.'

Mike agreed, but with him wearing the coat of Mr Generous, Tommy doubted Mike would say a word. Not that he gave a fuck. Yes, he was miffed that Jack had given them the slip, but now it looked like Jack wasn't as involved as he'd first thought. He wanted to catch the copycat without Jack Talbot's help, and although Bryan had made a good point about keeping Jack close, if Talbot wasn't smart enough to stick around the people best able to protect him, well, that was his stupid fault. He knew that Bryan didn't really want to use Jack as bait. They didn't know at this stage if Jack was even a target, though it was plausible.

After ten fruitless minutes across from the taxi rank, Tommy broke the silence, 'He'd have been here by now.' He fired the car into life, 'We're going.'

'What about the bus station?' Bryan asked.

'If I know Jack Talbot, he's probably on the piss somewhere. He won't be thinking about getting home, he'll be thinking about getting trolleyed.' Tommy replied, then sighed. He dragged the wheel in the direction of the bus station, 'Fine. Ten minutes. If we don't see him, we're off.'

Bryan seemed pleased. Why Bryan Dempsey gave a shit about Jack Talbot all of a sudden was baffling, but now wasn't the time to press the issue.

'I've got better things to do with my time than babysit a borderline alcoholic.'

Bryan said nothing.

It was fifteen minutes and one false alarm later before Tommy once again fired the car into life. 'We're finished here.'

Bryan, of course, remonstrated, 'Maybe we'll catch him at home.'

Tommy shook his head. 'We haven't got the manpower to post somebody at his house. If you are that bothered, when we get back me and Mark...'

'Mike,' the homeless man said.

Tommy corrected himself without missing a beat or acknowledging the correction, 'Me and Mike will go into the station and you can go and scout Jack's place, but if he isn't back within two hours, that's it.'

And so it was. Tommy and Mike went into the station, and Bryan sat outside Jack's house, and waited.

CHAPTER TWO

Twelve noon. Four and a half hours till sunset. Jack headed for the bus station on the edge of town. The obvious place to go would be the taxi rank outside the shopping centre; it was a small fare back to Finchley and much closer than the bus station, especially for a man with no coat. Those were the two reasons he was not taking a taxi. He knew that Bryan would press Tommy into looking for him. And he didn't want to spend any more time in Tommy's company than he absolutely had to.

He knew fine well that asking to see the files would lead to the situation that followed, and that situation was his 'out'. He didn't really need to see the case files. If he did, he could just go home, even if going home when a violent copycat killer was probably looking for him was a bad idea. The last thing he'd done at the station was to copy the case files. The fact was, Jack had the case files in his head. For the last twelve months since Jenny had gone, he played them over and over in his mind. Wondering if he'd done something differently earlier in the investigation, it would have saved Jenny.

He ducked into one of the high street clothes shops which didn't have wooden windows. He correctly guessed that about now, Tommy and Bryan were driving a bewildered Mike past the taxi rank and that their next port of call would be the bus station. There they would wait about twenty minutes to see if Jack showed. When he didn't, Tommy would suggest that Jack was probably "on the piss" and that they didn't have time to waste babysitting him. They would swing by Jack's place later and check for him there. As Jack had correctly deduced, he had ten minutes to kill. The jeans he'd put on had his wallet in the pocket. He would buy himself a nice new winter coat, stop at an off-licence, buy cigarettes and a four-pack of the strongest lager they had (which would probably be Stella Artois, the special brew was usually all gone by this hour). This would kill ten minutes. He could then take an eight-and-a-half minute mosey to the bus station, by which time the impatient Tommy would have given up on looking for a man he didn't even want to find.

Like clockwork, approximately one minute after Tommy had screeched away from the bus station, Jack arrived. He sat on the bus in his brand-new winter coat, a 100% cotton khaki coloured "casual jacket" plastered with pockets (which was basically a parka, sans fur lining on the hood). It reminded him of the one he'd had as a young Mod. Now, with his head gently vibrating against the cold window, he was ready to go. Ticket in his pocket, can of Stella in his hand. The second can that morning. The first he'd opened and drunk in one go. The other two sat on the seat beside him.

He leant forward and mulled over the events of that morning and asked himself if there was a chance the copycat knew who he was. If so, would he try to kill him? Yes. Going home was a bad idea. But what did the copycat want with the body of Laszlo Breyer? Body snatching after the days of the infamous Burke and Hare was incredibly unusual, and rarely publicised.

He needed more info. The bus he was on would take him to Stevenage, which was on the mainline from London Kings Cross station to Edinburgh. After about two hours, sometime just before sunset, the train would reach York. York was the home of Daniel Cross, the occult expert who'd acted as a consultant when Jack worked the Breyer case. The bus shuddered into life and set off. A weary Jack rested his head back against the window and recalled his last, and so far only, conversation with Daniel Cross.

2

Daniel Cross padded across his studio apartment in stocking feet. It was October and the wind that month was a bitter one. It flung dry, golden leaves against the window in the dark night. Inside, the apartment was a cornucopia of the bizarre. Bookcases lined the walls, each one crammed with leather-bound hardback editions on witchcraft, the paranormal, werewolves and the like. Stuffed birds perched upon the cases ready to swoop down onto whoever dared stand below. Black candles cast flickering light onto crucifixes and an array of jars, each home to a liquid in primary colour. In the liquid, stillborn farmyard freaks. A two headed calf, an eight-legged lamb. The mantel piece over the real fireplace had a human skull at one end, at the other, a case of silver bullets gleamed in the flickering light. An ornate clock ticked away in the centre. That is not to say the apartment was bereft of technology.

Cross cradled the mobile in his neck and tip-tapped away at the laptop on the writing desk, 'Hi, Jack... Yeah, I got your email.' He clicked on an email from Jack Talbot.

'You said that the murders were so savage that it didn't seem possible that a man would have the strength to do it.'

Jack sat at his desk at the police station in Welwyn, desk phone receiver in one hand cigarette in the other, 'That's right. I didn't want to send the photographs. It's a real horror show. But it looks like these people were attacked by an animal.'

Cross sat in his desk chair and leaned as far as the sprung back would allow, 'And all of the murders, how many were there?'

'It was six, it's seven now.'

'All of the murders happened on evenings when there was a full moon, is that right?'

'Yeah. The first night there were four. Three on the second night. Last night none. I'm working on some theories as to why there were no kills yesterday. The full moon thing was the reason I was given your name.'

Cross leant forward and scribbled notes onto a pad, 'Is there anything else you think could be relevant?'

Jack frowned a little, 'Just what I put in the email. You have read the email...'

'Yes, yes. I just like to hear it from the horse's mouth. I get a better sense of what the person thinks is, or might be, important that way.'

Jack wasn't convinced, but it sounded plausible.

Cross continued, 'You mentioned animal prints and fur?'

'That's right. Along with the full moon, it screamed "occult" from there so...'

'Any suspects?'

'A few leads. Nothing concrete.' Jack lied.

He had spoken with an anonymous source, a woman who said she recognised a man whose image had turned up on CCTV. The woman knew the man and his wife. Jack was planning to visit Mrs Laszlo Breyer within the next few days but didn't want to shade Daniel Cross's judgement.

Cross sensed this but wasn't angry. There could be any number of reasons Jack was holding back. Instead he offered a single word into the phone at let it hang there.

'Lycanthropy.'

Jack frowned, 'Come again?'

Cross repeated the word.

Jack said, 'I heard you. Lycanthropy. You mean werewolves?'

'Yes, but not literally. It's a mental condition in which the sufferer is convinced he is a wolf. A werewolf to be exact. It all adds up. The full moon, the animal hair.'

Jack interrupted, 'You want me to tell my boss I'm looking for Lon Chaney junior?'

Cross smiled. 'Not Lon Chaney. Or a werewolf. Someone who *thinks* he's a werewolf. In the middle ages it wasn't uncommon for lycanthropes to wear wolf skins. If the sufferer has mental problems, it may also explain the strength displayed.'

Jack had heard that a madman had the strength of ten, but he still wanted convincing. 'These attacks. They're are nothing that a man could do. Plus the animal prints...'

'If a man is capable of wearing a fur then it stands to reason he could have created some kind of weapon. A claw-like tool. One that would do the kind of damage you're talking about. If we surmise that a man would wear fur and use a weapon, then it isn't too much of a stretch to imagine he might have some kind of foot covering that would leave the prints you describe.'

Jack thought it over. Forensics said that the depth of the prints left indicated the suspect was at least six and a half feet tall. Number one suspect Breyer was just under six feet. If he was wearing an animal pelt, and using some kind of tool then he would obviously weigh more. The very odd pieces were starting to fit together to make an even odder picture. An involuntary "fuck me" escaped Jack's lips.

'Are you still there, Jack?'

'Sorry, Daniel. Was just thinking things through. You've been a big help. Thanks very much.'

'Don't mention it. If there's anything else I can help you with let me know.'

Jack thought about giving Breyer's name, but decided to hold it back. He wasn't sure how tight lipped this man was. He couldn't bring himself to fully trust a man whose reputation was as colourful as Daniel Cross's. There was a second reason. The last of three nights of full moons had passed. That gave him twenty-odd days to get more info and check back with Cross.

Cross broke Jack's train of thought. 'Is there anything else?'

He'd sensed Jack was toying with ideas.

Jack paused. 'No Daniel. Thanks again. I'll be in touch.'

Fading back to that freezing bus and a third can of Stella, Jack realised that he hadn't got back in touch with Daniel Cross to update him on the outcome. The case had somehow been swept under the carpet. Breyer was killed and his name was never released to the press. They cried foul, but the murders stopped. There was too much going on in the world for them to worry about a dead killer.

The bus arrived at the station in Stevenage and pulled up outdoor in a nook along a long, grey, three-storey building. The damp weather did the greyness of the area no favours. Jack thought he'd better do Daniel Cross the courtesy of giving him a phone call and apology. Had Jack arrived an hour earlier, he'd have seen the man with amber eyes in the blue jumper and grey tracksuit bottoms walking by. Headed in the direction of the A1. Headed north.

3

Kenny Mackenzie wailed tunelessly at the top of his voice along with the radio as his lorry roared out of Stevenage. The A1 back north was a dull but familiar route for him. The radio was decent company, but an affable Glaswegian, Kenny preferred human contact. You wouldn't think it to look at him. A bear of a man, arms covered in tattoos, he looked more likely to beat the life out of you. He was a problem solver back in his Glasgow days for whoever needed it, as long as he liked you. Hired muscle with morals. Since he'd moved south of the border to his wife's hometown he'd mellowed. The two kids had helped in that respect, too. He couldn't go around hellraising with two young boys dependent on him back home. He'd never go looking for trouble, but he'd never shied away from it either. Nowadays, if trouble took the time to look for Kenny, it would find him. He'd mellowed, but he still wasn't one to cross.

Cruising along the slow lane, sun at his back, he saw something at the roadside. He smiled and flicked the indicator switch, easing the break and steering wheel at the same time until the behemoth truck was at rest in the hard shoulder. He leaned over and opened the passenger door. He turned the radio down to a whisper as the hitchhiker jogged along.

Kenny smiled, 'How you doing, pal?'

He always picked up hitchhikers if he could. He'd heard it was dangerous, but he thought to himself it was probably more dangerous for them if they tried anything. Last month, the guy he invited into his cab had sensed this and made his excuses before running away. Kenny wasn't worried by the lean man tossing a thumb back over his shoulder on this day.

The man cracked a smile, 'I'm going north, I was wondering...'

Kenny interrupted, 'Nae bother. Jump in.'

He reached for his mobile and fired off a quick text as the hitchhiker climbed into the cab. He clumsily typed "Got a hiker. Should help pass the time. Back in a few hours. Love you xxx" and hit send.

Kenny looked across at the hiker and smiled again, 'I can take you as far as York. That Oright?'

'Perfect'. His passenger forced a smile. A troubled one which never reached his amber eyes.

4

Tommy sat at his desk and rubbed his temples with the thumb and middle finger of his right hand. A headache was brewing, and it was a beauty. The thought occurred that he might look as if he were meditating. He had Bryan on the phone.

'There's no sign of him.'

Tommy was waiting for the homeless man to finish with the sketch artist. He was sure Mark or Mike or whoever was stalling to get more tea, but as he watched the bitter wind swish flurries through the gloomy grey outside, he couldn't really blame him. Bryan's news about Jack hardly came as a surprise. What did come as a surprise was that he found the news disappointing. He closed his eyes and kept rubbing.

'Okay, mate, get yourself back here and we'll go over everything.'

Tommy heard the car engine fire up.

'Any word from forensics?' Bryan asked.

'Just about to speak to them now. Mark's still in with the sketch artist.'

Bryan said his goodbyes and freed up the line for Tommy to call the forensics team in charge of the case. The phone rang a few times before anyone answered.

'Hello?'

'This is Detective Tommy Wainwright at Finchley...'

'Oh, hi Tom. I was just about to call you.'

He recognised the happy-go-lucky tone of Steve Stewart. Steve was the man who'd handled the Breyer case, and for somebody who dealt in the most macabre part of the job, the nuts-and-bolts science of death, the bouncy, cheery character was something that always threw Tom off a little. Which was why today's less than usually happy tone came as both a relief and a concern.

'Steve, what have you got for me?'

'Well, it's the hair sample you found at the cemetery. Just doing the usual checks, length, width, medulla formation, cuticle scale pattern, blah blah. The hair's animal.'

He paused as if building up for some big finish. Tommy hated melodrama. Drum roll please.

'And we don't have a match.'

That was the thing you were about to call and tell me?

'We don't have a match with any animal common to this area. However...'

Here we go.

'And please remember that this is by no means conclusive, the closest match we do have is with that of the Eurasian Grey Wolf.'

Tommy's eyes sprang open. The Eurasian Grey Wolf. The name was familiar. Why did he recognise it? A chill washed over him. The hair found in the Breyer case. He sat up in his chair, now listening intently.

'Like I said it's not conclusive. There's more. Analysing the ring patterns the hair is consistent with that of the sample you found in the homeless man's hand in Bromley...'

Another pause. *Get on with it, Steve, for fuck's sake.*

'And from the Breyer case.'

Tommy grabbed a pencil and started scribbling notes for Bryan. 'Are you sure, Steve?'

'Like I said, it's not one hundred percent.'

'What about DNA from the hair, does it match the hair from the Breyer case?'

'We never tested the hair for DNA. It was animal.'

'Can you test it now?'

Steve took a sharp intake of breath. The kind a mechanic takes when he lifts the bonnet of your car as a harbinger of bad news. 'We could, but the thing is the sample's quite old now. Plus it would have to join a long queue of human DNA. The new sample would yield better results.'

'What about RapidHIT up in Cov?'

RapidHIT was a system of testing DNA which rather than needing experts to run tests, could be used by anyone with the basic training and gave results in a couple of hours rather than the usual 3-5 days it actually took to get results, or the weeks/months spent queueing. The system up in Coventry had been a Godsend on so many cases since its introduction.

'Sorry Tom,' the technician sounded as disappointed as Tommy felt at hearing the words, 'RapidHIT needs blood or saliva.'

'Okay, Steve. Thanks anyway.'

Tommy sat listening to the dial tone drone for a second before replacing the handset. He remembered homeless Mark/Mike saying that the killer had amber eyes, like Laszlo Breyer. It resonated, like it had some kind of significance to the hair. Then it was gone. Tommy took his pencil and scratched a circle around the words "family member" in his notes and stared at the wall, waiting for Bryan to return. And his headache to hit. He closed his eyes and rubbed his temples.

***

5

Jack walked through Stevenage hunting a payphone. It was harder than he had imagined. There again he couldn't recall the last time he'd used one. Times had changed. Across the road from the entrance to the train station, he managed to find one that hadn't been smashed; like all the others, this one was accompanied by the stinging reek of stale ammonia. He lifted the handset and wracked his brains for Daniel Cross's number. He'd always been proud of his elephantine memory. The problem here was that he had only dialled the number twice. Over a year ago. He grasped in the dark recesses of his mind and came back clutching something. He'd have to hope Cross was still living at the same address, and that he was at home. He held his breath and dialled. It rang for an eternity. Staring at the names scratched into the glass of the booth he began to wonder if Jonno still loved Stacey B when finally, someone answered.

'Hello?'

In the age of identity theft the days of giving your name when you answered were long gone. At least it was male.

'Daniel? Daniel Cross?'

'Who's this?'

Jackpot. Anyone else would have said "No".

'It's Jack Talbot.'

Cross plonked himself in the same leather desk chair he had over twelve months before. Now Jack could hear it creak as he reclined.

'The detective?'

'Former. Long story. How are you?'

'Fine thanks. How can I help?'

If he was pissed off at the lack of a return phone call last year, he was hiding it well. So far so good.

'I'm on my way to York and I was wondering if we could meet up.'

Silence.

'It's quite urgent.'

'Er, sure. What's going on?'

Jack explained the empty grave he'd been staring at earlier and that this was a weird one. Jack didn't realise but it was about to get a whole lot weirder.

Cross sighed, 'Body snatching? Wow. A rarity, thankfully. At least on these shores. Last one was 2006.'

Jack wondered about somebody who could recall that kind of information without double checking. The man was an expert, but... Body snatching? Cross went on to explain that a group of animal rights activists had stolen the body of a woman connected to a cosmetics company which carried out animal testing. Jack was a little impatient to cut to the chase and Cross seemed to somehow sense it.

'Before that we're going back thirty years. Not too far from my neck of the woods, actually. Small local church in a little village.'

Something resonated again within Jack. Like it had when he first saw the empty grave. And again when the first victims were found north of Finchley. He was no closer to putting his finger on what that something was.

'Controversy surrounded his death. He was supposedly shot and killed in a hunting accident. About twelve months later, his body went missing. Some thought it was because new evidence had turned up. Apparently, the victim of the shooting had murdered a little girl and the whole hunting accident thing was a cover-up and the body was about to be exhumed...'

Jack cut Cross off mid-sentence, 'Whose body?'

Cross thought for a moment. 'Unusual name. Hungarian. What was it?'

Jack's palm was sweating. He switched the receiver into his other hand and noticed that his knuckles had turned white. He held his breath. He knew exactly what Cross was going to say.

Unable to take it any longer Jack offered, 'Breyer.'

'That's it,' Cross sounded excited, impressed, and surprised all at once.

Three body snatchings in thirty years and two of them from the same family. That family. His mind swam. What were the odds on something like that? The further this case went on the deeper into the realms of impossibility it strayed. Jack's heart was thumping.

'Breyer. Yes that was it. Laszlo Breyer.'

'Laszlo?'

The ground fell away beneath Jack's feet. It was impossible. If Breyer had died thirty years ago, whose body had they buried in Finchley? Was it possible they had the wrong man for the murder spree? Had the same person taken the body from Finchley cemetery? It was impossible. Two body snatchings. Two Laszlo Breyers? Father and son. Undoubtedly. But why steal their remains? This changed everything. Jack had to contact Bryan. His semi-drunk mind raced to put together some semblance of a plan.

'Daniel, I can be in York around five. Could we meet?'

'Sure. My place. I'll give you the address. Got a pen?'

'Don't need one.'

Daniel relayed the address, 'It's right next to the cemetery, you can't miss it.'

'Great. I really appreciate this. I've got to go. Contact some colleagues on the Force. Could you find out as much as you can on this Breyer character? Relatives, ancestors, anything. And gather as much info as possible on body snatching.'

Daniel confirmed Jack's plan as Jack slammed down the receiver and dove back into his pocket for more coins. Notes only. No change. Shit. He remembered giving a handful of shrapnel to a homeless guy at the bus station in Bromley. Forgot that, could remember a phone number from a year ago.

'That's the beer, Jack,' he sighed.

He stepped out of the stench of the freezing phone booth and made a beeline for two teenaged boys. They sauntered along the street, hands and (somewhere in their cavernous hoodies) eyes glued to expensive mobile phones; the kind that adults working full-time would have to think twice before splashing out on. Jack was pretty sure that beneath the hoodies were T-shirts with slogans like "*Who cares*" lacking the requisite punctuation, and that mantra of the indifferent "*Whatever*", though this shirt might have had the missing question mark from the other. When Jack approached, he waved to break the hypnotic spell of the mobile phones. They peered at him from within the hoods.

'Yeah?'

'I need to borrow your phone. To call a friend.'

They parted to go around him. One, Jack wasn't sure which, offered, 'No chance.'

Jack stepped back and spread his arms. The boys stopped. Glared.

Jack said, 'I can pay you.'

'Fuck off.'

The boys parted again, faster this time. Barging through any attempt to block the way.

'Nonce.'

Jack thought of challenging them, then thought better of the idea. You never know. They all carry knives these days. Not like when he was a kid and you sorted everything out with your fists. He didn't have time to get into it, more pressing matters were at hand. He headed for the station. He would arrive in York, meet Daniel and call Bryan from there, or maybe he'd have more luck on the train. He checked his watch. It was half past two. Two hours until sunset.

6

The clock on the lorry dashboard flicked to two-thirty. By now Kenny was an hour from Stevenage, but time was dragging. His passenger wasn't as chatty as he'd hoped.

He reached out a meaty hand, 'Kenny.'

His passenger turned to him. His amber eyes came into focus as if he'd been thinking about something somewhere else entirely. He finally replied, 'My friends call me Larry.'

'Nice to meet you Larry. How are you doing?'

'Tired. I've had a hard few days.'

Kenny was talkative and certainly bigger than his passenger. More than most found Kenny imposing, but he didn't want to be intrusive. He always respected someone's privacy. 'Message received, loud and clear. Get your head down if you like.'

'No, no. I didn't mean...'

'It's alright. If you don't want to talk I don't mind.'

'Please. You misunderstand me. I was just saying. Actually, I'd prefer to talk, it will help me to stay awake. I don't want to sleep. I've been asleep for a long time.'

Kenny was relieved, though he felt a little awkward at his passenger's reaction. He never got used to people being intimidated by his size. It had come in handy in his past life; now it was a barrier. At least Larry was polite. Kenny liked that. He thought the best thing to do was to kill the silence.

He replied quickly, 'Glad to hear you want to talk. It can get pretty boring out here sometimes. The radio plays the same shite all the time.'

Larry half smiled.

Kenny fired another question at Larry, 'You going home? If you don't mind me asking.'

'Yes. I live close to York. Well, quite close. I'd like to get there before dark if possible. I'd like to make the rest of the distance today. What time do you think we'll arrive in York?'

Kenny glanced at the clock and drew in a deep breath. This was mostly for show. Even on Saturday, the traffic outside York at this time would probably prevent them arriving before sunset.

He offered a glimmer of hope to Larry, 'It'll be close. We'll have a go.'

His foot eased down onto the accelerator as he said it.

Larry offered a nervous smile, 'Thank you, Kenny.'

Kenny smiled as they sped for York. After a few seconds he spoke again. 'Nae bother.'

Larry glanced at the photograph Kenny had stuck in the sun visor. 'Your family?'

49

Kenny also glanced at the picture. Him with his wife Karen, and their two boys Callum and Paul at the beach. Kenny had to restrain himself from answering that it would be fucking weird if it wasn't his family. He knew that Larry was tired and friendly and that the joke would probably not be received as intended. The photo was a couple of years old now, (Callum, Kenny's oldest, was only seven in the picture) but it was still Kenny's favourite.

Kenny decided to take the polite route with the picture, 'That's them. My favourite photo. Marbella. Going back next week. Can't wait.'

'It's a nice photo.'

'You married, Larry?' Kenny cringed at the thought of his question making the conversation more awkward.

'Yes.' Relief. 'But I haven't seen her for a long time. I've been working away a lot.'

'Not to worry, you'll see her soon enough.'

The journey was starting to fly by.

'Would it be OK if I opened my window a little?'

'Aye, on ya go,' Kenny replied in thick Glaswegian. Larry's baffled stare and immobility forced a chuckle from Kenny. He affected an Anglicised version of his accent, 'That's fine.'

Larry smiled. Kenny recognised the old window-down-to-stay-awake trick. He reached down to the door and grabbed the warm metal of his flask.

'You wanting...' he stopped and modified his accent again, 'Would you like some coffee?'

Larry seemed eternally grateful. Kenny liked Larry and felt a little sorry for him. He knew someone in trouble when saw them. That was probably the reason why, at about quarter to four (roughly forty minutes before the sun set), when Larry finally succumbed to sleep, Kenny let him. He would wake him up just before York and give him a few of the caffeine tablets he always had on hand. He presumed that Larry didn't want to be drowsy when he was finally reunited with his wife.

He was wrong.

7

At twenty-five past two, Jack boarded the train and strode through searching anyone kind enough to lend him their mobile phone. He eyed the worn seats, replayed the shock at the cost of his ticket, and wondered when the government were going to admit that privatisation was a bad idea. At this time of day there was barely anyone on the train, nothing like the chaos of rush hour where commuters fought for a seat. The empty carriages made the job of commandeering a mobile a real chore. At the fourth time of asking, he was successful.

He sat across from the young couple and took the man's phone. He faffed around trying to get to the screen to input a number before conceding defeat and giving it back to the owner. The man navigated to the correct screen and handed the phone back to Jack, who noticed the young man badly hide his surprise at finding somebody who couldn't use an i-phone. Jack ignored it. He dialled Bryan's number.

It rang a couple of times before Bryan answered, 'Hello?'

Another success for data protection.

'Bryan is that you? It's Jack.'

Bryan took a second to answer. Jack guessed he was moving away from his desk, or, more likely, letting Tommy know who he had on the phone.

Bryan finally replied, voice lowered, 'Where the hell are you?'

'I can't really talk now, I'm on someone else's phone, can you call me back?'

Bryan agreed and Jack relayed the man's number to him. The call ended and a few seconds later the phone rang. Jack recognised the number and apologised to the young man for the time he was taking before answering.

'Hello.'

Bryan answered, 'We've got another lycanthrope. It's confirmed, forensics came back. The fur in the homeless guys hand was probably wolf fur. And there was a full moon last night. Tonight and tomorrow, too.'

'We can expect a busy couple of days then.'

Wolf fur. He knew that in the original case, Breyer was using an animal somehow, but a wolf? *Probably a wolf.* He kept his cards close to his chest. Tommy and Bryan didn't know of his theory because, well, in the end it didn't matter.

'I've got something to tell you, Bryan. You're not going to believe this.'

'Try me.'

'Laszlo Breyer. He died.' Jack tried to avoid looking at the couple as he mentioned death. He failed horribly then smiled reassuringly.

'Thank God for that. We buried the poor bastard. Great police work, Jack.'

'No. He died thirty years ago.'

'What?'

'I'm not sure if it's identity theft yet, or... or what we're dealing with.'

Bryan fell silent. Jack heard a muffled conversation from underneath Bryan's hand.

He came back, 'That doesn't make any sense.' He paused, waiting for the right time to drop the next question. He realised there was never a right time and went ahead regardless, 'Where are you now?'

Jack chuckled, 'No chance.'

'Jack, I realise it's far from perfect spending time with me and Tommy,'

Why does he give a shit about me all of a sudden?

'but there's a copycat killer out there and chances are he's going to be after you.'

'So you've managed to convince Tommy I had nothing to do with the business at the cemetery?'

Bryan lied, 'He never really thought that, he was just covering his bases.'

'Sounds like Tommy.'

'Listen, Jack, don't get too involved in this thing. Tommy will go apeshit if he finds out you're investigating.'

Jack looked up again at the man, who was trying his best not to appear impatient. Jack nodded at the man. 'Listen, Bryan, I've got to go. I'll call again later. Oh, one more thing... The footprints...'

Bryan cut him off, 'Forensics analysed the CCTV from the dog killing. It was somebody close to seven feet,' Jack was speechless. Bryan continued, 'OK, go. Call me later.'

Jack ended the call and silently handed the phone back across the table. He nodded a thank you and got up. He wandered over to another seat in a daze.

He couldn't wrap his head around the new information. He sat and tried to organise his thoughts. Laszlo Breyer was dead over thirty years ago. Which meant that if the guy that was buried in Finchley committed the murders, he was only two years old at the time. Impossible. So were they looking at father and son? More likely.

Then there was the copycat. Was he a blood relative? He knew his stuff, clearly. But he was caught on camera. The prints and CCTV analysis concurred: both came from an individual almost seven feet tall. And what did the copycat want with Breyer's remains? None of it made sense. Jack pored over the details in his tired mind. The journey to York passed quickly. The sun was about to set, and somewhere just off the A1 a lorry driver was about to experience something he'd find difficult to forget.

CHAPTER THREE

Announcements echoed through the cavernous station as Jack stepped off the train and into the cold York air. The station was a mix of old and new: digital arrivals boards and fancy coffee under huge arched ceilings. He weaved through bustling travellers, throwing a glance up at the ornate wall-mounted clock as he crossed from his platform, to the station exit. 5PM; twenty-three minutes after sundown.

Outside, car headlights gave commuters' warm breath an almost luminous glow as they puffed into the dark night. Jack sized up the queue of passengers waiting for taxis before impatiently turning towards the city centre, setting off along the twinkling frosted pavement. The queue was short, but he had to keep moving. That was the overwhelming urge, the part of his conscience that spoke the loudest. But as he marched further from the station, further from that glimpse of modernity, he recognised the fight-or-flight tingling building in his arms and legs.

Jack had walked the beat in the Meadows estate, Nottingham, before he transferred south. At the time it was one of a handful of beats in Britain where the police carried firearms. He'd drawn his weapon twice. Never needed to fire it, but he'd seen his fair share of dirty work. He didn't spook easily but was always acutely aware of his senses, and always smart enough to listen to them when they spoke. He had a feeling it had got him out of more scrapes than he'd ever know. Tonight he couldn't shake the feeling that he was being watched by unseen eyes. Something was wrong in York and he knew it. Just as he knew that tonight, more would die at the hands of the copycat. He abandoned his walk, about faced, and made for the taxi rank.

By the time he got back to the rank there was one taxi left. He hopped into the warmth, and was instantly hit by the sickly smell wafting from the tree-shaped air-freshener dangling from the rear-view mirror. His driver was in his fifties, though the licence hanging from the dusty dash showed a happier face than the one on display in the driver's seat; it looked like it had been a long day. He perked up as Jack climbed aboard.

'Where to, chief?' In a thick local accent.

'I'm looking for accommodation near the cemetery. Any ideas?'

The driver paused for a moment, hand rubbing his stubbled chin. 'There's a couple,' he said as he set off. He asked about Jack's budget and it was decided that a B&B would do the trick. The driver knew a good one, close to the cemetery. He swung the cab into the main road and headed at a steady pace through the winter evening.

He glanced in the mirror, 'Heard about the accident?'

'Accident?'

'A19. They've found a lorry all smashed up, no-one inside.'

Jack felt the same resonance as before. *Breyer.*

'Is that close to here?' Jack knew the answer before it came and his skin crawled.

'Not far. About ten minutes.' The driver had his own theory. 'Bet it was drugs. Bloody kids these days.' He shook his head as he flicked the indicator and swung the cab round a corner.

'So it was a kid?' Jack replied, humouring him, certain that all of the problems in the world received an identical analysis.

'They didn't say. But I'd put money on it.'

We can close the file on that one then. The conversation turned to the recent cold snap as they snaked through York, eventually pulling up outside a quaint semi-detached house that was to be Jack's home for the evening. Jack pulled a shrinking roll of tens from his pocket and handed one to the driver who, shoddy police work aside, Jack decided he actually liked.

'Keep the change.'

'Much obliged. Want me to wait, make sure they've got a room?'

Jack smiled to himself. He was rarely wrong about people.

'No thanks. I'm sure it'll be fine.'

It was. Jack was greeted by a genial lady who told him the rates. A little older than Jack, her dark hair was greying, but behind the horn-rimmed spectacles the eyes held a twinkle that hinted at a youthful mischief. He quickly took the first room offered, said "probably" to breakfast and that if it was a "no", he'd let her know later, took his key and went upstairs, getting the impression she would have liked a longer chat.

If the circumstances had been different, he may have obliged her.

His room was simple, clean, and almost exactly as he'd envisaged. From the pale green paint job, and solid old writing bureau wedged in the corner to the uneven, yet surprisingly comfortable bed. And that seemingly uniform B&B room smell. He entered the small, en-suite bathroom and splashed cold water on his face. Only now did he realise that he hadn't thought about beer since he'd polished off the last can just outside Peterborough. The buzz was back, and it wasn't for booze. It was for the work. He thought about a more thorough freshening up and realised that he'd need to visit a chemist. No toothbrush, no deodorant.

Not important now.

He freshened up quickly and headed straight back downstairs. In reception there was a case of colourful brochures advertising local tourist attractions (Vikings and dungeons seemed to be the order of the day). He grabbed the map and asked the landlady to point out Daniel Cross's street. Ten minutes' walk. Perfect. He bade the landlady a good evening and stepped back into the cold. He pulled the zip on his new coat all the way up, muttering a small thank you to himself as he strode up the path to the street. He consulted the map before turning left.

The high grey cemetery walls along which he would have to walk cut a foreboding sight against the leaden sky. And the discreet unease which troubled him outside the station crept back. He sped up. Despite having fallen out of shape since Jenny's death, he didn't slow until he reached the point marked on his map.

Cross's tree-lined street was eerily quiet, though that was to be expected. It was well out of the way – a cul-de-sac of ten houses on each side that led onto endless blackness of fields which stared back like the black eye of a shark. It was two degrees below zero, colder with wind-chill, and early evening. Not many would venture out – few did just after New Years' – and those that did wouldn't do so for another couple of hours.

Still, the desolation...

Claw-like fingers reached for him, cast by the wavering trees blowing across the streetlights above. He glanced over his shoulder down the tree-lined street and pulled his collar up against the cold, though he was unsure that the weather induced the shiver. He sensed movement up ahead and stopped. Twenty yards along the dark street, somewhere between him and that dead shark's eye. A black cat darted out, stopped in the middle of the street and stared at him, its green eyes reflecting white gold in the moonlight. It arched its back and with its mouth forming a sickening rictus, the cat hissed, before scampering into the darkness.

Jack froze. Not because of the cat. But because he knew that the hiss wasn't for him. Behind him, he felt a presence.

2

He didn't want to turn around but knew the longer he didn't the worse it would be. His skin crept and the sound of his heartbeat rose in his ears as his imagination filled the void of his knowledge. He span quickly and found himself nose to nose with a pair of staring eyes.

Jack leapt back. The thin, pathetic figure of a homeless man held out a hand. He can't have been older than twenty-two. Jack thought of the horrendous weather and immediately felt for him.

'Got any spare change, mate?'

'Jesus wept. You scared the living daylights out of me.'

The homeless man stepped back, 'Sorry. I didn't mean to.'

Jack reached into his pocket, then remembered that he'd tipped the taxi driver the rest of the ten quid left over from his cab fare. He'd paid forty-five flat for the room back at the B&B and his account was empty. His tired mind flashed back to the ceremonious act of cutting up the credit cards after Jenny died (she was the only one who used them). He did have an arranged overdraft, but that was only for a hundred pounds, which meant that the single ten- and five-pound notes in his pocket were all that he had. The young man looked at him. 'I haven't got any change, but I can give you some cigarettes,' Jack offered, hopefully.

'No, it's OK. I don't smoke. But thanks.'

This poor bastard. Jenny used to look at homeless figures on the streets and complain. "Look, they're always bloody smoking" or "He can afford to keep a dog and yet he's got no money. It's animal cruelty". She always did care more for animals than she did for people. Jenny couldn't complain about this kid. Jack reached into his pocket, pulled out the crumpled fiver, and handed it to the young homeless man.

'No that's too much.' Surprise painted on his soft features.

'It's fine. I want you to have it or I wouldn't have offered. What's your name?'

'Danny.'

'Happy New Year, Danny.' Jack smiled.

Danny smiled too, 'Thanks so much, man. People don't usually even acknowledge me.'

'Call me Jack. What's the money for?'

'I've got a mate in Donny. It's for train fare.'

Jack looked at the kid, 'How long have you been on the streets, Danny?' Guessing from the relatively clean clothes, it hadn't been too long.

'Couple of months. But they've been cold ones. Plus some places have started putting them studs down. So it's getting harder to find places to kip.'

Jack remembered seeing an article about the studs on one of the rare occasions he'd splashed out on a newspaper: stainless steel, about an inch and a half tall, dozens placed into the ground in shop doorways, to deter the homeless from sleeping in good shelter spots.

'I've seen those things. Barbaric. We treat pigeons like that.'

Danny nodded in agreement. 'What can you do?'

'The guys who invented them want to be careful,' Jack continued, 'karma's a bitch.'

Danny smiled.

'Take care of yourself, Danny.'

'Thanks again for the money.'

Jack shook hands with the young man and they went their separate ways. The meeting with Danny had distracted Jack from his feeling of unease, but as soon as Danny went, it started to creep back in. He turned back again and watched Danny shrinking into the night, and the further he got, the worse Jack felt. Jack about faced towards Cross's place and trudged on towards the dark emptiness of the windswept grassy fields. Up ahead a streetlight flickered before fizzling out, leaving a patch, about thirty yards across, of pitch darkness.

As Jack stepped into the circle, he felt something. His stomach fluttered. Using the numbers on the houses as a guide, Jack guessed that Cross's place was about a hundred yards from the faulty lamppost, next to those blackened fields.

From somewhere up ahead, came a sharp snapping sound. Jack froze. Ice-cold fingers traced a line down his back. The bushes at the foot of the broken light seemed to be the source of the sound. Jack squinted at the bushes, sensing movement within. A gentle buzzing came from above. Against his better judgement, Jack glanced up. The streetlight flickered on and fizzed before again going out. Jack looked back down at the bushes and the clouds parted above, revealing the ethereal glow of the full moon into the streets below. Into the streets and into the bushes, illuminating a pair of gleaming eyes that were locked onto Jack. Jack and this creature seemed frozen as they stared. Then, without warning, the creature leapt.

'Fucking cat.'

It sped across Jack's path. Once again it stopped and hissed at Jack. He lifted a boot, threatening to kick the animal. It darted away down the road and vanished over the wall into the cemetery.

'Go on, fuck off.'

On another night, he'd have brushed it off as nothing. Nerves. Coincidence. But not tonight. Tonight, even before the walk to see Daniel Cross, from the very moment he set foot in York, in fact, he'd sensed something. No, tonight it wasn't just nerves. Tonight it was a sign from nature. A sign that all was not well. Tonight, it was a warning.

3

Jack jogged the few remaining yards to Daniel Cross's place, peering back down the dark street as he entered the small garden. Nothing stirred. The moon reappeared from behind a cloud again casting into the street an unsettling, other-worldly fluorescence. He ran to the door and jabbed at the doorbell. Through the frosted glass an outline silhouetted against the soft yellow light. It grew until the door opened. A tall man, in his late thirties stood in the doorway.

'Jack?'

Jack nodded and held out a hand. Cross took it in one of his own hands. A delicate hand, like that of a pianist.

'We meet at last. Please, come in.'

He was nothing like Jack had expected. He thought of an occult specialist as someone who looked like a seventies Doctor Who but dressed top to toe in leather like a character from the Matrix. Cross looked more like a slick stage magician. Not one of the smoke-and-mirrors-saw-a-woman-in-half ilk. More that of the witty, intellectual, mind-reading kind.

Cross smiled at Jack, a genuine, warm smile that touched the eyes. 'I look different from what you were expecting.'

'I suppose,' Jack smiled. 'You said you've moved?'

'Yes,' Cross wondered why Jack was so interested, before it dawned on him. 'The phone number.'

'Right.'

'I'm on the same phone exchange so they let me keep the number. Huge ball ache. I've had three numbers in the last two months. I almost gave up. If you'd called last week, you wouldn't have got me.'

The last taxi at the station. Now this. Maybe his luck was changing. Jack smiled as he entered the hallway. Neutral colours. A hat stand. All very... *normal*. Nothing like he had been expecting.

'Shoes off?

'If you don't mind.'

Jack removed his shoes and was relieved that the pair of socks he had on not only matched but lacked the ventilation holes that would have allowed Cross to see his toes. Cross led him through to his study. More like it. *This* was what he'd expected. The weird contents of his studio apartment now took up residence in a cosy room at the back of the house Jack guessed was designed to be a dining room but was now a study. A very weird study.

'It was the dining room,' Cross confirmed, in that eerie way of his like he was reading your mind, and who knew, maybe he *was*, 'but I eat in the living room on a small table where I used to keep my television. When I had one. Can I offer you a drink?'

I could murder a beer.

'Beer perhaps?' Cross said, smiling.

'Beer would be great.'

'It's your lucky night.'

Cross disappeared and Jack heard the sound of a fridge being opened and the clinking of glasses. Moments later Cross reappeared with two blue cans of ice-cold beer.

'Belgian. Just had it delivered today. The Rolls-Royce of lagers.'

Jack stared at the can. Maes. He'd never heard of it. Cross handed him an ice-frosted glass marked with the Maes crest and the word itself raised running vertically down it. He and Cross opened their cans one after the other. That satisfying sound of instant refreshment. He poured and drank. *The Rolls-Royce of lagers; he wasn't kidding.* He liked Daniel Cross immediately.

'You sounded quite urgent on the phone,' Cross said, his friendly features clouding with concern.

'Laszlo Breyer's body went missing.'

Cross nodded, 'The eleventh of July 1978.'

Jack shook his head.

'I looked into his background as you asked.' Cross frowned.

'Laszlo Breyer's body went missing late yesterday evening.'

'What?' Cross slumped a little, not unlike a puppet with its strings cut. 'That's impossible.'

'That's why I'm here.'

Jack and Cross sat in silence for a moment, each trying to calculate the odds on the strange events each had described. Out in the night, something stalked. Something from the fires of hell. From the dawn of time. Yes. Something stalked. And it was heading this way.

4

A few miles away, inside Colin's Café, Alison Steven, a pretty twenty-three-year-old waitress, and Colin Davis, the portly 38-year-old cook, were debating whether or not to shut up shop for the evening.

The diner was a goldmine in the summer. Lots of passing trade came from the A19. Before that many had been on the long haul of the A1. It might just be a case of miscalculating the capacity of their bladders that brought customers inside, but whatever their story they came. And those who came, ate, and invariably came back. The cold dark winter nights were a different story. Tired drivers were more likely to stop at services on the A1 for refreshments than at Colin's Café. Colin knew that better than anyone and gave Alison the nod to lock up.

Not that Colin was lazy. He was never one to shy away from hard work. He had big plans. His parents *were* going to retire early with the impressive takings of the little café. They had bought it as an investment ten years ago thinking of it as a retirement package to keep them busy after quitting the hotel trade. But business boomed, Colin's cooking skills gaining fame from those who regularly took the route past. They would return not only for Colin's cooking, but for his cheeky brand of customer service. All of that meant he was soon to become owner of the diner.

The diner itself was a squat redbrick building just roomy enough to squeeze seven four-seater tables. The red vinyl and chrome furniture gave the look of an American roadside diner, though the menu was anything but. Fry-ups, bacon butties, and tea given primacy over coffee on the menu meant you could only be in the north of England. But this part of the world was deathly cold and unnervingly quiet at night.

Colin threw the keys to Alison so that she could perform the locking up duties. She was pleased. A full day at college had left her knackered. She knew Colin would pay her for the three extra hours she was supposed to work anyway. Plus she got to finish early, which meant she could meet her new boyfriend early. That was what she had told her new man Jason at the start of the shift when she left for work.

It was a plan that would never come to fruition.

As she approached the door, keys in hand, it flew open. She stumbled backwards. Colin turned to see what the commotion was. In the doorway stood a brawny, tattooed man. His eyes wild and his skin pale. He gasped for air as he closed the door behind him and bolted it, top and bottom.

Colin's mind raced. This was it. The moment he'd been dreading. He had always thought that because of the success and the relative remoteness of the place, it was a prime target for robbery. But the week had been a slow one and there wasn't much to steal. He hoped the man wouldn't be too angry at the meagre returns for his trouble. Colin wanted to set expectation levels to avoid disappointing the man, but he turned around before Colin got a chance to speak.

'Call the police,' he said in a broad Glaswegian accent, stressing the first syllable. *Po*-liss. It was Kenny.

Petrified, Alison glanced sideways at Colin for guidance. He looked as pale and shaken as she felt.

Colin replied, 'What's going on?'

Kenny pointed to the windows, 'Have they got shutters?'

Colin was too dumbfounded to reply.

Kenny repeated himself. 'The windows, have they got shutters?'

Colin snapped out of his trance. 'Yes.'

'Can you shut them fae in here?'

Alison finally spoke, her dark eyes wide with terror. 'No, you have to do it from out there.'

Alison felt angry. Angry that there were no cars on the road. There had been a few passing by twenty minutes ago, where the hell were they all now? Kenny was about to speak, but was abruptly cut off. An ungodly howl drifted from somewhere in the distance. Everyone spun to the windows trying to see where it came from.

The noise had clearly shaken Colin, 'What the fuck was that?'

That was the first time Alison had ever heard Colin swear.

Outside there was nothing but moonlit fields and the empty road.

Kenny replied, 'I've seen it. And if we don't close those shutters it'll be in here.'

Colin couldn't imagine what had shaken a tough looking Scotsman like this, but whatever it was he knew he didn't want it in his place of business. Colin strode round the counter and without looking, said to Alison, 'Call the police.'

Alison nodded as Kenny snatched back the bolts and led Colin outside. The chill of the wind sent dark, wispy clouds scampering across the surface of the full moon. Colin tried to focus on the job in hand, so scared that he didn't feel the cold.

'How many windows have you got?' said Kenny breathlessly as they dragged the first shutter over the window.

'Four. Two at the front, one on the end and one on the far side. The others are too sm...'

He was about to say 'small' when the terrible howl rose through the night. Closer now. Both men knew it as they raced to the next window. With a clatter the shutter slammed into the housing at the bottom of the window frame. They ran to the third.

'This one sticks,' Colin warned.

'Fuck's sake,' came the broad Glaswegian reply.

Both men jumped and held the shutter, before dropping back to the floor. Colin wished he'd taken the few minutes to WD-40 the damned thing like he'd been telling himself for the last few weeks. He wondered if there was enough time to run inside and grab the can. The howl rose again. Again it was closer. Kenny and Colin didn't hesitate. They jumped again. This time, with a reluctant squeal, the shutter screeched into position. The fourth was no problem when they went to the back of the building. As they came around the final corner, Kenny saw the windows on the final wall. Two mere slits at the top. Too small for a man, let alone the thing which was on its way.

Inside, Alison in her panic had run past the landline to get her mobile. She fumbled with the zip on her favourite bag when the howl came again. Closer. Her shaking hands tore at the zip and it finally gave way. She dialled emergency services and tried to explain the bizarre situation that was unfolding between the squeal of steel shutters and that approaching, ungodly howl.

'I don't know, the owner told me to call. A man burst in and this horrible noise keeps coming from outside. Howling.'

'OK calm down. Can you tell me your location?'

As the question was asked, Colin and Kenny came back in. Colin told Kenny to close the final shutter over the door. About a foot from the floor, it jammed for a second, until Kenny kicked it into position. They were shut inside. Alison wondered why she felt no safer, but she was relieved to see them. She spoke to the emergency service operator, 'The owner's just come in, I'm putting him on.' She held out the phone for Colin, 'It's the police.'

Kenny shut and bolted the door. Colin reached for the phone.

From the darkness outside, somewhere close to the door, came a growl. Deep, throaty, vicious. More lion than dog. They quickly turned to face the door. Alison dropped the phone. It separated on contact with the floor, battery and casing going in opposite directions.

'What the hell is it?' Colin said, the pitch of his voice high and rising.

'The lights!' Kenny said in a hushed voice.

Colin traversed the café floor to the switches. Instant darkness. Faint snarling emanated through the shutters at the back of the café. The three span round.

'Oh Christ, It's circling us. Is it circling us?' whispered Colin.

Huddled together, back to back, the three held their breaths in the dark. They slowly rotated trying to sense the creature's location.

'What is that thing?' Alison whispered.

'I don't know.' Kenny said, eyes glued to the windows.

'What the hell do you mean?' Colin asked.

'Shh!'

They stopped dead.

Alison's voice trembled, 'I think it's gone.'

They stood motionless, listening, in the pitch darkness.

Colin whispered, 'I'm not risking it. I'm calling the police.'

The others nodded, too afraid to realise that there was no way that Colin would be able to see them. He edged in the darkness towards the counter. The hatch in the counter was next to the longest window, the one with the sticky shutter. Just as Colin was passing it, the window exploded. Alison screamed at the incredible noise.

Splintered glass shards showered Colin. The steel shutter was bowed in the middle by a huge dent. Moonlight filtered through the thin slits at the sides where the damaged shutter had come away from the frame. Kenny ran and dragged Colin away from the window. Colin was covered in blood and either unconscious, or dead. Kenny wasn't sure which. When she saw the horrific injuries Alison let out another scream.

Kenny grabbed Alison from behind and covered her mouth. She tried to scream again when, between the gap in the window frame and the damaged shutter, she saw the beast launch itself once again. Tremendous noise rang out as the muscular creature slammed itself against the steel. The damage was terrific. Kenny and Alison backed against the door. The beast's face jutted through the opening. Snarling, bloody jaws, and piercing amber eyes burst through in frenzy. The shutter rattled as the beast fought to gain entry. Kenny surveyed the battered shutter. One more hit and it was done for.

Kenny span and unfastened the bolt at the top of the door. Then the bottom one. The monster had disappeared. Ready for another run-up, Kenny thought. The front door shutter squeaked as Kenny raised it. A foot of moonlight was showing when it stuck.

'Go!'

He shoved Alison down. She squeezed through the gap and dragged herself to her feet on the other side. Behind him Kenny heard that terrifying clatter of beast on metal and then a louder crash as the shutter gave way. He was already on the floor and halfway through when it happened.

'Run!' He shouted to Alison.

In floods of tears, Alison burst across the road. She sprinted and didn't stop until she reached the shadows of the lane opposite the café. She glanced back to see Kenny dragging himself through the gap in the door. He stopped. His belt caught on the shutter. She saw his face drop in almost serene disbelief and his mouth move: 'Oh no.'

Alison turned and ran into the darkness. She wouldn't be able to help. She was powerless. Between her sobs she heard a high-pitched scream. She didn't have to look back. Kenny must be dead. Colin, too.

The lane she ran down was flanked either side by tall thicket lit only by fleeting glimpses of moonlight that shone through scattered clouds. She could see the lights of Fulford in the distance, glowing like treasure in an old cartoon. When she heard the sound of the great creature ploughing through the steel shutter on the front door, she wondered if she would make it alive.

5

'Let me tell you everything I know about Laszlo Breyer.'

Jack thought to himself the second the words left his mouth. It wasn't going to be *everything*. He wasn't ready to share his darkest secrets with someone who, in the most basic terms, was a total stranger. Even if his taste in lager was exquisite.

Cross watched Jack drain his glass. 'Another?'

'Please.'

Jack noted that Cross still had half a glass left and that he ought to better pace himself. Cross left and returned shortly clutching two more frosted blue cans. Jack's mouth watered. Cross handed a can to Jack and sat.

Jack thought about how much to reveal. How much to hold back. He'd give Cross the basics of the case, carefully, then stop when it was getting too personal. Cross didn't need that much. Jack swigged his fresh beer and gazed at the dancing flame of the candle reflected in the heads of the ultra-realistic silver bullets on the mantle, all the while wishing he was in the countryside somewhere, instead of this museum of the outlandish in York. His mind drifted back to the previous year when summer turned to autumn.

When Jenny met Laszlo Breyer.

6

The summer had not been the best, so far. His twelve-year marriage to Jenny hadn't been a happy one for the last few years, now it was falling apart. They'd met through Tommy shortly after Jack was transferred down to Welwyn from Nottingham, but over time they began to drift, in spite of Jack's determination not to become another cliché cop with a failed marriage. Jack's response was to do the thing he did best – his job. The extra hours he'd been putting in had been a symptom rather than a cause, and Jenny would have been the first to admit it. They'd been together in Lemsford Village, a half hour walk to Welwyn Garden City and Hertfordshire Constabulary HQ (where he worked with Tommy), for two years before they wed.

The village was a small one in picturesque Hertfordshire – Jack wondered how it was somehow impervious to the drug problems plaguing nearby Welwyn. Maybe it was too small, too quiet for the types involved in that world – with its main street which branched into more minor ones but went little further – though, typically of an English village, it managed to find room for and sustain two pubs. The idea had wormed its way into Jack's thinking that a break might do the marriage good when fate intervened.

Jenny's father fell ill. He'd been struggling for some time with kidney problems, but recently he'd become bed-bound with a need for constant dialysis. With her mother already dead, the only option was for Jenny to move back to her hometown of Finchley.

Jack threw himself into his work. So much so that even battle-hardened Tommy worried for his health. The case they were working together was reaching a climax, which meant Jack's visits back to Finchley became even less frequent. One day, within the space of ten minutes, Jack received two phone calls that would change everything.

The drug problem in Welwyn Garden City was well documented and, after a two-and-a-half-year struggle, the net was finally closing in on the main supplier. They'd have to deal with the smaller dogs fighting to become the new Alpha, but it would be a huge start. Jack sat hunched over his desk in the dark empty office. He scribbled onto a notepad; phone cradled in the crook of his neck.

'And you're certain it's going down next weekend? Can you narrow it down to a specific day? A time...? No, no, that's great. Next weekend. Thanks a lot. You've made an old man very happy.' He stared into space unaware of the stupid smile on his face. It lasted a second before he threw the phone down and punched the air.

Tommy entered smiling. 'What's this?'

'That was it, mate. Next weekend. We've got the bastards now.'

Before they could absorb the news, the phone rang again. Jack beamed at Tommy as he answered. He'd been waiting for the previous call for so long that he'd completely forgotten about the call he was dreading. Now it was here. Tommy mirrored Jack as he felt the smile fall from his face. Jack slumped as he listened to his wife sobbing into the handset.

'I'm so sorry.'

He spoke to his wife, but his eyes never shifted from his friend. Tommy squeezed his eyes closed. He knew exactly what the call meant.

'Yeah, he's still here.'

Jack handed the phone to Tommy, giving him a squeeze on the shoulder as he did. Tommy nodded acknowledgement.

Things moved quickly. Later the next afternoon, Tommy ended another call from Jenny.

'Funeral's next Saturday.'

He and Jack looked at one another, both realising the implications. Jack held his tongue, in the name of sensitivity.

'Well?' asked Tommy. 'What are we going to do?'

'You should go.'

If anyone should suggest that Tommy should stay to close the case, it certainly wasn't going to be Jack. If he was lucky, the whole business would go down in time for him to make it for the funeral. *If* was sometimes a big word.

Tommy tried his best to smile, 'And let you take all the credit?'

'Everyone knows how much you've put into this case, Tom.'

Tommy nodded.

'Besides,' Jack said, 'your old boy never did like me that much.'

Tommy and Jack shared a chuckle. Many a true word spoken in half-jest.

7

Cross stared at Jack's glazed face in the dim half-light of his occult-themed living area, 'Jack!' he said, with a tone that suggested it wasn't the first time.

Jack's eyes cleared and he looked back at Cross and curled his lips into an embarrassed smile.

'Sorry. Miles away.'

'You were about to tell me about the Breyer case.'

'Right,' said Jack chasing the memories from his mind. 'The case I wanted your help with last year? The ritualistic murders, the full moons, the animal pelt – that was Breyer. Turns out the lycanthropy lead was a red herring. I think. That's another story. Anyway, he, Breyer, was killed at the scene of his last murder.'

Cross's eyebrows drew together over his dark eyes, which focussed nowhere in particular. His research must have confirmed he really was the man taken from the grave in '78. Well someone with the same name.

'He was buried in an unmarked grave in Finchley cemetery eleven months ago. Until last night. Now me and my former colleagues are trying to track down a copycat killer. He killed a guy's dog close to the cemetery, maybe for practice, and a homeless man further north.' *Further north.* 'And we think that, as it's a full moon, he'll kill again tonight.'

Cross *hhhm*'d, thoughtfully. Jack swigged the ice-cool beer and savoured the smooth liquid as it flowed into his stomach. He enjoyed a moment's silence before asking, 'What did your research on Breyer turn up?'

Cross's eyes came into focus quickly, 'My research,' he started, 'threw up some fascinating information. Through census records, I've been able to trace Breyer's ancestors back as far as the early 1800s. They showed up in York in 1831. Then again in 1841. Parents Zoltan and Eva, and a son, Laszlo. Then something strange happens. They drop off the grid, as it were, until another Laszlo Breyer – a descendant – turns up in the 1971 census.'

'And you're sure it's the same family?'

'Well I can't be one hundred percent certain, but they are the only Breyers to appear in UK census records. But that's not the strange part. It was his body that disappeared from the cemetery in Carwick in 1978. The death was shrouded in mystery. All manner of speculation and conjecture prevail, including witchcraft. And lycanthropy.'

Jack leaned forward in his chair, totally captivated by Cross's narrative.

'Rumour has it that he killed a little girl, on a full moon, and then hearsay takes over. Some say that the locals avenged her death, others that he was shot at close range by the girl's father. Whatever happened he was buried in an unmarked grave in a corner of the cemetery. Nine months later, the body was gone. I checked the date. It was a full moon.'

'Fuck me,' Jack muttered under his breath. 'Relatives of the little girl? The body snatching.' Jack ventured.

'Unlikely. It was an unmarked grave, as in Finchley, so they couldn't be sure which grave to rob. Plus the father was the last surviving relative.'

'It couldn't have been him?'

Cross shook his head as he swigged at his beer. 'He went a little la-la. Deemed mentally unsuitable for prison and taken to a secure facility for the criminally insane in Nottinghamshire.'

Breyer's body has gone missing twice. It couldn't be. The first time was over thirty years ago. How many more members of the Breyer family were there? Could it be that a young relative of Breyer was responsible for the new killings? If the copycat was a relative, it would explain the likeness between the later version of Breyer, and the man who stole homeless Mike's clothes. His train of thought was on loose rails these days. The drink wasn't helping. Maybe he should think about quitting.

Cross broke his contemplation. 'Ready for another?' he said, shaking his empty glass at Jack.

Jack gave his can a shake. Another couple of mouthfuls inside. *Who am I kidding? Of course I'll say 'yes'.*

'That'd be great, thanks.'

Cross disappeared into the kitchen and again Jack's thoughts turned to the strange case of Laszlo Breyer.

8

The chill evening did little to soothe Alison Steven's stinging legs as she raced along the dirt lane towards civilisation. Towards salvation. Her way was peppered with stones big and small, each threatening to turn her fragile ankles. To put a conclusive end to her escape bid. The dim, distant lights did nothing to illuminate the pitch-black path. Every few seconds her only source of light vanished behind dense clouds, plunging the treacherous road into desolate darkness.

The wind died to a murmur until the only sound was her own panicked gasps and the frantic scrabbling of shoes on dirt. Then, from somewhere behind her, through the darkness, rose a savage, harrowing howl. It sounded close. Much closer than when she heard that thing crash through the steel shutters of the café. Glancing up, her heart sank as she saw a solid wad of cloud moving inevitably through the night. Her heavy legs burned from the exertion but she was driven on by the image of those wild amber eyes burning from the bloody face that stared through the gap in the shutters. More than anything, she wanted to turn back to see how close that thing was.

She glanced back up to see the edge of the cloud glowing white with the glare of the moon. In a few seconds she could see. See the beast. But that meant *it* would be able to see *her*. The sound of her own feet scraping against the dirt was the only sound she heard; no growling, no footsteps following her own. Light filtered into the lane and the temptation was too much. She started to turn her head to see back where she'd came.

By the time she felt it, it had already happened. She hit the dirt track hard, knees and heels of her hands stinging from the fall, before the pain of her twisted ankle exploded along her calf. She quickly raised herself to her haunches and peered back down the lane. It was just before the light faded completely that she traced the outline of the creature's hulking figure. Not sprinting: stalking. She stifled a scream and scrambled into the thorny bushes for shelter.

She gasped for air trying to control her breathing. A cold bead of sweat trickled its way between her shoulder blades as she peered out into the darkness, her pulse beating a manic rhythm in her ears. Throbbing in her stinging hands. At last, she managed to gain some control of her breath, until there was silence. A silence so complete, it almost overwhelmed her. At least she was alone, and it felt for a strange moment like her ordeal was over. That the beast had gone. She would be rescued. Help would come from the night and transport her home. Safe.

From a few yards away, a sound crept through the quiet. A rasping, hungry breath.

She clasped a hand to her mouth and stifled a whimper. She stared into the pitch darkness of the narrow road before her. The cold wind sighed, shaking the bare branches above. Through the noise she heard small stones displace in slow, deliberate footsteps. White light from the emerging moon cast small shadows off pebbles in the road. Now she'd be able to see where it was. To try to locate the beast. Where the idea to move came from, she didn't know, she just knew the urge was stronger than her will to resist it. She carefully placed a hand forward, trying to see back along the track. Again darkness fell. She froze.

Then, from the infinite blackness, came a low, menacing growl.

She clasped her hand tighter to her mouth. The moon revealed the creature's huge, blurred outline through her tears. It was close. Had it seen her? She thought not. Once again cloud rolled over the moon, and once again she was plunged into darkness. She felt around her and placed a hand on something cold and jagged. A rock which barely fit into her fist, just small enough to lift, large enough to do damage. She grabbed and lifted it, ready to swing.

A whirring 8mm home video montage of regrets snapped into her mind. How she'd never told her parents how much they meant to her. How grateful she'd been for their support. How she'd regretted taking life so seriously, spending too much time and energy on things with little real significance. How she'd spent too much time staring at a screen instead of appreciating the beauty of the real world around her. How she was going to change things, if she ever got out of here. She'd stop to enjoy the simple things: the cool tickle of grass under bare feet; a gentle breeze on a hot day; the smile of a familiar face. She was suddenly aware of the 8mm video playing memories and wondered if this was what it was like when you died, and at that moment, the video was over and she was back in the cold desolate blackness of the alley and she knew she'd never make it out alive.

Her large dark eyes scanned the void. She leaned forward again. Beneath the weight of her burning hand, she felt the frail outline of a spindly twig, though her reactions were too slow to prevent it from snapping. She froze. The feeling of impotence enveloping her was absolute. The desolation total. Even the restless breeze held its breath.

There was no sound from the road. Utter silence. For a moment she wanted to scream out. To shatter the stillness. The silence made the coursing of blood through her veins almost deafening. It were as if she could hear the individual cells of her being vibrate. There was no wind. No snarling. No howling. That thing that had emerged from Hell must have gone. She waited a moment, the tension gently released. The rock lowered to the ground. Then, and only then, on the back of her neck, she felt a warm breath and smelt its metallic stench of blood. And from that moment, Alison Steven felt no more.

9

Chandu glanced at the address scribbled on the plain brown bag as he pulled into the estate, the car full of the magnificent aroma of spices and warm naan bread. It was the same estate which Alison had been running towards. A quiet, peaceful area sat on the edge of York. York had several estates like this. Most of the residents were middle-aged or approaching retirement. It had its share of divorced businessmen, whose wives had long since grown tired of throwing cold dinners in the dog. Every now and then there was a young professional. Single. Too focussed on work for a serious relationship. Too busy in the pursuit of money for a life of any real meaning. Chandu approached a house near the edge of the estate and pulled to a stop.

Delivering food was just to help his uncle – usually his head was full of numbers: measurements, prices, dates. All information for the latest property he was developing. That was his real passion, and even though it was at times difficult, he couldn't bring himself to call it work. The latest property had run into planning permission problems and tomorrow he had a meeting with Sonya from the council with the tiny waist and an arse like two huge dinosaur eggs stuffed into a skirt. But it wasn't numbers or even Sonia's strip-club physique which occupied his mind tonight. No, tonight, what was on his mind was the trouble.

The quiet on this particular estate had been broken three months ago when one of the divorcees had decided to put his house up for rent and three young men moved in. Working professionals. At first. As time went on, their true identities surfaced. They worked by day, but nights and weekends, they got more and more out of control. A constant menace to the neighbourhood, they threw loud, wild parties, arrived home drunk at all hours, and cared little for their neighbours. Tonight all he could hope was that the boys were out on one of their marathon drinking sessions.

The house he was to deliver to, like the others on the estate, was a large bungalow. This one in particular ran parallel to a long dirt track. He knew the track well, because about two miles away at the opposite end was the A19 and (more importantly) the café with the cute little waitress which served the best breakfasts around. The bungalow belonged to Mr Ross, a regular customer who Chandu genuinely liked (good tipper too, which never hurt).

He grabbed the brown paper bag and stepped into the fresh winter night. The waft of spices made his mouth water as he strode up the path. He checked over both shoulders before he reached the door and jabbed at the doorbell. A few seconds passed before a middle-aged man in comfortable clothes appeared beaming a wide smile.

'Evening.'

'How are you tonight, Mr Ross?' Chandu, third generation Englishman, answered in perfect English and flashed a perfect set of white teeth.

'Happy to see you, young man. I'm starving.' He mirrored the delivery driver's smile, 'How much?'

'Same as always,' said Chandu, checking over his shoulders.

'Don't worry,' Mr Ross said, 'they're out. Went at about eleven this morning. Christ knows what state they'll be in when they crawl home.'

Chandu rolled his eyes.

'Listen, sorry about last time,' said the man.

'It's not your fault.'

'I know, I just feel someone should apologise. Fucking English Defence League idiots,' he muttered the profanity as he handed the cash over. 'They'll be gone soon I hope. Think the police had a word with the landlord. Anyway, thanks again, keep the change.'

Chandu nodded and turned back up the garden path. He rounded the car and slid the key into the lock (he always locked the door on this estate since the boys moved in). Somewhere in the distance he heard something; carried on the wind from the direction of the track. A lingering, piercing scream.

He paused, listening intently. He took the key from the lock and pocketed it. Another, longer scream came up the track. Still faint, but there was no mistaking this one. It sent him cold. It was pain and terror rolled into one chilling outburst. He moved from the street to the end of the alley and peered into the infinite black. The halo extending from the streetlights only cut fifty feet into the darkness making it impossible to see, but the noise was definite.

'Oy!' came the shout from his left. He turned.

His head broke into a cold sweat as the last person he wanted to see in the world rounded a corner. In a thin white T-shirt, bracing himself against the cold was the shortest, mouthiest of the three idiots that had ruined the estate.

Despite this guy being the shortest of the three idiots, he was no stranger to the gym, but Chandu thought about standing his ground. His worry was that if he went to the deck, this guy wouldn't stop. Chandu wasn't the fittest either. Maybe this guy focussed totally on weights and ignored cardio. He looked stupid enough to do that. Perhaps he could outrun him.

They stared in silence, Chandu contemplating running, but still wanting to help whoever the owner of those terrified screams was, when, just then, the idiot's two buddies rounded the corner. The other two grinned as they set eyes on him. He stared back. Nothing new or special about them. The same as any group of clowns the world over; Tall, Venti and Grande. Dicks no doubt, but still a triple threat.

'You Paki bastard,' sneered the shortest, his face contorted into a caricature of hatred.

They were fall-down drunk, but they were also in hunt mode. They were ready to go as they strode along the street, sniggering. Shorty happened to have the biggest build, though all of them looked like they lived in a weights room. Decked in designer jeans and T-shirts, despite the freezing weather, they swaggered along the quiet street. The one on the right was tallest. Over six feet and a good six inches taller than Chandu.

'Going for a shit, you dirty black bastard?' he shouted.

He chose to ignore the slur, 'I haven't got time for your bullshit. There's someone in trouble down the lane.'

Shorty repeated what he'd said in a terrible attempt at a Pakistani accent.

'And you're going to run down that lane to help them, are you, Paki?' Shorty again.

Venti turned to Tall and Grande and said, 'I wouldn't run down that lane if I were a dirty Paki, would you, lads?'

'I wouldn't dare.' Tall replied.

'No chance,' said Grande. 'Liable to get your Paki face kicked in down there.'

Agitation tore at his stomach, 'Look, you fucking idiots, firstly I'm English, and second my family are from India.' He paused. They'd slowed, but the louts were still closing in, and it looked like it didn't make much difference to them that he was English. If he went, he might not (probably wouldn't) make it out.

But that scream...

'Someone's in serious trouble down here,' he paused again. This was it. Now or never. He stared at the three idiots. After a second, he turned to go down the lane. 'And I'm going to help them.'

'You fucking dare, you black bastard. It'll be the last fucking thing you do.'

He wasn't sure who said it, and it didn't really matter. The screaming had stopped but his mind was made up.

Chandu glanced at the movement in the bungalow window and caught sight of Mr Ross on his mobile. Ross nodded. The international signal for "I've taken care of it". He knew the police were on their way, and that Mr Ross would tell them where he'd gone.

'Don't do it.' Grande said. He could hear the taunting smirk plastered on his face in his voice.

Fuck them.

He sprinted into the alley. The three drunks gave chase, shouting after him.

He wasn't to know but after the second, longer scream, Alison was already dead. Later that evening, after a long search when Jason the worried boyfriend reported her missing, the police would find what was left of her body.

He was being chased headlong into a death trap. Only a miracle could save him.

10

Daniel Cross stared at Jack in the candlelight flicker of the study of his house. They swigged at their fourth Maes.

'What can you tell me about lycanthropy?' asked Jack.

'Well,' said Cross after a swig of beer, 'just the things I mentioned to you on the phone last year.' Jack noticed Cross's words had acquired a gentle fuzziness around the edges.

Jack interrupted, 'The dressing up, acting like a wolf on full moons, that kind of thing?' slightly surprised by his own equally fuzzy speech,

'Precisely. You said this wasn't lycanthropy?'

'Just curiosity. Where do they find out about the behaviour though? I mean, if somebody knows nothing about werewolves...'

'Aha! Good man. That's precisely the point.'

Jack realised Cross liked the word "precisely".

Cross continued, 'For an individual to display the characteristics of a werewolf, he must first understand the mythology of the werewolf. The mythos, if you like. The recorded cases of lycanthropes taking on the mannerisms of a wolf-man without this prior knowledge are nil. It's usually part of some obsession with the mythology.'

Jack nodded, but not wishing to interrupt the expert, didn't speak.

'The book "Werewolves: The Myth and the Reality" by Victor Magyar is widely considered the best on the subject. Magyar, as the name would suggest, is a Hungarian, though thankfully his works have been translated into English. In his book he discusses the main traits of the werewolf, and separates the traditional mythology from Hungarian history, from the Hollywood mythology.'

He paused; Jack sensed to allow a moment for him to speak. He didn't speak, but he was leaning forward, forearms rested upon his knees. Cross's eyes were alight, like he knew Jack was absorbing his every word.

'The main points you see in the Hollywood productions – the full moon, silver bullets, being bitten to become a werewolf – these are, according to the book, part of the reality. The full moon, though, does not last for three days. That's Hollywood's influence.

'It's not well known, but the full moon lasts only for a moment. Though on the day, and for one day either side, it appears full, so the sufferer would be unable to distinguish this small difference and therefore display symptoms on these days. There are other things. The lifespan of a werewolf is much longer than that of a man. Although nobody knows how long. The strength of a werewolf is incredible. In the book, Magyar sites one case.'

'What do you mean sites a case? A real case?' Jack interrupted.

'Of lycanthropy. Lycanthropy is very real. Werewolves...' he paused. The tone with which he'd said "werewolves" led Jack to believe the next words were to be "on the other hand". Cross had deliberately stopped himself. It barely had time to register, but it was jarring.

'Unfortunately, it was over a hundred years before the book was written. So it has been passed down and embellished by each new generation. Speculation mostly. But it's not too difficult to imagine the circumstances. From the village next to that of the author. A famous case. A werewolf was captured at sunrise, after he'd returned to human form. He'd killed forty people from the village. The remaining villagers had managed to somehow fend him off until the sun came up. He was captured, chained, and tortured. They tortured him all day, thinking that when the full moon appeared, he'd be in too weak a state to do anything. The moment the sun set, he transformed into a wolf. Though he was near death, he managed to escape. He broke free of the chains and managed to kill another twelve villagers before he was killed himself. Stabbed by a silver blade.'

'So the silver thing, that's real?'

'According to the book. I was asked once if I could provide real silver bullets.' He gestured to the case on the fireplace, 'So I had those made.'

'They're real?' Jack was shocked. Convinced they were a gimmick to add a further dash of weird to the place.

'Afraid so.'

'Afraid?'

'They cost a small fortune and as you can see, the bloody buyer never turned up.'

Jack gestured to the bullets, 'Can I?'

Cross waved at them to signal his indifference. As Jack stood and stumbled the short distance to the bullets Cross continued his narrative.

'The wolf-man in human form also displays traits connected with the animal instincts of his brain. Lust for revenge and a strong streak of jealousy are prevalent. Another thing is cell regeneration.'

'What's that?' Jack answered without looking, transfixed as the flickering candle performed a mesmerising dance from the shiny surface of the bullet he inspected.

Cross downed the remains of his lager, slowly raised a finger which involuntarily waved from side to side, then forced himself to his feet. He wobbled across to a drinks cabinet, pinched two heavy glass tumblers between the fingers of one hand and choked a bottle in the other before staggering back to the small table beside Jack. He plonked the glasses down, getting Jack's attention, and removed the cap from the bottle with a flourish. He presented the bottle to Jack. Wild Turkey. He motioned to pour then stopped.

'Ice?'

'No' Jack said in a perish-the-thought tone.

'Thank God for that. You'd have broken my heart,' smiled Cross.

He poured a healthy three fingers into each glass then slumped heavily back into his chair. He raised his glass. Then frowned.

'What was your question?'

Jack thought for a second, before both men almost shouted, 'cell regeneration!' in unison.

Cross chuckled, composed himself, then continued, 'The example in the book is of a wolf losing a paw during an attack. It ran away. Limped away,' he corrected himself, 'never to be seen again. Or so they thought. The man in the village everyone suspected wasn't seen for a fortnight, but when he did return, his hand was heavily bandaged. A week later, the bandage was gone.

The man claimed he'd injured his hand whilst cutting down a tree.'

'Plausible.' Jack said slumping back into his own seat.

'Of course. The strangest part of the story is, next full moon, the wolf was spotted crossing a river. It was shot, the body floated downstream and out of sight. The man was never seen again.'

Jack sat in silence thinking about it.

Cross broke the silence, 'Of course, it's probably bollocks. Just coincidence.'

'Let me ask you something,' Jack said, sitting up straight and serious, 'this hospital. Where they've got the father of the little girl...' Cross nodded. 'Is it far from here?'

Cross thought for a second, 'About an hour's drive. What did you have in mind?'

'Thought it might be worth paying him a visit. He could give us something Uncle Google can't.'

'It would be hard to set up. Plus, as I say, it's all conjecture. About the father killing the...' he paused, train of thought well and truly derailed, 'I haven't got anything concrete on the man. The name might not even be right. The whole thing could be poppycock. It could all be cock at its absolute poppiest.'

'So we cross it off our list. If it is poppycock.' Jack almost spat the word out, clearly not in his common vocabulary. He went on, 'What do you think?'

'I suppose,' Cross considered the idea before his thoughts trailed away. Another silence followed. 'Can I ask you something, Jack?'

Jack shrugged in a way that said, "Give me this much free booze, you can marry my mother."

'Go for it.'

'If it's too much, just say.'

'Go on.'

'It's a little personal.'

'Are you going to ask me or not?'

Cross shook his head, 'Forget I asked.'

'Christ's sake, Cross.'

'Call me Daniel.'

'Christ's sake, Daniel.'

'Or Danny.'

'Christ's sake, Danny,' Jack's eyes wandered for a second. The name "Danny" the cause.

Cross blurted out, 'Why aren't you a detective anymore?'

Jack drifted deeper into wherever his mind was.

Cross frowned sensing Jack's discomfort, 'Forget I asked.'

'Danny,' Jack slurred, 'Danny, it's fine.'

The tension lifted from Cross's shoulders. Jack was surprised to find that he wasn't just saying that to comfort him.

'It's a long story. But it's fine.'

11

Chandu Sharma sprinted along the narrow dirt track where, less than a mile away, Alison Steven lay dead. He was no longer sprinting to try and save the owner of the terrified screams he'd heard moments before; now he was sprinting to escape the three meatheads that chased him.

Chandu was a fast runner. He was at one time also well versed in distance running. He'd finished first in the 1500m at the high school athletics meeting and fourth in the county. But he hadn't run since then and was out of shape. His running days were long behind him, and he certainly wasn't used to sprinting down dark dirt tracks. Underfoot he felt large stones. Landing an inch one way or the other could mean a twisted or broken ankle, and a broken ankle wouldn't save him a beating from the drunken thugs behind. He cast an eye over his shoulder. The three men were twenty or so yards back, still shouting racial abuse. Despite their alcohol intake, they seemed to be gaining.

The bright full moon played hide-and-seek with the thick banks of cloud that rolled across the dark sky. He saw before him the jagged terrain which threatened to derail his escape. His feet danced between large stones and lumps of frost-hardened dirt which littered the path. Behind him, one of his pursuers stumbled and cursed. Now he could see what he was running on, he knew that turning back to check which one had stumbled was a bad idea. Another thick cloud drifted across the moon and the lane again fell into darkness. He thought he might be able to outrun the drunks, if the rough ground didn't interfere. What he didn't know was that he was running towards a creature so savage that in the last twenty minutes, it had killed two people and torn another man almost in two.

Sweat started to run down his face and the cold air chilled it against his dark skin. The abuse from behind was further back now, fainter, as if in a dream. Something felt strange. A threat. Not the chase. It was nothing physical; his arms pumped and his legs felt strong, despite the exertion. But there was something in front of him. It was nothing he could see; the lane was pitch dark. He could feel a presence. He just knew he couldn't afford to slow; that would be verging on suicide.

The mothership cloud finally drifted away to reveal the full beauty of the moon. The white disc reflected a glow of light to the countryside below. That's when he saw it. About thirty yards ahead in the narrow lane, it lurked. A mass. Something huge on all fours, about the size of a bear. The moonlight glowed in its amber eyes and its breath formed in clouds from its bloody jaw. Chandu slid to a halt. A sneer came from behind. Chandu barely heard it, his eyes locked onto those of the great beast before him. He edged backwards as the creature stalked towards him, snarling.

12

The chase. He loved it. All the hours in the gym weren't to look good. That was a side effect. "Just a bonus, Andy." That's what Matt always said. This was what it was all about. Having the knowledge that you could outrun and catch someone, even if you had been on the piss all day. Adrenaline took over. Pakis were usually small anyway. Weak. The weak always run. Blacks were bigger. Stronger. There usually wasn't a chase then. They stood and fought. That's where the weight room training came in. Small ones always ran. And they always caught them. This one could run, credit where it was due. He was fast. For the first time since he could remember, he thought about giving up. There'd be other times. Other, slower victims.

Then he stopped.

Andy didn't know why he'd stopped. But he had. Maybe he'd had enough. Now he was going to get the kicking he deserved. Quitter. Last time he'd told them his name. Chandu. Now Chandu had his arms outstretched in a non-threatening posture, but he was facing away. Andy was closer than the others. They were certainly bigger than he was, he was always faster. He launched himself in mid-air, right arm cocked. As he descended, he unloaded the punch, full force, onto the back of Chandu's head. He was unconscious before he hit the floor. Matt and Keith laughed. Andy landed a few feet in front of Chandu, staring straight into the eyes of a creature he could not comprehend.

'What the fuck is that?' He panted.

Matt and Keith flanked him, kicking up dirt as they ground to a halt. They knew they were in trouble. They stood face to face with a monster, and gasped for air, knowing that escape on foot was not an option. The *fight or flight* debate already over. The ten feet separating them, and the beast meant the time was almost upon them.

Andy took up a fighting stance. 'Come on then, you ugly fucker.'

Blood dripped from its jaws and matted the dark grey fur of its barrel chest. The creature slowly, deliberately moved, one huge paw in front of the other, a low growl emanating from deep in its throat. Eight feet away, it stopped.

It shifted its bodyweight. Back, ready to pounce. It growled again. The men, frozen, watched their meaningless lives flash before their eyes. The creature snarled, poised, ready to spring. Then the lane went pitch black.

Andy was used to the screams a person makes when fearing for his life. He never imagined that tonight that he and his friends would be the ones screaming. And he had never heard screams like this before. The screams when under attack at the hands of a wild animal were different. The pain makes it high in pitch. The fear makes it guttural. The combination is something Andy would find difficult to forget, if he lived long enough. It was a sound which drilled itself into the mind and took root. Rooted itself in the darkest corners and lingered, waiting for the time you least expect it to sneak upon you, knowing that when it did, the exact same emotions would flood back.

It is impossible to uproot anything without leaving a mark of what once was.

The lane was dark for a handful of seconds. Andy heard the screams of the others and turned. Ran. His legs now felt heavy. As he went, stumbling over his own feet, the wild eyes of that thing burning from the bloody charcoal face haunted him. His friends had stopped screaming and he knew instinctively that they were dead. All he heard was his own gasping, panting breath and his feet scraping from the surface he had just been chasing down. Now he was the hunted. This wasn't fun anymore.

From the darkness he felt a huge force pin itself around his legs. First one calf, then the other. He'd never broken a bone before but knew exactly what had happened. Like a ragdoll, the beast flipped him onto his back. He threw his arms up to protect his face and throat and felt the weight of the animal's strength as it tore its claws in a deep burning gorge to the bone on his chest. He fought back and the beast retreated, back into the invisible cloak of darkness.

When the moon reappeared, he saw Matt and Keith. Both were dead. Torn limb from limb by the raw strength of the creature. It was surreal. The lane had been dark for a matter of seconds, now it was awash with thick bright red blood. Andy crawled, dragging his shattered legs behind him. The left foot dragged lifelessly, flip-flopping around as it bounced from one stone to another. He felt the numbness of bone dragging on the dirt where the foot of the right leg was missing completely. *This can't be real. There wasn't enough time.* The open wound where the creature had slashed at his chest collected dust as he drew himself back along the dirt track in tears.

Andy clawed at the earth and stared at the unconscious figure of Chandu as he passed. He seemed so peaceful, not like a man who'd been running for his life, just as if he'd fallen asleep face down. The thin film of sweat on his brow the only sign he'd been running at all. Andy envied him. He despised him. He'd slept through the horror. Even if he died, he'd know nothing about it. And yet, that's exactly what he wanted. Andy wanted him dead. What he had to do now was to crawl past Chandu, so that the Paki bastard would be closer to that thing, and that thing would do to him what it had done to Matt and Keith.

He gritted his teeth and left Chandu behind. He glanced back. The beast shook a tattooed arm, though it was almost impossible to tell whose, both of his dead friends had full sleeve tattoos. Then Andy recognised a tiny detail. In the midst of the bloodied ink he saw a bluebird. It was Keith's arm. Andy realised that both of his friends were dead, and spotting this detail brought the horror home, forcing a choked sob from his throat.

The beast looked up. It turned its head to inspect the two figures before it. It watched one dragging, trying to escape and one closer, motionless. It walked over to Chandu, growling. The growling caused Andy to descend into deep, uncontrollable sobs as he crawled away, his raw legs collecting dust which burned his open wounds.

Andy knew he couldn't escape. He didn't want to anymore. Now all he wanted was to watch Chandu get what he deserved. He stopped. He turned back and saw the mess where his legs had been. The searing pain of his broken bones and open wounds faded. Every muscle, every sinew in his body was tense. The monster's snarling fell away, dimmed to near silence by the sound of his heart thumping in his ears.

Fuck it. Let me watch him die. It can kill me. Just let me watch it do to that black bastard what it's done to me. I'll die happy then. The beast stood over Chandu. It sniffed at his ear. Andy watched it nudge Chandu's unconscious hand, then sniff at his neck.

'Eat him.' Andy said, his voice low and rasping.

The beast turned and fixed its amber eyes on the man, like a judge handing down a death sentence.

'Fucking eat the bastard! Do to him what you did to me.' His voice broke into sobs. Fear, anger, frustration. 'Fucking eat the cunt!' he screamed.

A new sound rose in the night. Faint, but there all the same. Andy recognised it at once. Sirens. The police. For the first time in years they brought relief. The last time was when they came to take his dad away after he'd nearly beaten his mum to death. Once again, they brought relief. Was this it? Was he saved? The monster looked up, as if trying to source the noise. Suddenly Andy realised that he didn't want to die. Even if he would be disfigured. Deformed. Any kind of life would be better than the nothing Keith and Matt had. Maybe the beast would be spooked by the sirens. Maybe it would leave him here. His eyelids felt heavy. The labouring thud of his heart faded in his ears and the faint sounds of that blackened alley returned. Along with the sickening agony. Blood transfusions could help. Save him. They can do all sorts these days. Perhaps he'd be OK. Momentarily, he drifted into black unconsciousness. He snapped awake.

Peering along the alley, he saw the creature looming over Chandu. It snarled. Snarled and pounced. Effortless. Graceful. In one leap it moved from Chandu's body to Andy's. He screamed that high pitched, unforgettable scream. All he could do was watch. Watch as the beast disembowelled him. Watch in numb horror as the beast dragged his entrails into the lane until he felt a sick tugging somewhere inside. Then it finally wrapped its jaws around his throat. The last sound he heard was the snapping of his neck.

At the end of the lane blue flashing lights bounced off the walls of the surrounding houses. Two men off in the distance shone a torch into the inky darkness of the country lane. It was time to go. The beast stepped through the bushes and vanished into the empty, endless blackness of the fields.

13

Jack swilled the two fingers of Wild Turkey around the bottom of his tumbler and seemed lost in it. Daniel Cross eyed him. Jack's eyes refocussed, he was trying to control his breathing. He sat back in his chair, still avoiding eye contact.

'Jack. I'm sorry I asked. Let's call it a night,' Cross said. 'I've got to be up early anyway.'

Jack didn't look up from his drink. He looked down and away from Cross. But he started to speak.

'The case I was working on. The murders. Breyer,' Jesus, he wasn't even sure if it was him, 'or whoever it was.'

Jack had spent the last year focussing his anger towards Breyer. Now he knew that the real Laszlo Breyer was killed thirty odd years ago he felt empty and strange.

'I got too close. Too involved.' He continued, 'Breyer. The killer. Found out who I was. Where I lived. Who my family were.' Jack finally looked up from his drink, steel blue eyes settling on Cross's. 'He killed my wife.'

Now he was looking at Cross, Jack knew he had questions. He tried to pre-empt them and hopefully fill enough holes to stop the *really* difficult questions before they came.

'It was a beautiful day. Early winter, late autumn, but one of those sunny days where it looks like summer is back. Not a cloud in the sky. That crisp winter air that everyone talks about. I'd been up here, well, close. And I was driving back. I remember feeling optimistic for the first time in ages. Despite... well, I had some personal issues, but...'

He'd never spoken about this. He hadn't been near enough to anyone since Jenny's death to tell them. Not that there hadn't been opportunities. He had been invited by friends to this event or that one, but of course when the time came, he didn't feel like going. How could he? The stares, the sympathetic gazes, endless condolences. Sometimes he felt the stares were accusatory, even though only he and Bryan knew the truth about what had happened. If they blamed him, he could understand. *No. It wasn't my fault.*

He glanced up and realised that Cross was waiting for the rest of the story.

'If it's too difficult, Jack...'

Jack shook his head. Cross didn't have that same sympathetic gaze. Not that he wasn't sympathetic, Jack felt it was more a case of Cross sensing that everybody must have given him that same look. He was right. Jack liked Daniel Cross immensely.

'Jenny's brother stopped me at the end of my street and I knew something was wrong. It just hit me in the gut. The world seemed to fall away around me. I'd never seen Tommy scared. Ever. He was chalk white. I knew then it was Jenny.'

Cross gazed at the floor.

Jack stared back into his drink. 'My colleague was coming to visit me with information on the case and he heard the screams. By the time he got upstairs she was already dead. Bryan caught him. There was a struggle. He killed him. Jenny was Breyer's only kill in broad daylight.'

'Jack, I'm so sorry.'

Jack continued as if he hadn't heard. Maybe he hadn't.

'Anyway, she died. I quit the job. That was when I hit the bottle.'

'That wasn't your fault, Jack. She was murdered.'

'How can I expect to protect people if I can't protect my own wife?' Jack snapped. There was an uncomfortable silence. 'I'm sorry, Daniel.'

'Not at all,' said Cross. He looked at Jack and held up his glass. A thin layer of bourbon sloshed around the bottom.

'I used to have a problem with this stuff, you know?'

'Used to?' Jack smiled.

Cross laughed, 'I know, I know. I've got a handle on it now. I drink whenever I feel like it and stop whenever I don't. I drink once a month, at the most.'

Daniel Cross's brow knotted. His eyes glazed over as he reminisced.

Jack recognised the tinge of nostalgia when he saw it. 'Can I ask what happened?' Jack said.

'Of course. It was a long time ago now.'

He raised a finger from the glass and pointed to a framed photograph on his desk. A young boy, no older than six grinned back. Huge pools of blue eyes and messy straw-coloured hair. He held a bag with a goldfish gaping at him. It was at a fairground.

'Nathan. He was five. He was diagnosed shortly after that picture was taken.'

Jack wanted to say something, but what can you say? What words could possibly offer comfort to somebody who has lost a child? He decided to say nothing.

'It was a short battle. He was always a small boy. Too delicate for this world.' Cross tailed off.

He spoke without anger, or bitterness. His eyes beamed a pureness of love for his son that only a parent can imagine. He was proud that this delicate child was his boy. And he was proud to have known him. When Jack saw that written Cross's face, he realised what pure love looked like.

Cross snapped from his contemplation, 'The marriage didn't last long after that. Difficult to put into words exactly why that was the case. Some things just happen I suppose. That's when I hit the drink. Everything seemed to be falling apart. Including me. It damn nearly killed me.'

Jack gave a sympathetic look to Cross.

Cross's eyes refocussed and landed back in the present. 'The reason I say this, Jack, is that I wasn't alcoholic. I didn't crave the drink. It wasn't addiction. I was trying to process everything and didn't know how. So I drank. It was a spiral.'

Jack thought about the reason for his drinking. He hadn't drunk every day since Jenny's death. Sometimes he just slept for days. Others he would drink until all the booze in the house was gone. He'd heard of people drinking aftershave or anything they could get their hands on with an alcohol content. He'd never thought about that. He remembered the journey up here, when his mind was on the case. That's all his mind was on. He realised quite quickly that Cross was right. It was a mechanism. For coping. He thought about stopping. How he was tired of feeling like this, physically.

'You're probably right, Danny,' Jack said.

Cross sat back in his chair and finished the last of his drink. Jack looked at the last of his. Less than half a finger, if such a pathetic measurement existed, slopped about the bottom of the heavy tumbler. He stared at it for a moment. He set the glass upon the table and smiled.

Cross looked at him. 'You OK?'

Jack nodded, 'I think it's time for bed.'

'There's a spare room upstairs,' Cross offered.

'No,' said Jack, reaching into his pocket, 'I've got a room at the...' he stopped shaking the keys to check the key fob, 'Minster B&B.'

Cross nodded. 'Do you still think we should try Rampton tomorrow?'

'Rampton? Oh the hospital.'

Cross nodded.

'Absolutely, Mr Cross, absolutely,' Jack said, checking his watch. 'Meet you here at ten?'

'Very well, sir.'

Cross led Jack to the hallway, watched him clumsily put on his shoes, and bade him good night. Jack stepped out into the street. The drink had given him an extra layer of warmth, but as he regarded the cemetery walls and the black circle beneath the broken lamplight a hundred yards ahead, he shuddered.

14

Every now and then, Constable Anthony Burton got a bad feeling. The last time it was an old woman, Vera, mugged for her pension. Random call out in the middle of the afternoon. Nothing special. She died in the hospital two days later. He got a bad feeling before that call out. Now he had one again. He did not want to be here. Here was dark. And freezing. He was enjoying a nice hot coffee in the nice warm station before they got this call. After New Year's was quiet. It was always quiet and that's how it should be. Now he was getting called out and the pubs hadn't even chucked out yet. More than anything he wanted to be back home in bed with Debbie. No fooling around. Not this close to the due date. Just cuddling. Instead he was freezing in some fucking alley because the three idiots from number 26 had chased some poor delivery driver along here. He strode along the uneven terrain, sweeping the beam of his torch for a sign, for, well, anything.

From the end of the lane there had been no sign of life, so Burton had volunteered to check things out alone. Keep moving. Keep warm. That or stand dealing with the neighbours and freeze your bollocks off. Just as the idea that this was pointless crept into his head, he saw something. In the distance he could make out shapes, bulges on the surface. One larger, and several smaller ones. The light glistened as it hit the dark surface of these smaller objects. About fifty yards away he slowed. He squinted at the shapes, before reaching a shaking hand for his walkie-talkie.

At the end of the alley, Burton's partner, Steve Clarke, chatted with Mr Ross. Burton had taken the option to scout the lane and left him with crowd control. Despite the twitching curtains, the cold weather had restricted tonight's "crowd" to one.

'It's best for you to stay inside, Mr Ross. Call us again if there's any trouble.'

Mr Ross said he was concerned about Chandu's safety and that he wanted to wait before going inside. The moment he finished the walkie-talkie coughed a static buzz. The young officer went for the walkie-talkie and before he could speak a shaky voice interrupted.

'You'd best come down here, Steve.'

Burton's tone set an alarm bell ringing, faint and distant, but the word choice turned the volume up to a screaming siren. Burton was always one to follow protocol, to do things by the book, so his partner was concerned by the lack of routine displayed in the message. "Steve"? It were as if the man on the other end had forgotten he was a police officer. Now he was not Constable Burton, just Tony.

'On my way,' the young officer replied.

'What's going on?' Mr Ross asked, peering into the darkness of the quiet lane.

'Please, sir, if I could ask you to stay inside,' the young officer said sternly as he set off to meet his partner.

Burton felt the blood draining from his face as he surveyed the carnage before him. He'd got the heebie-jeebies at the end of the lane. He knew that there was more to this call. Danger hung in the air, and it was still lurking somewhere, maybe those black fields the other side of that thorny hedge. This wasn't a breach of the peace anymore. Usually he was glad of a bit of action, but this was too much. Now he *really* wanted to be back home in bed. It almost looked like an explosion had hit the narrow lane. Of the four bodies in the lane, only one was intact. The only way to recognise that there were four victims was by counting the remaining heads. A twenty-foot area was strewn with raw, bloodied limbs.

Clark approached. Sure he was out of earshot from civilisation he muttered, 'Fuck me,' under his breath, now understanding why Burton had forgotten himself before.

'Watch where you're standing!' shouted Burton.

Clark checked under his feet for evidence. He cast a gaze back at the end of the lane and saw a figure, probably Ross, talking to a neighbour. Now it's a crowd. He shook his head before turning back. Burton was stooped over the one complete body in the lane. He checked the neck for a pulse.

Steve was agog. 'We'd better radio this in.'

Burton glanced over at his partner. 'He's alive,' he said, his voice pitched higher than usual. The thought had entered his head that the unconscious man could be the perpetrator of the crimes, and that he and Clarke would gain no little reward for such an impressive collar.

If Chandu could talk, he'd tell him that the real killer had just slipped through the bushes. The real killer could be anywhere by now. He might still be watching. Standing on the other side of those bushes in that empty field. Or he might have gone towards the city. In this time, he could have made it as far as the cemetery.

CHAPTER FOUR

Jack closed Daniel Cross's gate and breathed in the cold York evening. He eyed the dark patch underneath the dead lamppost along the street and shuddered. He turned the collar of his coat up and set off for the B&B. The journey home would take a couple of minutes more than the one there, due to Jack's newly adopted Wild Turkey Walk. He didn't mind. He wanted time to try and process the new information.

He ran through what they had: if Laszlo Breyer had been killed in 1978, who was the man responsible for the killings last year? If not Breyer, then who? How was it possible that on two occasions, a man calling himself Laszlo Breyer had had his body stolen from unmarked graves? Was it some kind of ritual? To what end?

His thinking was cloudy, and the thought entered his head that he should stop drinking. It was then that he remembered the pledge he'd made to himself before putting the remains of his drink firmly on the table at Cross's place. He allowed himself a smile.

He entered the darkness surrounding the broken light. The bare branched trees above shook in the bitter breeze as the shadow fingers reached for Jack. The cemetery wall was somehow taller, more imposing. And there was also the feeling that something lurked within. He stopped; turned. He looked back at the warm lights cascading onto the street from Cross's place, expecting to see Cross himself standing there. He was not. The gentle light spilling from his front room looked warm, comforting and inviting: the road ahead foreboding. Jack sensed he was not alone.

'Bet it's that fucking cat,' he muttered to himself.

The swirling wind sent clouds speeding across the moon, the winds stronger in the higher reaches on that dark night. Around him the pavement went from total darkness, to the roadmap of branches, and back again. He turned back and set off again for the B&B.

He sped up now, sure he'd heard something moving behind him. He glanced back, looking for the cat. The street seemed empty. It was not. He was sure of it. He marched alongside the cemetery wall. Just fifty yards ahead was the corner, and around the corner the lights were better. Plus from there it was a straight walk, five minutes give or take, to the warmth and safety of the bed and breakfast. He moved faster still.

He threw another glance back along the street as he got to the corner. He was certain he'd see something. Only now he realised that the talk of Breyer had put him on edge. He glanced back along the street, but it was empty. He took another step forward.

'Whoa! Watch out!'

Jack stopped dead. He almost screamed out. He turned to see homeless Danny standing almost nose-to-nose with him.

'You scared the life out of me. Again.'

'I can see that.'

'How come you're still wandering around out here? It's freezing, Danny.'

'Couldn't find anywhere decent to doss. Wind's coming in at all angles. Anyway...'

He set off towards Cross's place. Jack grabbed his arm.

'Don't go that way.'

'What do you mean?'

Jack couldn't explain it. How could he? This poor guy was just looking for a sheltered place to sleep. Jack wanted him to go back the way he'd just come from, where he knew there was nowhere to go, just because of a feeling?

'There's nothing along there. Really windy.'

'Well, thanks, but I've tried all my usual spots. It's that or nothing.'

'Just...' Jack stopped. The cat, the full moon and Cross's talk of werewolves had him uncharacteristically on edge. Danny looked on expectantly awaiting the end of the sentence.

'Just... I don't know. Just be careful, Danny.'

The young man smiled at him, 'I will. Thanks.'

Danny strode off hunched against the wind and Jack watched him disappear around the corner. Towards the inviting warmth of light that spilled from the houses of those still not in bed. Towards that darkness where the streetlight had gone out.

Should have warned him.

'About what? Werewolves? Twat.'

Jack straightened his collar again for maximum protection from the elements and pushed on. He got about twenty yards, stopped and turned back. He ran to the corner.

'Danny!'

He burst around the corner, but the street was empty.

'Danny?' he shouted again.

No reply came. The shadows seemed darker and the road more deserted than ever before. Jack turned once more and headed for the B&B with the bright full moon for company, all the way back wishing he'd convinced Danny not to go down that road.

2

Chandu Sharma's head had settled into a percussive throb. His closed eyelids protecting from the bright light beyond. Something wasn't right. He sensed motion - driving. He was lying down. He peeled his eyes open. He came to and recognised the inside of the back of an ambulance. What had happened? He couldn't move his arms or legs. He glanced down and saw thick leather straps binding him to the gurney. He glanced over to the paramedic at his side and saw a young policeman beside him.

'What's going on?' he asked, his voice faint. 'Where am I?'

It was the policeman who replied, 'I'm Constable Anthony Burton. We found you unconscious. We're taking you to the hospital to get you checked out, and then we have some questions for you.'

'Questions? What about?'

'Your friends in the alley there.'

He thought for a second, then his eyes hardened.

'Those bastards,' he tried to raise his head, flinching as pain surged up the back of his neck. He started again, 'Those bastards aren't my friends.'

The paramedic placed a hand on his chest, easing him back down onto the trolley, 'OK, let's try to relax.'

Burton seemed to be suppressing a smile. He was surveying his dusty white T-shirt, the brightness of his eyes faded. He took a deep breath through his nose and discretely eased it from his mouth, 'Better not to say anything until after the doctors have had a look at you.'

The ambulance journey continued in silence. He lay back, his eyes half closed. He noticed the paramedic and Burton exchange glances. The paramedic looked like he had seen a ghost. He wondered what was going on. The straps over his chest; the uncomfortable silence; the exchanged glances when they thought he wasn't looking. Did he notice a tinge of sympathy from the paramedic as they pulled up outside A&E?

His eyes opened. The cloudiness had seemingly gone. 'Are we here?'

The paramedic replied, 'Yes we are. How are you feeling?'

'Better. Do I have to go in on this thing?' he said, gesturing with his head to the gurney.

The paramedic turned to Burton for confirmation. The officer nodded his approval and took his hand cuffs from his belt. Handcuffs?

'What're they for?'

Burton slipped the cuffs on, 'Safety.'

He protested as the paramedic undid the straps. 'I haven't done anything wrong. They were chasing *me*.'

Burton helped him to his feet, 'Let's go.'

He manhandled Chandu down from the ambulance and frogmarched him through the sliding doors and into the shocking fluorescent glare of accident and emergency. He struggled against the officer in protest. Not too much; just enough to let him know how he felt at the rough treatment.

Ten minutes later he sat in the dazzle of bright hospital lights. The flimsy turquoise curtain drawn around the bed did nothing to stop that sterile hospital smell reaching him. A doctor who looked like he'd not seen a bed in days gave him the once-over as Burton stood guard. The doctor was young. He had a kind face but was somehow supressing something. For a moment he thought that it could be fear.

Pausing at the back of his head, where it really hurt, the doctor said, 'Yes, there's quite a lump here. You can't remember what happened?'

'I was running,' he started.

'From the men?' Burton asked.

'Yes.' He paused. He glanced from side to side as he scanned his memory. 'No. Not from them.'

'From who then, if not the men?'

'I wasn't running from something. I was running *to* someone. A woman.' He turned to the police officer. 'I heard a woman screaming, down the lane. Did you find her?'

Burton stopped scribbling shorthand into his notepad. 'The report was three men chasing a fourth. No woman was ever mentioned.'

'That's why I was going down there. I wasn't running from them.'

Burton eyed him. 'We'll have to go back to the lane. You're one hundred per cent certain about this?'

'Yes!'

'Because if you just want us to spend another few hours out in that weather... Wasting police time is a serious matter.'

'I heard somebody scream.' The pain surged as he tensed, forcing him immediately to relax.

Burton finished the note and then looked back at him, 'Then what happened?'

'I was running down the lane, then... Then I woke up, in the ambulance.'

'You don't recall what happened in between? It's very important.'

He strained to find the answer, another wave of pain surged from the back of his head which he shook, as gently as possible.

Burton tried to jog his memory, 'You look like you're in decent shape, Chandu. You a good runner?'

He nodded. 'Used to be.'

'Now, these guys following you, according to the call we received, were pretty drunk.'

It started to come back, 'Yeah. Yeah they were smashed.'

'If they were drunk, and you're a good runner, how did they catch you?'

'I said I used to be...'

He wasn't sure how true it was. The only thing he was sure about was that he couldn't remember. Not really. Whatever had happened to the guys, he sensed that Burton didn't think he was guilty. That was why the paramedic was looking at him. The sympathy. He was a suspect for something.

'Did you fall?'

He thought for a moment. 'No.'

'Did you stop to fight them then?'

His answer was quicker this time, 'No. They'd have killed me. I'm no coward, but I'm not an idiot either. No way I'd have stopped.'

'You must have stopped for something.'

He felt his lips tingle as the blood emptied from his face at the same time an image flashed into his mind. Burton's face changed as he saw it register. The doctor placed a hand on his shoulder to steady him. He looked up at the constable.

'The others. Are they OK?'

The doctor gave the policeman a look. It was clear that he didn't think he was ready for the truth.

Burton crouched in front of him, 'Why, what did you see?'

His eyes blurred as he searched for the memory. Something appeared in his mind's eye. And it didn't make a bit of sense.

The thin turquoise curtain surrounding the bed was snatched open. A man in a cheap suit entered. Officer Burton stood and the man called him over. He watched the uniformed officer and man in discussion. The man in the suit was in his late thirties and carried an air of authority. As the young constable whispered, the man in the cheap suit looked over at Chandu with piercing eyes, then at the officer. The man said something to Burton, who shook his head. They both strode over and looked down at him.

'I'm detective Wheeler,' said the man. 'My colleague here says you saw something in the alley. Can you describe it to us?'

He stared straight at the detective, 'It was a wolf.'

The doctor and police officers exchanged glances. Wheeler looked at Burton, then back at the shaken young man.

'A wolf?'

'It was massive. Not like a wolf. More like a bear. It had blood all round its face. I think it killed the girl I heard screaming.' He cast a concerned look at Burton before looking back at the detective.

Wheeler hardened his gaze, 'Are you sure?'

He started a hesitant explanation, 'I was running from the men, and I was getting away. The lane was pitch black. Then the moon came out. That's when I saw it. Covered in blood. These eyes. Amber eyes. Almost gold.' His brow had drawn over his eyes. He'd seen something, but his mind was having trouble processing it. 'I stopped. They can't have seen it; I think that's when they hit me.' He turned back to Burton, 'Are they dead?'

Burton nodded. Wheeler stared at him.

He pleaded with the detective, 'It wasn't me. I swear. It was a wolf.'

Wheeler nodded and left the cubicle, 'Burton.' The constable followed. They hushed their voices, but he could still hear them.

'I think he's telling the truth, Sir,' said the constable.

Wheeler gave a small nod. 'Get on to the station. We're taking him there. Go back to the scene. Find the girl.'

Burton nodded and turned to go.

'And Burton,' the detective shouted. Burton stopped and turned. 'You'd best tell them to get hold of Daniel Cross.'

3

Jack turned and squinted at the door to his room. A thin horizon of light shone underneath, broken by two patches of shadow. Feet. There was another bang on the door. Jack frowned at the digital clock. 2AM; he'd only been asleep for twenty-odd minutes. He realised he'd fallen asleep fully clothed. The banging continued.

'Open up, Jack.' A voice Jack immediately recognised. 'It's Cross.'

'OK, OK.'

Jack's mind switched straight to the young homeless man. Was this somehow connected to him? A sick feeling of guilt wrenched his stomach. *Idiot. Should have told him.*

Jack reached the light switch and readied his eyes for the illuminated assault that awaited. He flicked on the light. His preparations were not enough. A tsunami of light slammed against his tired retinas. He unlocked and opened the door. Cross stood there, collar squint, out of breath, clearly tipsy, the frowning landlady at his arm.

'Danny?' Jack asked, thoughts still on the homeless man.

'Yes, it's me,' Cross replied, misunderstanding.

Jack was relieved. Despite the crossed wires, he knew looking at Cross that there was something else going on. It was impossible that Cross would even know about Danny. He cursed his scrambled thoughts before his focus shifted to the dressing-gown clad landlady.

She fumed at the interruption to her sleep. He realised that he was the only guest, and the poor woman probably didn't get much peace, let alone a free weekend. Jack felt guilty again, but this he could live with. Jack turned to the red-faced landlady, 'I'm very sorry for the disturbance.'

She turned and marched down the hall, shaking her head as she went. *There goes breakfast.*

'What's going on, Cross? Have you driven here?'

'Ran.' He spoke in breathless syllables, his lungs unprepared for full sentences.

He came on foot. He had walked the same streets as Jack. Had he felt the same menace which Jack had felt? There was something outside; Jack knew it. Again, Jack's thoughts turned to Danny. *I should have stopped him.*

'Did you see anyone?'

Head shaking, 'No.'

Jack shrugged, still squinting out as much of the hallway glare as possible, 'So?'

He panted, 'Just got a call from the police. I think your man's in town.'

A car horn beeped outside.

'That'll be our taxi,' said Cross.

When they stepped outside, the night was still. The sizzle of electricity hung in the air, tugging at the tiny hairs on Jack's neck. He was here alright, whoever he was. As they strode up the path to the waiting taxi, Jack spotted movement in the background. He slowed as he opened the door, eventually stopping, open door in his hand. Cross stopped and shifted his eyes to where Jack was staring.

Jack closed his door. 'Two minutes.'

Jack half jogged to the figure huddled by the cemetery wall. The figure was a bundle of clothes, from inside a pair of eyes peered out. The young man's face appeared.

'Danny.'

'Alright, mate?' he said, sitting up.

Jack felt around in his pocket and produced a key. He tossed it at Danny who caught it in cupped hands.

'What's this?'

'Bed for the night,' he said, cocking a thumb over his shoulder at the B&B. 'I'm not going to be needing it. Got work to do.'

'Are you sure?'

Jack nodded, 'Don't cause problems.'

'I won't,' he smiled.

'It's only for tonight,' he said, and then, thinking of the angry landlady, 'doesn't include breakfast.'

Danny jumped to his feet, 'No problem.'

Jack turned back and he and Cross got into the taxi. They sat staring out of opposite windows as the taxi pulled away. Jack smiled as Danny threw a wave at them from the gate. He'd be safe tonight. Soon he'd have the money together for the train ticket. A fresh start. For Jack, this was only the beginning.

4

Twenty minutes later the cab entered what looked like a quiet, well-to-do neighbourhood. Jack surveyed the rows of quaint bungalows, faintly aware somewhere in his subconscious of some recent disturbance: twenty-odd years a policeman, you can just sense it; like the change in the air at a pub a few minutes before a fight kicked off. The cab turned a corner and stopped at the end of a country lane in a cul-de-sac. In the street sat three police cars, blue lights flickering off bungalow walls. Curtains twitched around the squad cars which looked entirely out of place in these pleasant surroundings. Twenty past two in the morning and everyone in the neighbourhood was awake. This, however, was the last time the boys would be to blame for such a kerfuffle. A shaken young constable emerged from the warmth of the nearest car.

'Constable Burton.'

Cross approached hand outstretched, 'Daniel Cross.' They shook hands. 'And this is Jack Talbot. He's a consultant.'

Cross's authorisation wasn't questioned, and they set off for the scene.

'What have we got?' Jack asked.

Burton replied, 'Four dead. Three men, and one girl. We also have one young man who somehow escaped unharmed.'

Jack and Cross exchanged a glance.

The young officer stopped. He checked over the shoulders of the men before him, and in turn, looked each of them in the eye. Again Jack and Cross shared a glance.

Cross spoke, 'What is it?'

The young constable's eyes flickered to each man in turn again, 'He said he saw the killer. He said it was a wolf.'

The earth fell away beneath Jack's feet. Jesus. The killer had found him. Hundreds of miles of travel couldn't distance Jack from fate. They followed Burton's torchlight into the black abyss of the alley, and now, more than ever it felt like the killer could burst from the hedgerow any second.

When they arrived on the scene a familiar sight met Jack. An explosion of bloody limbs strewn; ragged red flesh torn from pure white bone. Cross wasn't expecting this level of slaughter. He gulped air to suppress his gag reflex. It worked for about five seconds.

'There's another body further down,' Burton said, shining a silver beam of light towards the A19. 'The girl.'

It felt as if Jack were watching from outside himself. That he'd wake up at any moment. Enveloped in a fuzzy unreality, Jack followed the others to the second kill site. In the darkness, as they stood over the remains of a once pretty girl, Jack pinched himself. Nothing changed. He was still here. She was still dead. She lay prone, deep red gorges ploughed across the width of her narrow back, leaving a mess of raw tissue. Jack looked at her blank expressionless face. A good-looking girl. He shook his head. No matter how many times he saw death he never got used to the loss of an innocent.

His lips tightened. He looked at the young constable. 'Well, what do you think?'

The constable's eyes widened; Burton was clearly not expecting a direct question. He cleared his throat, 'Our witness said he heard screams, which would put this murder first. Which explains him coming face to face with the... killer back there,' he shone the torch back to the other scene, then back to the girl, 'and, by my reckoning, means she came from the direction of the A19.' He stopped.

Jack concurred with the assessment so far. He pressed the young officer, 'What about the killer?'

'Nobody saw him...' he corrected himself, '*it* leave the other end of this lane which means, that it either came back along here, or left through the bushes back there.'

'Which do you prefer?'

'Back there.'

Again the torch shone on the scene of the multiple murder. Again, Jack agreed, but remained silent.

The policeman spoke, 'Some of the branches were broken near the scene there and the size of the hole fits with the description we were given by the witness.'

'Impressive, constable.' Jack said, before silence descended.

Cross looked at Jack, 'Well?'

He stopped short of saying "Is it him?" but Jack had already finished the thought.

Jack circled Alison's body, 'Same frenzied attack, no apparent motive, similar wounds. Looks like our man. So... what's down there?' Jack pointed to the A19.

Burton glanced at Cross. The expert looked pale and splashes of vomit marked his shoes. Burton's own face had washed over blank for a split second before his oversight in deduction dawned.

'Shit.'

Cross realised they'd be going to see what was at the other end of the track.

'Shit.'

Jack smiled, 'Let's go.'

As they neared the end of the dirt track the squat redbrick construction of Colin's Café came into view. Jack noted the missing front door, its shutter almost folded in half from a huge impact, and in its place a man lying across the threshold. Through the open door, the faint torchlight revealed chaotic scenes of strewn furniture, yet another dismembered body, and another larger, folded shutter.

'Fuck me,' Burton said, low, but loud enough for Jack to hear.

They peered along the empty road and crossed. Jack and Burton leaned into the café, the thin beams of light from their torches scanning the carnage, while Cross crouched over the mangled figure of Kenny in the doorway.

'What a fucking mess.' Jack muttered.

The torchlights revealed huge animal prints in the blood. Cross spoke beneath them, but Jack couldn't believe what he'd heard.

'What?'

'He's alive. Burton, get an ambulance.'

Burton nodded and barked into his walkie-talkie. At the other end of the radio came the same disbelief. Burton repeated himself, 'There's somebody alive, get me an ambulance to Colin's Café now!'

Cross was in action trying his best to stop the man in the doorway from losing any more blood. 'Jack, put your hand here.'

Jack looked down to where Cross was pressing his scarf into the hole in Kenny's back. He replaced Cross's hand.

'Press hard.'

Jack nodded. He couldn't believe the man was still alive, the only thing that saved him was probably the shutter. The worst injuries were below the waist. The wolf had probably attacked him then realised the girl was escaping, switching focus midway through the assault.

'Shit!' Burton was angry with himself.

'What is it?' Jack asked, pressing the sodden scarf into the wound in the dying man's back.

'The lorry.'

'What lorry?'

'It all makes sense now. There was a lorry. Three miles from here. All smashed up. Empty. I bet it's his.'

The A19. His taxi driver from the station had mentioned an incident with a lorry, and when he had, Jack knew it was Breyer. Now, after the conversations of grave robberies with Cross, he didn't know who it was.

Twelve minutes after the call, the ambulance arrived and the paramedics took over, complimenting Cross on keeping the man alive. Jack felt a twinge of guilt at hoping the man would survive only so he could provide clues as to the identity of the assailant. As it was, Kenny Mackenzie knew more than Jack could comprehend. The three men watched as the ambulance pulled away, blue lights dancing off the trees, but sirens silenced. Three more squad cars came down to secure the area.

Cross looked at the young officer, 'Thank you, we'll meet you back at the car.'

Burton nodded and made his way back down the alley towards the car. Jack and Cross followed, slowly.

'Is it possible this copycat of yours knew you were coming here?'

Jack had been asking himself the same question ever since Cross picked him up. 'It's possible. If he knew the case well enough, he'd have known that I spoke to you first time around.'

'You think he's here because of me?'

'He might have thought that I'd meet you.' Jack thought it unlikely, but Cross blanched a new, whiter shade of pale.

'So this is a warning?'

'Perhaps. It's all I can think of now, but that doesn't mean much. I've drunk too much and not slept enough to think straight. It could be a coincidence. It's too early to say. For me at least.' He said the words to reassure Cross more than anything. He couldn't shake the feeling that somebody could have put this psycho onto him.

'How would he know that we met in the first place? It wasn't publicised.'

Jack looked at Cross, 'Exactly.'

Cross frowned. 'Good God, Jack. Is it possible? Is there somebody who would betray you like this?'

He hadn't left the force on the best of terms with Jenny's brother, Tommy. *Was that why Tommy wanted to get you to the cemetery? So the killer could see you?* And Bryan had acted strangely towards him, although these days he was friendlier. A little *too* friendly sometimes. There were a few cliques within the station, but Jack couldn't imagine somebody trying to get him killed over loyalties. He didn't want to think about it now. He changed tack.

'This witness, the guy who survived, says he saw an animal. Let's meet him and see what he's got to say. Then we'll see if your friends can help us meet the old man in Rampton.'

5

A warm feeling of optimism filled the car. It wasn't just the autumn sun. For once I felt at peace. Problems Jenny and I had had in the past didn't seem to matter anymore. It might have been more natural to feel sadness. Guilt even. But the only thing was calm. Everything was going to be OK. For the second time that day I was approaching the house; the colours had a fullness to them, a vibrancy, as if somebody had been playing with the saturation on the television.

Then I realised. It was a dream. The same dream. I realised at the same point I always do. At the same time my feelings changed on that day. For it wasn't just a dream, but a memory, though now I can't tell you if it's a memory, or a memory of a memory. Replaying. My old life flashing before my eyes as my former self died. As I reach the end of my street, everything is wrong. My optimism dissipates and turns to dread. I feel my throat tighten. I turn the radio off and reach for my top button, surprised to find it already unfastened. I slow to a crawl when I see Tommy, his blank eyes staring under a wrinkled brow. Time seems to slow as a hundred questions flood my mind.

He approaches as I draw to a stop. I peer down the street around the parked cars as I lower my window. The end of my street around my house is wrapped in blue police tape. This can't be happening. A lonely male figure sits, knees huddled up to his chest, on one front lawn. My front lawn. He stares as two paramedics load a body into the back of the awaiting ambulance.

Jenny.

Tommy's ashen face tells me everything I need to know. One look at him and I know that she is dead.

'What happened?'

Tommy looks at me, his usually hard stare softened around the edges. I've never seen him like this before, and I never wish to again. 'I'm sorry, Jack,' is all he can manage.

'Breyer?' I say. Though it's more of a statement than a question. He nods.

The sounds of that day fade as I start towards my house. An unsettling mixture of blank faces and sympathetic gazes watch on as the car nears the huddled figure on my front lawn. My presence drawing whispers and nudges among the waiting neighbours. The police officers on the scene just stare.

As I draw closer, I recognise the huddled figure as Bryan. He stares as the ambulance passes me, locking eyes when mine meet his. His blood soaked-shirt contrasts with his pale face. I reach the police tape and stop. Bryan stands up with all the grace of an infant deer. I struggle to my feet from the car and lurch towards him. Before I can speak, he grabs my elbow and leads me away from the investigating officers. From the crime scene.

He glances over his shoulder and, content we're alone, stops. 'We need to talk,' he says.

6

At the police station in York, Jack and Cross strode along the dull grey corridor led by constable Burton. The buzz of excitement in the air had Jack's stomach doing cartwheels: the butterflies were having a real shindig in there. These were the moments police officers lived for. Bad guy out there? Bring it on. Though judging by the odd skin tone Burton's face had taken, he sensed that not everybody was excited as he was. He glanced down at Cross's sick-splashed shoes, then up at his face. It was the same colour as Burton's. Burton stopped outside Interview Room 1 and knocked.

Detective Wheeler stepped out and shook Cross by the hand. His eyes shifted to Jack.

Cross spoke. 'This is Jack Talbot,' he said as Wheeler reached out a hand, 'he's a consultant.'

Wheeler looked none too impressed.

'He'll be working with me on this case.'

Wheeler softened when the realisation dawned that any help Cross could offer was much needed.

'Come in,' he said, opening the door to reveal a tired looking Chandu Sharma.

Twenty minutes later, Jack, Cross and Wheeler sat around Wheeler's untidy desk slugging black coffee.

'We'll see what Chandu and the sketch artist can come up with, but what do you make of it?' Wheeler asked.

Cross replied, 'The young man is clearly shaken, but it is possible that the trauma of what he's experienced has caused him to exaggerate what he's witnessed. Inadvertently, of course.'

'You don't mean to say that it wasn't an animal that's done this?'

'No, no. Not at all. It almost certainly was. I simply mean that this could just be a case of misidentification. Ninety-five per cent of my investigations are simply mistaken identity. UFOs that are planes or planets. Hauntings that are old pipes and draughts.'

Jack raised his eyebrows. *UFOs? Hauntings?*

Wheeler brought Jack back down to earth. 'What do you think, Mr Talbot?'

'The story Mr Sharma is relating is very similar to a case from the late seventies. There's a man who could be a big help in this,' Cross tried to control his widening eyes, 'if you could arrange a visit?'

'A visit?'

Cross took over. 'In the seventies, a man shot and killed a similar creature to the one Chandu Sharma describes,'

Jack now felt his eyes widen. Cross had just fibbed to a detective to get what he wanted. *Full of surprises this one.*

Cross continued, 'I think if I could speak to the man, I could determine if there are any similarities between the two cases.'

Wheeler's tired face showed no expression. No emotion. Cross pressed on.

'The man I wish to speak to was taken to Rampton Secure Hospital. He's still there now. If you could arrange a visit...'

Wheeler sat motionless. Then snatched the receiver from his desk phone with such gusto it made Cross jump, 'I'll get onto it right away. When would you like to go?'

Cross and Jack deliberately avoided looking at one another.

Jack replied, 'First thing tomorrow?'

***

7

Another taxi shuttled Jack and Cross back to Cross's place. The journey was silent as both men gathered their thoughts on the singular events of the evening. In the warmth of Cross's study, they sat over steaming mugs of green tea, silently reviewing the case as they tried to unwind.

'Back at the station,' Jack said, rousing Cross from his contemplation, 'when Wheeler asked about what you thought.'

Cross nodded, as if to say, "go on".

'Why did you lie?'

Cross seemed surprised.

'You don't believe the Sharma boy saw a big dog and confused it for a wolf, do you?' Jack asked.

'You saw the mess it had made of the three young boys. That wasn't the work of a dog. Or a madman.'

'What are you saying? That there was a wolf in York earlier tonight?'

Cross paused before answering, 'We've got an eyewitness...'

'In a dark country lane,' Jack interrupted.

'Six bodies torn to pieces,' he continued, calmly, 'and the damage done to the roadside cafe. It didn't much look like the work of a dog to me.'

Jack countered, 'The mess at the cafe was significant, but we'd be looking at an animal more like a tiger in size.'

'Isn't that what Chandu described?' Cross said.

Jack stopped arguing as his eyes glazed over. 'Shit.' He recalled his previous theory silently. His "Baskerville" theory he called it. That the killer was somehow using a wild animal. Didn't this fit? He didn't know up from down at the moment. Too many variables. Too much drink. He felt glad he hadn't discussed it with Cross earlier.

Cross must have sensed Jack's disquiet. 'We'll see what the interview at Rampton turns up. For now we should get some sleep.'

After what felt like too few hours' sleep later, Jack awoke in the spare bedroom at Cross's place. Like the other rooms outside the study, this one was thankfully normal. The dark winter morning outside formed a black vertical line through a crack in the heavy curtains. In the hours that had passed three more unfortunate souls had met their end at the hands of the wild whatever was out there. Wrong place, wrong time. Life is seldom fair.

Jack found his way to the bathroom and was eternally grateful at the sight of a bottle of purple mouthwash on the sink. He took a leak before helping himself. He cupped his hands under the rush of freezing water from the tap. Without pause he threw it on his face with a sharp intake of breath. Not perfect, but it was as close to human as he was going to get this morning.

He tottered downstairs, the smell of bacon filling his nostrils, and lurched into the study. Cross was waiting, standing in rather ridiculous jogging gear.

'I was just about to come and wake you.'

He pointed to the cup of coffee and bacon sandwich sitting on the table.

'Life saver,' Jack said plopping into the chair.

Cross was unsure if Jack referred to him or the sandwich, but his demeanour made him smile.

'Polish that off, and we'll get going.'

Jack nodded and ate while Cross disappeared upstairs to change. The moment he finished his sandwich (bacon slightly overdone and crispy, just as he liked it) the two men braved the cold for the short journey to Cross's car, jumped in, and set off for Rampton hospital.

Much of the journey was taken in silence. Countryside mostly, with the occasional snapshot of peaceful village life. Jack surveyed the greens and yellows of the gently undulating fields which weren't blanketed in snow, playing the events over in his mind. Two thoughts dominated. Firstly, who was the man who killed Jenny, using the handle Laszlo Breyer? And secondly, was it possible that a colleague with a grudge had deliberately put a violent copycat killer on his trail?

'You still think we're dealing with a real wolf?' He asked Cross, half smiling, thoughts on Cross's reference to UFOs and hauntings.

Cross eyeballed him sideways, 'Why not? I just think we should keep an open mind, that's all.'

That was the only conversation until they reached the hospital grounds.

8

Malcolm Baldwin stumbled out of the shop transfixed by the newspaper headline he was staring at. It was the same shop he'd come to every day for the past sixteen years, with the exception of one week in September of 2002 when Sarah had been in the hospital with women's troubles. He'd seen everything in the headlines over the years. Positive stories like Royal Weddings. Royal Births. Sporting victories. And not-so-nice things. Celebrity deaths. Terrorism. Wars. Though none of those things had shaken him like the headline he stared at now.

He staggered back to his house, his knees felt the way they did after he'd been gardening, kneeling too long, lost in memories of happier days. He stared at the paper, ignoring the stares from passing neighbours. He stared hoping that he'd misread the headline, or that it would magically change before his eyes. Just when things were getting back to normal. Use-by dates. Doctor's appointments. DIY. Now he'd have to go through this nightmare again. He was too old for this. He'd taken early retirement last year and things were supposed to be easy. Things were maybe going too well. That's why this was happening now.

Julie, the shop assistant who'd worked in the paper shop for as long as he could remember, hadn't greeted him with her usual cheerful smile. That was the first clue. He thought at first that something had happened to her. Until he saw the newspapers. Each one carried the same story.

He drew a deep breath as he swung the gate back. It squeaked and normally such squeaks went straight to the top of the to-do list, but now he barely noticed it as he rehearsed what he would say to his wife. He slid the key into the lock, pausing for another deep breath before turning it.

He found Sarah sitting in the dining room poring over yesterday's crossword. Coat, shoes, gloves on; ready to go. She looked smaller. Vulnerable. As they'd grown older, he'd noticed this progressive change, not day by day, but in photos of family gatherings at Christmas and birthdays.

Without looking at him she said, 'Transmogrify.'

'What?'

'Transmogrify. Eight down – "Change in framing story". It's an anagram.' She finally looked up, 'Good God, Mal, what is it? You look terrible.'

She rose to stand, but he gestured that it wasn't necessary. She sunk back into the dining room chair.

'Where is she?' he asked, voice barely above a whisper.

'Still in bed. Why?'

He sat next to her and placed the newspaper on the table, headline facing down. He turned it over.

'Oh, God. No.'

The headline read "Full Moon Copycat Killer Slays Eight", with the sub-header: "Another fights for life in intensive care after attack in York".

She looked at him. He'd held it together pretty well up to this point, but the way her mouth trembled made him want to cry.

'What are we going to do?' She asked.

'We'll discuss it on the way.'

'We have to tell her, Mal,' her voice raised.

He nodded. 'Not now. We're going to be late.'

Sarah's face fell into a gape, 'Fuck the hospital, Malcolm.'

He reached for her hand and placed his over the top of hers. He sensed that she wanted to pull her hand away at first, but didn't. It felt small and fragile and he gave it a gentle squeeze.

'Listen. We will tell her, but you've waited four months for this appointment, and we're not going to miss it. We're already late. On the way to the hospital, we'll discuss the best way to tell her. She's not in any danger. Nobody knows she's here. It's just the emotions she'll have to deal with. It's not something that we can do in a few minutes. OK?'

The bedroom door at the top of the stairs opened.

'OK?'

Sarah's face had gone from shock, to fear, to understanding. She nodded.

As gentle footfall whispered from the stairs Malcolm rose and helped Sarah to her feet. He kissed her nose and smiled. She smiled back. He snatched up the newspaper. They made for the door as their daughter appeared around the corner.

'Morning.'

Malcolm smiled. Sarah too. Malcolm spoke.

'Good morning, Lucy love.'

She seemed a little shocked, 'You're going already?'

Sarah smiled, 'We're already late.' She kissed her daughter on the cheek. 'We'll be back in a couple of hours. What will you do?'

Lucy smiled at her mother and hugged her. 'Don't worry about me, I'll be fine. I've got some painting to do. You just get going.'

Sarah smiled, a weight had lifted, Malcolm watched it go. He kissed Lucy's cheek as he and Sarah headed for the door.

'Take care love. There's veggie lasagne in the fridge for later.'

'That's great. Now get going you two, you'll be late.' She smiled in a way that reminded Malcolm of a younger version of his wife. He felt doubly protective, and the urge to tell Lucy came, before the same reasoning he'd used on his wife kicked in and he thought better of it. He held the door for Sarah, and then they were outside.

Lucy crossed the dining area to the window and watched them pull out of the drive. Her mum said something to her dad, and her face became serious, then she looked up and saw Lucy and the look melted away as she smiled and waved.

Lucy waved back, thinking how her parents had been affected by her life. Her stomach fluttered with guilt. They'd never turned their backs on her. After everything. She remembered ignoring her mother's pleas for her not to marry Laszlo. That was why she couldn't tell them. They'd worry, and of that, they'd had enough. Besides, it wouldn't take long. As long as her mother had waited for her hospital appointment, Lucy had waited longer. It gave her the best window. Now she could go back. If there were the usual delays at the hospital, Lucy could be on her way back here before they knew she'd gone.

9

All Jack knew about Rampton Secure Hospital he'd seen in a controversial documentary twenty – maybe thirty – years ago. The patients were "inmates" and treated brutally; bullied or even tortured by the very people put there to help them. Grey skies brooded over the two imposing redbrick columns topped with what Jack thought looked like white stone football trophies which stood guard over the entrance. As they turned onto the road, Jack shuddered. The road to the hospital itself was long, straight, and undulating, the redbrick three-storey building behind the tall black fence seemed to challenge anybody to enter. The two-minute journey to the gate taken in nervous silence.

They approached a security gate, the road beyond it snaking to the building. At the gate, they both showed a stony-faced attendant their identification. As they wound up the drive Jack was struck by the normality of the surroundings, though he couldn't help but feel disquiet at the knowledge of those who walked within. Some of Britain's most infamous. The ones that stole the headlines. *Like Breyer.*

Cross finally broke the silence, 'Rampton Hospital is home to around three hundred and fifty patients. Of these, two hundred and eighty are convicted criminals. It is home to some of the most dangerous criminals in Britain. Mass murderers. Child killers. Serial killers. Serial rapists.' He let the words sink in before adding, 'Keep your wits about you in here.'

Cross pulled up in the car park, already filling up with the cars of the two thousand staff employed here. Both men leaned towards the windscreen to take in the full height of the sinister redbrick structure. The white grill windows reminded Jack of Belgian waffles. The black fence, twenty feet tall, solid at the bottom, a mesh at the top, added to the gloomy atmosphere. CCTV cameras mounted on tall poles surveyed every corner. It was clear somebody wanted these people to stay exactly where they were. They sat for a moment, just looking. Jack knew that Cross was as nervous as he was.

'Well...' Said Cross drawing a deep breath. He reached for his door handle and paused.

Jack reached for his handle and opened the door, Cross finally opening his. Gusts of wind grabbed at them as the crossed to the first of two huge revolving doors. Go through the first and you're beyond that fence. You're inside. Jack felt the heavy oppressive difference immediately. He couldn't wait to get out of here.

They stepped through a revolving door and into a short passage with dark blue carpeting which led to the next revolving door. On the other side the white walls would have given the place a lighter feel, if not for the airport style security.

A squat guard in an all-white uniform adjusted his dark-rimmed spectacles and cleared his throat. He passed deep grey plastic trays over, the light playing on the fine blond hair on his bare forearms as he did.

Cross addressed him, 'I'm Dr Daniel Cross and this...'

'I know who you are. We've been expecting you. You'll need to leave some items here.'

He pointed at a list of forbidden items, from the obvious sharp objects and glass, to the less obvious; mobile phones, and maps of the local area. One item caught Jack's eye.

'Chewing gum?' He offered to the guard, an attempt to warm the frosty atmosphere.

'Same as Blu-tac.'

'Blu-tac?'

'And Sellotape.'

'Why aren't you allowed chewing gum?'

'Could be used to get an impression,' He said. 'From a key,' he added, in case they'd missed it.

'And the Sellotape?' asked Cross.

The guard looked Cross dead in the eye, 'Could be used as a garrotte.'

So much for ice breaking.

Jack was slightly embarrassed at having nothing to leave. Cross left his car keys and both men headed a short distance to a second man who was staring a hole in his watch. This one as welcoming as his colleague, in blue shirtsleeves and grey trousers. His black hair flecked with grey and thinning.

'I'm the Ward Manager.'

Cross held out a hand, which was promptly ignored as quickly as it was offered. Instead the man about turned.

'Follow me.'

He led Jack and Cross through Rampton's labyrinthine corridors, shoes clipping dully off the same thin, dark blue carpet that seemed to cover every inch of these notorious halls. Jack did everything to keep pace with the anonymous manager and Cross, glancing up at every single CCTV camera they passed, expecting to hear the agonised screams of those kept within this strange place. But there were no screams. Just an ominous, unsettling silence. A silence broken only by their footsteps and the occasional chirp of the card key passes which sat beside every door they passed through. Yes, Jack wanted to get out of here as soon as possible.

The Ward Manager stopped abruptly outside a door and used his key pass for the final time. The electronic lock chirped and he swung the heavy door open.

'Please.'

Cross entered, Jack at his heels. The only furniture within its bright white walls a table and four chairs. Cross turned.

'Will somebody...?'

He was cut off by the door slamming. They raised eyebrows at each other at pulled up a chair facing the door. They stared at the opposite wall, Jack trying his utmost not to look at the camera that stared at him. Jack was about to speak when he became alert at the sound of footsteps in the hall. The door swung open and an officious looking man, tall, thin, draped in a suit that matched the dark blue carpets, stood before them. He pressed his glasses back onto the bridge of his nose before sitting across from Jack.

'I'm Dr Knowles.'

Before Jack could tell the doctor how pleased they were to see him and that they were very grateful to be given this opportunity, he continued.

'I'm told you're to be given full access to one of my patients.'

'Mr Charlie Sweeney,' said Cross.

Knowles shifted his keen eyes between Jack and Cross as he spoke. 'What is it exactly that you wish to ask him?'

'It's in connection with the killing of Laszlo Breyer.'

Knowles didn't respond. He waited for Cross to continue, but the uneasy silence spurred Jack into action.

'In 1978 Mr Sweeney shot and killed Laszlo Breyer. Mr Sweeney didn't go to prison. He came here. Before the crime, Mr Sweeney had a few minor transgressions on his record, but nothing in the line of murder. Something happened. We believe he saw something that led to his state of mind. So we'd like to try and find out what that is.'

Knowles was unimpressed. Jack sensed the discomfort in the doctor.

Cross's tone of voice suggested he felt the same, 'Has he ever spoken of what happened?'

'Never. He flat refuses. He becomes very agitated when pressed on this.'

'That may be the case...' said Jack.

'My sole purpose here is to protect the welfare of my patients.'

Cross – 'We respect that, but lives could be at stake here, doctor.'

'I've been informed of the seriousness of the situation. But I must tell you, if, at any time, I sense my patient is too distressed, or displays any overt signs of being so, then this interview shall be called to an immediate halt, and you shall be escorted from the premises. Are we clear?'

Jack rubbed his forehead to hide his disbelieving eyes as Cross replied. 'Certainly'.

'Good. Then we can start,' he said, rising from the seat.

He disappeared through the door. Jack eyed Cross. Cross shrugged. His circus. His monkeys. It felt like they were in the headmaster's office. Again they sat in silence. It was a full five minutes before footfall echoed back down the corridor, but this time it wasn't just one pair of feet. Knowles stood holding the door open as a bear of a man in white uniform led a frail, pathetic looking creature into the room.

Charlie Sweeney trembled as the guard gently lowered the old man into his seat. Sweeney was in his late sixties, with thin white hair swept back from his old features. He appeared closer to his nineties, such was his frailty, and Jack wondered if the incident in '78 had led to the swift deterioration of the fragile man before him.

Knowles eased himself into the chair alongside Sweeney. In a raised voice he said, 'These gentlemen would like to talk to you, Mr Sweeney.'

'You don't have to shout,' came the reply in a thick Yorkshire accent. The body was frail, but the mind inside was alert. 'I'm not deaf and I'm not daft.'

'We'd like to ask you a few questions, Mr Sweeney.'

Jack spoke as if he were addressing anybody, keen to get the old man onside.

'About '78, no doubt.'

The old man's mind was sharp indeed.

'That's right. My name's Jack Talbot and this is Dr Daniel Cross. In your own time, Mr Sweeney, can you tell us what happened?'

The old man fell silent and the only sound in the room was the shaking of his scrawny hand in its sleeve. His faded eyes glazed as he called the memory to the front of his mind. He stared at the floor. 'Nobody's asked me about that for a long time.'

Knowles turned and fixed eyes on Jack. Jack stared at Sweeney. Whatever had happened last time, Jack knew if it happened again their interview would be over. Jack could only hope that time had dulled the edge of the feelings. For the first time since he entered the room Sweeney looked up.

'If you want to know, I'll tell you.'

Knowles's mouth fell open. He quickly closed it again clearing his throat, though his reaction had done nothing to change the heavy atmosphere that seemed to fall as the old man spoke.

'I've bottled it up for long enough. And I suppose I because somebody's at it again.'

Jack nodded, 'That's right.' *Very sharp indeed.*

'If you reckon it'll help, I'll tell you.'

Jack felt the hairs on his neck rise, and judging from Cross and Knowles's reaction, they had felt something similar. The old man paused for a second, recalling the moment. Jack drew his chair closer to the table, but quickly sat back, not wanting to pressure the old man. Finally, he spoke.

'It were summer. A nice one at that. Anyway, the days were long so Linda, that's my daughter, well she loved it. I could never get her in the house of a night. I spent most of the day working, so I wouldn't see her for hours. It were normal. There were never nobody about. It weren't something you thought about back then. You know, you could leave your door open. This one night, not long after sunset, so it woulda been about half nine, I'd just managed to get her back to the house an' she was crying. She loved being out, but there were never any hysterics from her. So I asked her what was wrong. She said one of the sheep was stuck. She was upset at the sight of blood. I told our lass that I'd have to check it out. A month before, I'd lost three sheep.'

'Lost?' asked Jack.

'They'd been attacked. Wild animal. Maybe,' it came out *mebby*, 'a big dog or something.' *Summat*. 'It had been nearly a month since, so I'd about forgotten it. Anyway I grabbed the shotgun just in case, and asked her to show me where this sheep was.'

'You took her with you?'

Jack cringed at the insensitivity of his question. The old man stopped in his tracks, just for a moment, but it had registered with him.

'This one had escaped she said. It weren't in the field. She were begging me to help it.'

He stopped, replaying the moment. Jack knew what he was thinking. If only he'd told her to wait until morning. All for a fucking lamb. Wrong place, wrong time. Sweeney drew a deep breath that trembled as he fought back the tears.

'So off we went. It were dark, but the moon lit up the fields and it was a warm night. I remember that. I can still see the long grass swayin in the breeze.

'We walked for about ten, fifteen minutes and found this sheep. There's a stream down that way, trees along the banks. It'd got its leg stuck between some rocks, don't ask me how. I set the gun down and started to move the rocks. This lamb made a right row, it did. Anyway, I finally got it out, and...'

The old man stopped. His hand was shaking quite violently now. A black cloud descended in his mind and his bushy eyebrows twisted into a deep frown. Jack, Cross and Knowles sat transfixed. Jack noticed that he and his colleagues had all leaned forwards. It was clear from Knowles's face that he'd been waiting a long time to hear this story.

'I turned round, expecting Linda to be happy I'd got this lamb free, and... She was gone.'

His eyes darted, trying to comprehend the memories.

'At first I thought she was hiding. Playful thing, she was. Always messing about. It had been a long day,' he blinked tears down his shirt, 'and I weren't in the mood. I just wanted to get back home. I was about to shout her, and I heard this scream.'

His voice raised shrill.

'I can hear it now. Pure terror. I grabbed the gun and ran towards it. I shouted for her. The screams carried on. It were coming from down the stream. I ran. I ran so fast. Shouting "I'm coming, Linda, I'm coming". Then she stopped. I knew then, that was it. I got to her and...' He stopped. His tone had suggested he still couldn't believe what had happened.

Just as Jack thought the story had finished, Sweeney went on, 'I was too late. It had ripped her throat...' He swallowed a deep sob, 'It had ripped her throat out.'

Jack leaned forward in his seat, 'What had?'

'So I shot it,' he sobbed. His face twisted into a snarl.

'It's OK Mr Sweeney,' said Knowles.

'What did you shoot?'

'I fired, hit it in the chest. The noise it made. I'll never forget it.'

'What was it?' Cross asked.

Charlie Sweeney's mouth was a snarl, but the eyes were wide under the furrowed brow as if, thirty something years later, his mind still couldn't make sense of what had happened.

'It growled. Looked straight at me,' he sprang to his feet sending his chair clattering against the wall. 'Those eyes.'

The guard leapt at him, grabbing him in a bear-hug from behind. Jack, Cross and Knowles all jumped to their feet.

Sweeney's voice trembled as he yelled, 'I shot it again. In the face.'

'That's enough, Mr Sweeney!' Knowles hit an alarm as the guard struggled.

'What was it?' Jack asked.

'What did you see?'

Sweeney cried out, but his words were swallowed in the commotion. His whole body tensed, then went limp. He sobbed, held in the guard's vice grip.

His eyes opened wide and he tensed again. He shouted. 'It was twitching. I reloaded. Shot it again. And again. A wolf.'

Footsteps of half a dozen sprinting down the hall. They burst in.

'Take him away,' said Knowles.

They dragged the frail old man. He kicked and screamed. Sweeney's eyes glazed with mania, 'He changed.'

Cross followed, 'What do you mean, Charlie?' He was manhandled to the floor by the bear-guard. 'Changed how?' he shouted.

'That's enough!' Knowles screamed.

Knowles blocked the door off as Charlie Sweeney's voice faded into the corridors. His chest rose and fell rapidly as he glared at Cross.

'I think you had better leave.'

Cross stood and straightened his ruffled shirt.

'Don't worry we're going,' Jack said leading Cross from the room. Knowles followed and escorted them to the entrance in silence.

'I shall report this.'

Cross wanted to reply; Jack got there first. 'You do whatever you see fit, Dr Knowles.'

Jack nodded a farewell. Knowles just glared. Small and officious but backed by two huge guards. The two men crossed the short distance to the car in silence, watched all the way by Knowles. They sat in the front seat, Cross clutching the keys.

'What was that?' Jack asked.

'You heard the man. He saw the same as Chandu Sharma. A wolf.'

'That man... That *old* man, was clearly disturbed.'

'By what he saw, Jack. He was fine before the incident. You heard him yourself. He changed.'

'Are we talking about the same thing here?'

Cross didn't answer. He didn't need to. It was clear what he was driving at.

'Come on, Cross. Werewolves?'

'Have you got a better suggestion?'

Daniel Cross was a quiet, unassuming man, which made this passionate outburst all the more powerful.

'Well?' He pressed.

'It's insane.'

Jack thought to himself. Telling Cross about what he'd seen would mean telling him everything. Why Jenny was dead. Why her brother Tommy hated him. Why he thought that somebody with a grudge could have put the copycat killer on his trail. It would mean facing his past.

'Jack,' Cross said, calmly.

Jack looked at Cross. He knew he'd have to tell him eventually. Face his demons. Acknowledge his guilt. He breathed deeply.

'Remember I told you that Breyer, or whoever it was, killed my wife?'

<u>CHAPTER FIVE</u>

The station in Welwyn was buzzing. Only when faced with death did this place really feel alive. If not for the 'wanted' posters surrounded by pictures of leads and associates, and 'missing' posters ringed with suspects and persons of interest dotted around the walls, the place could normally pass for a regular office. Now phones ringing off the hook, excited chatter, and the lack of banter meant that it was go time.

Jack sat on his messy desk facing Tommy, 'It's going to be weird without your smiling face around here.'

Tommy was facing the other way, and though he was trying to hide his feelings, Jack could see Tommy's cheek swell in a smile.

'Bollocks.'

It was two months to the day after Jenny and Tommy buried their father. Jenny was still alive. Tommy had just had his transfer back to Finchley signed off and was packing the last of his stuff from his desk ready to go. Oh, and he didn't hate Jack's guts.

He was taking the piss, but even though he was a man of few words, Jack really was going to miss Tommy's presence at the station. They'd been partners for five years, that wasn't something you forgot in a hurry. It was also good to joke a bit to lighten the mood. Six days had passed since the first murder of what would come to be known as the "Breyer Case", and by now, the killer had moved north and killed again, then disappeared as quickly as he'd turned up. Jack Talbot was lead detective in Hertfordshire, and his posting on the case would lead to the death of his wife Jenny in two short months.

The large cardboard box looked smaller in Tommy's arms as he lifted it easily from the desk.

'Well,' he said, finally looking over at Jack, 'that's me.'

Jack felt a ping of sadness. He'd joked it was the "end of an earache" since Tommy's transfer came through, but now it was real and he was actually leaving, Jack felt he was getting further away from Jenny, too. While Jack was never happy that horrible crimes were committed against the public, it was a welcome distraction from the mess of a private life he had. The visits back to Finchley, and Jenny, had become less frequent. When they did happen, he spent the nights in the cramped spare room. He mentioned none of this to Tommy, but Jenny never got over the fact that Jack had missed their father's funeral. Yes, it was fair to say that the Breyer Case was a welcome distraction. It was also a difficult case with few clues.

Jack tried to keep it light, 'Can I carry your books?'

Tom shook his head, feigning exasperation, 'Come on, nobhead.'

He was gesturing outside with his head. Then, Jack's phone rang.

'I'd better get that.'

Jack answered the phone, and after a minute of talking, Tommy got bored, dropped his box of belongings with a thud onto his old desk, and slumped into his chair one last time.

Jack put the phone down and leaned around the cardboard box to talk to his former partner, 'Gold, Tommy. We've struck fucking gold.'

Tommy smiled back, '*You've* struck gold. I'm out of here, remember?'

'Come on. One last job. For old time's sake.'

Tommy's smile widened. 'What have we got?'

Jack grinned. 'The appeal we put out. Not only did somebody see him,' said Jack, jumping to his feet and slinging his arms into his jacket, 'they've got him on CCTV.'

They had appealed to the public to call in with any information of people acting strangely near the date of the crime. Jack's witness had somebody on tape the morning after. It was a gift from the Gods.

Tommy jumped up, 'Fuck off. Where?'

'Petrol station, just outside Stevenage.'

'Let's go.'

Tommy grabbed the navy suit jacket he'd thrown over the back of his chair a minute before, and they raced outside, without the box, for one last adventure.

2

Within the hour Tommy was standing next to Jack, staring at the gormless attendant at the petrol station. The pimply youth, Jason, according to the askew name tag, peered at Jack from beneath the curved peak of his standard issue baseball cap. He seemed happy just to have the time off work and let the manager cover for him while he spoke to the detectives.

'We nearly got rid of the tape. We tape over them after a week.'

'So it was last Wednesday?' asked Tommy.

'Yeah, it was Wednesday, and I remember this guy being proper weird. His clothes didn't fit proper and he seemed well shaky.'

'Anything else you noticed, apart from his behaviour? Any unusual features?' Jack asked, in a shameless display of what would be known in a courtroom as "leading the witness".

Jason took the bait. 'Yeah. Definitely. His eyes. He had mad eyes.'

Tommy chipped in, 'Can you define "mad" for us, Jason? I mean, was he angry?'

Jack fought a smile at Tommy's teasing of the boy.

'Nah, man. Not mad like angry. Mad as in, weird.'

Jack again – 'What was weird about his eyes?'

'The colour. They was like, gold.'

'Very good, Jason. Anything else?'

Jason beamed a set of crooked teeth at the comment. Jack guessed a young petrol station attendant didn't get many compliments.

'Yeah,' the young man said, 'he was five foot ten.'

'Exactly five ten?'

'Yeah,' Jason broke into a proud smile, 'Five ten exactly.'

'How can you be so sure?' asked Tommy.

Jason's chest puffed out, 'Coz the posters next to the door, I put the tops at six feet, and as he walked out, I clocked he was an inch under, then with his shoes off...'

'Nice work, Jason,' Tommy said, genuinely impressed.

Jack thought the boy would explode with pride.

'Thanks very much, Jason, you've been a big help,' said Jack.

Jack and Tommy strode out of the petrol station leaving young Jason with a smile as wide as it was unattractive, or as Jason himself might put it "proper beaming". Jack clutched the VHS tape with WEDNESDAY printed along the edge.

'Now all we have to do is dust off the video player.'

They sped back to the station and went straight into the dark, cramped video room and wound the tape forward to 8AM. They'd forsaken the usual coffee and biscuits. It wasn't uncommon to spend hours in here. The shoddy heating, uncomfortable plastic chairs. Jack hated it. But today was different. They'd got good info. If it was as good as Jack hoped, they'd be done in a few minutes.

'Right, our boy Jason says it was just after eight so any second now...'

Jack stopped in his tracks as, on the grainy video before them, the doors slid open and a man with shoulder length hair and ill-fitting clothes walked in.

'Pause it!' said Tommy.

Jack hit the pause button. 'Fuck me, it's perfect,' he said in a low voice.

'Could be his passport picture,' Tommy replied.

The very moment Jack had hit pause, the man in shot had turned his amber eyes and looked straight into the camera.

3

Jack sat in the dark of the station, staring at Tommy's desk. He had scoured the case files with a meticulous eye and still unearthed nothing new. He needed another break. After the CCTV revelation from the petrol station the case had developed fast, despite the killer dropping off the radar. The murders had gripped the nation: Full Moon Killer, murders six in two nights, three in Hertfordshire and three in the Harrogate area, then disappears without a trace; not something the great British press won't squeeze for every inch of column they can get. The Welwyn branch had sent a copy of the tape to the police in Harrogate and the still image of Breyer gazing down the lens went nationwide. The phones had been red hot ever since, but sadly with false reports made by those with a grudge against neighbours who bore a passing resemblance to the man in the video. Jack Talbot was running all of this through his mind when the phone rang.

His hair stood on end. He couldn't explain it, but he knew straight away that the call was key to the whole investigation.

'Detective Talbot?' A deep female voice.

'Speaking.'

'I've got a lady on the line who says she has information regarding the CCTV picture.'

'You didn't take any details?'

'She insisted on speaking to you, detective,' she said.

'OK, put her through.'

The line fell silent. Jack thought the call had been disconnected.

'Hello?'

'Detective Jack Talbot?'

The voice was English, though something was a little off. Jack struggled to say what it was. He hoped to finger it as the call went on.

'Speaking.'

'I'm calling about the man on the CCTV. The killer, I know him.'

Misplaced article. Slightly elongated 'i' in 'killer'. Hit the aitch in 'him' a little too hard.

'May I ask who I'm speaking to?'

'My name is not important, but if you want to catch this man, you have to go to the North Yorkshire moors.'

'North Yorkshire moors?'

Jack squeezed the phone to his ear with his shoulder and tapped the info into Google.

The voice continued, 'There is a wood. Carr Wood. To the north there is a house...'

Jack zoomed into the map. Trees like broccoli stretched across the barren remoteness of North Yorkshire. There were lots of woods. It could be anywhere. Then Jack spotted it. Carr Wood, and to the north, as the voice said, there was a house.

'The woman who lives at that house can tell you about the man in the CCTV. His name is Laszlo Breyer.'

'How do I know this isn't...?' Jack didn't bother to finish the sentence to a dial tone.

He replaced the receiver and sat silently. Was this it? Was this how he caught the Full Moon Killer? The whole thing could be a wild goose chase. There were more than enough members of the public willing to give the police the run around. Some clown in the North-East of England mocked the police for years pretending to be the Yorkshire Ripper. His little prank cost three women their lives as Peter Sutcliffe took full advantage of the averted police eyes. There again, what if it wasn't a prank? Something about the call felt real. Maybe that's what Jack wanted to believe. This person had asked for him in particular. The female voice had lured him into a false sense of security, but it didn't lessen the chance of a set-up. Either way, he couldn't justify a three-hundred-mile round trip on a hunch.

He stared at the screen and the low-res image of North Yorkshire. Something caught his eye. At first, he was unsure if it was some sort of fault with the picture resolution. He scrolled and zoomed. It wasn't a fault. Close to the cottage in the woods was a clearing. And inside, what looked like a small building. Perhaps a cabin. If you're on the run from the police, an almost perfect hiding place.

The next day, he walked into his boss's office and asked for leave, using his disintegrating marriage as a valid reason. Twenty minutes later, he was on his way to Carr Wood.

4

The journey to Carr Wood was four hours first of dull motorway, then repetitive dual carriage way, and finally snaking country road, to the incessant beat of windscreen wipers.

He felt guilty for using his crumbling marriage as an excuse for leaving the office,

Why? It's not like she'd care.

but if this panned out as he hoped, it would be more than justified. In the back of his mind a nagging voice told him that it could be a set-up. He also couldn't help but feel that the woman on the phone and the woman living at the house near Carr Wood could be one and the same. The state of his private life saw Jack including ever-increasing risk in his decision making. During the minutiae of daily life, it mattered little. It is only when the cold hand of death reaches out from the shadows that we acknowledge our own mortality.

Swollen dark clouds hung in the grey skies over the imposing hills of Yorkshire's North Riding and swathes of woodland spread down the hillside that rode the horizon. He peered through huge raindrops that burst on the windscreen between the dull rhythm of the wipers. As the car wound up the rolling tarmac of the Sutton

Bank Road, larger and larger trees loomed alongside, as if to warn the lone traveller that this was the gateway to isolation extreme. As Sutton Bank turned into the oddly named Main Street (Main Street of what, exactly?) the trees to the left fell away revealing an endless expanse of viridescence.

For five miles the road weaved out of the official boundary of the North York Moors, but once it snaked back in, it switched from two lanes to one, road markings to cattle grids, civilization to isolation. The deep green rolling hills had a melancholic beauty of their own, but they also cast a warning. Jack shuddered at the thought of a break down. Being alone here would have a suffocating fear, being lost would mean tragedy.

He eased on the breaks and drew to a stop. It had been over an hour since he'd seen the last car. The last signs of life. He reached for the road map which sat in the passenger seat. The GPS had given up a long time ago. His mobile phone was rendered an elaborate timepiece. No missed calls. No messages. No signal. Neither use nor ornament. Not that it mattered; the battery was a few hours from exhaustion. He was truly alone, with only the bleak surroundings for company. As he ripped a bite from his service station sandwich, he studied the map. Twelve noon now, another hour to the house; half by car, the rest on foot.

Jack pulled over at the north edge of Carr Wood. The patter of rain on the canopy of leaves rose as he opened the door and ran to the boot of the car. He pulled on his poncho, snatched up his leather carry-all, locked the car, and set off. He knew that sticking to the north edge of the trees would see him eventually arrive at the farmhouse on the image he'd seen. But he was heading somewhere else first.

In the images he'd found on the Internet it was the cabin that caught Jack's eye. Close to the house. Through the woods, about forty minutes on foot, in the centre of the clearing. If this Breyer character was hiding out anywhere, it was there.

The dirt track was surprisingly well worn for such a remote place and the top layer had turned to a sticky brown slush. Rain fell through the leaves overhead and gently tapped out a staccato beat on the hood of the poncho as Jack trod the path, each step feeling more likely to suck his shoes off altogether. He knew that if Breyer was there things could get hairy pretty quickly. He wished he'd brought something other than lock picks to defend himself and scanned the ground for a stick large enough to offer protection. The adrenalin levels surged with each step: every step forward moving him further from safety and closer to danger. It was exactly the time he checked his watch thinking he'd gone too far that he spotted something through the trees.

Thirty feet by fifteen and surprisingly well maintained – a cabin. Somebody had been here all right. Recently. He reached down and lifted the thick wet branch that lay at his feet. He was careful now not to make a sound. He stalked slowly to the cabin, aware now of the rising sounds of rainfall on the hood as he left the shelter of the trees and entered the clearing. Feeling vulnerable and exposed, he lowered the hood so he could see all around. He knew he'd have to circle the building as there were no doors or windows at this side. His silent strafing had him up to the cabin wall. He raised the branch, ready to lower it with devastating effect, should the need arise. Upon reaching the far side he saw a small padlocked door, large enough for him to stoop through, and next to it a small window. He moved quickly to the window only to find it shuttered from the inside. Moving back to the door he now had to deal with the padlock.

As with the rest of the cabin, this too was surprisingly new. Somebody had been here very recently, and if the cottage did belong to the killer, then this cabin was surely his. Somewhere behind him a crow cawed a throaty salutation, or warning, and took off through the trees. He silently set the branch and briefcase down and reached into his pocket for his lock pick, aware that the killer could be watching. He got to work, shuddering and stopping when he made the slightest noise. He'd used the lock picks maybe three times since he got them for a birthday gift from Tommy five years ago. Tommy got them as a bit of a joke, but Jack never felt more like a detective than when he was using them. He flicked the metal tongs inside the lock for a moment until there was a satisfying click. He was in. He pocketed his tool and grabbed the branch. Better safe than sorry.

He flung the door open and burst inside. He was greeted by nothing more than a musty smell and cold darkness. The room was fifteen feet square with a low wooden table against one wall and a rickety old bed against the far wall. The tiny window was less than two feet square, clumsy shutters closed across it. He reached for the shutters and gently swung them open. The dim light revealed a chess board on the table and worn acoustic guitar beside it. The window offered little in the way of light, but just enough to expose something in the far corner, opposite the front door. A second door. Jack peeked outside and, sure that he was alone, headed towards it.

He placed a hand flat onto the rough wood of the door and gave it a shove. Stepping inside he stopped dead and gasped. He took another step and reached out a hand to touch, unable to trust his eyes. Inside the windowless room, reaching all the way from the far wall to the door, from floor to ceiling, was a heavy, black, cast iron cage. It lay empty save for the heavy shackles inside. His mind boggled at how whoever it was got the damned thing here. It must have been assembled piece by piece and then the cabin built around it. It looked like something from a travelling circus. Then it hit him. The savagery of the killings. It appeared they were carried out by an animal. Possibly a huge dog. This was where he kept it. The first real clue in this bizarre case. It also meant that the cottage almost certainly belonged to the killer, and as Jack Talbot stared at the cage, he felt the cold hand of death reach from the shadows.

***

5

Lush green landscape coloured with purple heather rose behind the white two-storey cottage, set against the foreboding black skies. A solitary handsome oak tree stood alongside the old building, rising just above the grey slate roof. Chimneys at either end of the house gently puffed white wispy clouds into the dark skies. It was difficult to imagine that somebody could live alone and survive the winters in such a remote, unforgiving environment. Was it possible that this faraway place could be home to a woman with knowledge of a brutal serial killer? Jack cursed the stupidity of this mission as he stared at the cottage before him. He should never have come here, and certainly not alone. Now he was miles from civilisation, with no contact to the outside world. There was somebody at home, the chimneys proved as much, but now Jack wasn't sure that was such a good thing. He longed to be back in Lemsford, but now he was here, he had to check it out.

The tapping of rain grew, both in volume and frequency, as Jack left the relative shelter of the tree line and headed the hundred or so yards to the house. As he walked the slush to the house, he wondered how he could explain his being here to the occupants. *Jesus, Jack. What are you doing?* He reached out a hand to the smooth wood of the heavy door, paused, then knocked. Nothing. He knocked again, louder, the rain tip-tapping on his hood. He cursed under his breath and, head bowed, turned back to the woods. He'd taken four steps when he heard the door behind him open. He spun around to face them.

A young woman, no more than thirty, stood in the doorway. Her delicate frame silhouetted in the gentle light from behind. Her soft features looked upon her visitor, her dark, sad eyes staring sympathetically. Her cute button nose reminding him of...

'You look freezing,' her soothing voice music to Jack's ear.

'Sorry to disturb you,' Jack said, quickly surveying the beauty before him, 'I'm having a spot of car trouble,' his eyes fixed on the wedding ring on the delicate hand that fidgeted with her dress, *Of course she doesn't live alone*, 'I was wondering if your husband...'

'My husband?' she answered, the softness falling from her features.

Jack pointed, 'The ring.'

She did her best to bury the ring finger into the clutches of her other hand, 'He's not home at the moment.'

There was a pause. Jack tried his best not to stare at her. He could never have imagined seeing a woman so beautiful in such a remote place.

'You should come in,' she said. 'You'll catch your death.'

She moved from the doorway and held the door back, inviting the soaked stranger inside. Jack smiled and edged into the warmth. The door opened directly onto a small foyer with an old staircase set against the right-hand wall. To his left and right were short passages, a little too narrow for comfort, that led to two rooms. The door shut behind him, closing out the sound of rain. He stood just inside the door. The surroundings were everything he'd expected when he saw the outside of the house. Solid old furniture and beams in the ceiling. The pleasant smell of wood and thick rugs on tiled floor.

'Take your poncho off and come through to the kitchen, we'll get you a cup of tea.'

Her soft voice could soothe the most savage of beasts, but the accent was not a local one, nor was it the same voice from the phone call Jack received.

Jack raised the poncho over his head and gestured at the coat pegs. His host nodded. She led him left, through to the spacious kitchen. He sat at the old table, big enough to seat a large family. It was like a snapshot from ideal homes, from the old Aga oven in the recess fireplace, to the rifle which looked like it hadn't been fired since Moses was a boy hanging above it.

'Where are you from, if you don't mind me asking?' Jack said.

She put the kettle (a real kettle, whistle and all) on the stove. She answered over her shoulder.

'The short answer is London. My parents are from York originally.'

'I'm Jack Talbot, by the way.'

She left the cups and walked over to Jack, small hand outstretched, 'Lucy.' A little smile touched her face. Her dark eyes twinkled as she gently shook Jack's hand. 'Lucy Breyer.'

Jack felt his poker face slip. He tried to recover. 'Breyer? Unusual name.'

'It's Hungarian. He's Hungarian. The name's Hungarian.'

Her tanned skin flushed a little and from nowhere Jack's mind went to an image of her outside in the summertime, sunbathing nude. It was almost like she saw the image too as she turned quickly and continued preparing the tea.

'I'm afraid I won't be much help with your car,' she said, composure regained, 'but I do make great tea.'

Jack couldn't help but stare as she made the tea. The way her dress clung to her hourglass frame. That was the way he used to look at Jenny. He shook the thought from his head and averted his gaze.

'I think my car's just overheated,' Jack lied.

'What brings you to North Yorkshire, Mr Talbot?' she shouted over the rising whistle of steam.

'Please, call me Jack,' he smiled.

The whistle sent him back through time to his childhood. His parents had had a similar kettle before it was replaced with the bubble and click of progress.

'So what brings you here, Jack?'

Jack was trying hard not to notice Lucy's flirtatious little smile, 'I'm actually here on work. I'm a detective.'

'A detective? That sounds exciting.' The softness fell away from her features and was replaced with a glint of suspicion, only for a second, but long enough for Jack to have noticed.

'It's not as glamorous as Hollywood makes out.' 'I'm investigating a triple murder at the moment, you've probably heard about it, it's all over the news.'

143

Lucy brought the steaming cups of tea over to the table and sat close to Jack.

'I don't have a telly, or the internet,' she wore a frown. 'You think the killer is from around here?'

'Mrs Breyer...'

'Call me Lucy.'

'OK, Lucy. I've got a photograph of somebody we need to speak to. Would you mind having a look at it?'

She shook her head. 'How did you know to come here?'

'I received a phone call.'

A look of revelation fell across her face, as if she knew exactly who the call had come from. Jack wouldn't press the issue. He reached into the carry-all and produced the photo from the petrol station.

'Now, I want you to keep in mind that this man is just somebody we'd like to speak to.' He handed the photograph to Lucy.

The colour drained from her face. 'Oh Jesus.'

'You know this man?'

'It's him. It's Laszlo,' she said staring at the photo.

'Lucy,' Jack said, snapping her from her shock, 'we're not saying he's done anything; we just want to speak to him.'

She nodded, biting her bottom lip as tears formed.

'Are you OK to answer a few questions?'

She nodded, wiping the tears away from her cheek with her sleeve.

'Have a drink of tea, it's OK,' said Jack, doing his best to keep her from completely losing it.

She took the cup in both hands and sipped. She drew in a deep breath and slowly eased it through her gentle lips as she set the cup down on the table.

'When was the last time you saw Mr Breyer?'

'I haven't seen him for over a week. He works away a lot.'

'How much is a lot?'

'Every month he goes away. For a few days or so.'

'What is it exactly that Mr Breyer does?'

'I'm not sure,' she started to cry, 'I've asked him before, he can't tell me.'

She drew in a deep staggering breath.

'I never asked in the beginning,' she continued. 'We were young and in love, and I just trusted him. He was so kind and loving. So gentle. He said he had to work away from time to time and I accepted it. Later when I asked him, he used to say, "This and that" and smile. That smile of his. Oh God.'

The last words came out in a whine as if she'd shaken the missing pieces of a jigsaw from the box and when placed into the puzzle, they'd formed a perfect, horrifying image.

Jack reached over and gently touched the top of her arm. She welcomed the human contact, her breath slowing.

'But what about money? For food and so on?'

'We're self-sufficient out here. Completely.'

'And this working away... Is it the same time every month? The beginning of the month? The end?'

'It changes. It's never the same time,' her face darkened. She drew a deep breath, 'We've been having some problems recently.'

Jack instinctively reached for his ring finger, the tan line the only reminder that a wedding ring had ever been there.

She continued, 'I started to question why he was going away so much. He could never give me a good reason. I was sure it was someone else.'

Jack looked at the beautiful woman in front of him. It seemed impossible that someone could not find her enough. 'You said you've been having problems recently. How recently?'

She thought about it for a second. Again Jack saw realisation. Perhaps it had been much longer than she thought. She started to cry again.

'Did he ever display any unusual behaviour? Violence, aggression? Anything like that?'

Lucy was shaking her head before Jack finished the sentence. 'He might be a lousy husband, but he's no killer, Detective.'

"Detective" now. You're losing her.

'I have to ask,' Jack said, deciding not to press her on the lousy husband comment for now, 'I'm sorry.'

'It's fine,' she said, still on guard.

'Do you have any record of the times he was away at all?'

She shook her head, 'Only a mental record.'

'If you could give me anything, it would be a great help.'

'He went away last Tuesday. That was the last I saw of him.'

Jack scribbled into his notebook. It fit with the killings.

'It doesn't matter to him when he goes,' she said, her voice rising. 'He just fucks off whenever he feels like it. He missed my birthday last month. It wasn't the first time, either. Christmases, anniversaries. He doesn't care, he just goes. I'm sure it's somebody else.'

'When is your birthday, Lucy? The date.'

'The second,' she said, her voice cracking.

Jack looked up from his note pad in time to see her rush to the window. She gently sobbed into the hand she'd buried in her sleeve. He wondered how somebody could do this to such a delicate, beautiful woman, then he realised he'd been doing the same to Jenny for years. He'd never cheated on her, but his devotion to his job outweighed the attention he'd paid to his wife. He'd justified it as trying to improve their lives, knowing deep down that it was selfish. He cursed himself.

He looked over again at Lucy. The resemblance to a younger version of Jenny was striking. It wasn't complete, but enough to stir feelings that he shouldn't be having towards a key witness. It had been so long since he'd held Jenny that his urges were difficult to fight. The way she'd looked at him though...

Got to get out of here, Jacky boy, before you do something really *stupid.*

He stood up to leave, dropping a business card on the table.

'We can do this another time. I've left my card.'

'No,' she turned, 'I'm fine. We can do it now.'

'Mrs Breyer...'

'Please, Jack. Don't go. He's been away for over a week, but I've been alone for months.'

She sobbed again. Jack moved closer. He placed his hand on her shoulder. She turned and threw her arms over his shoulders, burying her face in his chest. He put his arms around her. While he felt for the woman, Jack couldn't help but find her extremely attractive. It would take a soulless man not to.

She regained control of her tears and spoke, head pressed against his chest, 'I'm sorry, Jack, I've got your shirt wet.'

Jack went for his default setting of humour to ease the tension and searched desperately for a witty comeback. None was forthcoming.

'Don't worry,' he said, 'one of the dangers of the job.'

He cringed. She looked up, and her huge dark eyes met Jack's. He wanted to say something else, but all he could think of was how beautiful she was. He lowered his head. He held her gaze until the moment his lips touched hers.

Stop, Jack.

But he couldn't. An uncontrollable tidal wave of passion surged over him. His mind was a mess, but he wasn't sure if he was using that as a justification to himself. A lame excuse to get what he wanted. What he *needed.* It had been so long since he and Jenny... Jenny.

She doesn't care, remember?

For a moment the passion evaporated from his kiss. He wondered about Lucy. Was she doing this just to get her husband out of trouble? But the kiss felt *good.* She was in it. It wasn't forced. Lucy broke off the kiss and stared into his eyes. At the second he thought it was over and the moment had gone, she unbuttoned the front of her dress, revealing tanned unblemished skin. She grabbed him and started kissing again.

He undid his shirt and she tore it off and threw it to the floor as they moved from the kitchen into the hallway, all the while Jack's conscience battling with his animal urges. Before he knew it, they were in the bedroom, a trail of clothes in their wake, and by then the battle was lost.

Day had become night; strangers, lovers. Jack gazed through the upstairs window into the darkness of North Yorkshire. The waning moon cast its eerie half-light onto the surrounding hills and Jack sensed some unspeakable danger from the shadows. He'd forgotten about the presence he'd felt at the cabin until now.

'What are you thinking about?' a soothing voice said behind him.

He turned to see Lucy; her head propped on a hand as she faced him.

'Isn't it lonely out here? How do you pass the time?'

She giggled.

'What?' he smiled.

'You look so serious.'

'That's because I am,' his smiling eyes belying his frown.

A deep belly laugh rose from within Lucy.

Jack smiled, 'That's a filthy laugh.'

Lucy's contagious laughter grew. Jack started to laugh himself, 'You still haven't answered my question.'

Lucy controlled her giggles for long enough to speak, 'Sorry, Detective,' she said between chuckles, 'but I can't remember what it was,' her laughter rising again.

Jack laughed, 'Oh God. What do you do to pass the time?'

Her laughter subsided before she replied, pointing at the wall. 'That.'

Jack turned his eyes to an oil painting of the rolling hills that he was looking at moments earlier. It was photo realistic in its detail, the brush strokes capturing the unique loneliness of the surroundings.

'Wow, that's yours? I mean, you painted it?'

'A Lucy Breyer original,' she said.

'You sell those?'

'Not that one, it's my favourite. But every few months I drive out to the coast and sell them to shops. Enough to keep a girl in clothes. That's where I was when I saw Laszlo's picture on the news. The lady in the shop, Greta, she must have recognised it and called,' she said in a cold, matter-of-fact way. 'They'd be worth a small fortune if I were dead,' she smiled.

Jack stared in admiration at the picture. She stroked his chest and tugged gently at the hair.

'Hey!' Jack said, shifting his focus to her mischievous eyes.

'Enough about me, what about you, Detective?'

'You like that word, don't you?' He smiled. She smiled back, blushing. He pretended to be all serious, 'What would you like to know?'

'Hmm,' she said in faux thoughtfulness, 'Let's see. How long have you been detecting?'

'Eight years.'

'Where are you from?'

'Nottingham, originally, now live in a little village called Lemsford in Hertfordshire.'

She blushed and became serious herself. 'Is there a Mrs Detective?'

Jack paused, 'At the moment, yes, but not for long.'

'I'm sorry.'

'Don't be. It's been on the cards for a long time. We'd both be better off apart'.

Lucy's features had drawn into a frown. Jack turned to face her and cupped her chin in one hand, focussing her eyes on his. 'Don't worry about it'.

'Will you stay? Until morning. I don't want to be alone.'

Jack nodded. He leaned forward and kissed her. They made love again and slept until morning.

***

6

The rain had finally stopped and bright sunshine glistened off the droplets of rain on Jack's car. A hand reached out and touched the car as if to check it were real. Laszlo Breyer rubbed the water between his fingers, his head turning to the direction of the house. If the position of the sun was anything to go by it was around nine in the morning. He quickly set off.

His weary legs ached as he approached. The house appeared through the trees as he neared. Just before he broke the treeline, it happened. The door to the house opened. He ducked into the long grass at the side of the muddy path. Through the ferns that lined the path Breyer observed as a tall, handsome man left his kitchen, said goodbye to Lucy and strode up the path. It couldn't be true. In his house? His bed? He felt his whole body tense. He waited till the bend in the path took the man out of sight before launching from his hiding place.

He reached the front door and pushed it open. Lucy turned, smiling. The smile fell away when she saw who was in front of her.

'Laszlo, where have you been? Where did you get those clothes?'

He could feel a furnace of heat building inside of him. 'Who was that man?' he said. Fists clenched; he took a half step towards Lucy.

She backed into the kitchen units, 'He was a detective. The police are looking for you Laszlo, what's going on?'

Laszlo glared into Lucy's wide eyes, 'Why was he here in the morning? Did he stay the night?'

'Did you hear what I said? The police are...'

'Answer me!'

She shrank back in horror as the yell reverberated around the house.

Tears formed, 'Laszlo, please tell me what's going on.'

He stormed towards his cowering wife. He grabbed her wrist and yanked her to her feet, 'Did you sleep with him?'

'Laszlo, please, you're hurting me.'

'Why won't you answer me?' His voice was an unrecognisable growl.

'I didn't. I didn't sleep with him.'

He didn't recognise the woman in front of him as his wife. They had been drifting apart since she'd grown suspicious of his comings and goings. His parents had warned him that this would happen. His wife had never lied to him before. Until now. When she said that she hadn't slept with the stranger who'd left the house. That was a lie. He just knew it. His heart sank. He released his grip and dropped to his knees.

'Why? Why did you sleep with him?' His demeanour had changed from raging monster to little boy lost.

She was crying. 'Laszlo, please'. She sank to her knees beside him. It was his turn to shrink away from her. She became more upset at his rejection. 'Laszlo, the police think you've killed somebody. Where have you been?' She paused. 'I've been worried.'

His heart pounded in his ears. 'Stop lying to me!' he jumped to his feet, the sudden movement and harshness of the voice made Lucy shrink back. He wondered if she had thought of going with this man when he left. If he had seen them leave together, they'd probably both already be dead. He turned and a bright object caught his eye against the dark wood of the kitchen table. He marched over to it.

He reached and snatched up the business card. He read the name out loud, 'Jack Talbot'.

'Laszlo, wait...'

She wants to protect *him*. In a second a vengeful cloud had descended upon his thoughts. It was clear what he had to do. He was going to punish Jack Talbot. He raced from the kitchen and through the front door leaving his shrieking wife in his wake.

Laszlo Breyer raced through the woods towards the car he'd seen. He ignored the path, choosing to make a beeline for the vehicle, remembering exactly where he'd seen it. With little effort he jumped fallen trees and ducked low branches as he raced for his target. The car appeared through the trees ahead. He narrowed his eyes. With renewed energy he sped at the gleaming wet metal dead ahead. He'd got there in time to stop the car driving away down the straight road to escape. Thoughts of what he'd say to Jack Talbot raced through his mind.

Then he stopped. He ducked behind a tree and watched as Jack Talbot strode towards the vehicle. The vengeful cloud in Breyer's mind had stopped him. Killing this worm would be too good for him. This man had taken the only thing he'd ever cared for and destroyed it. His sweet, delicate Lucy. There was no way they could ever go back to the life they had before, now this man had defiled her. The Lucy he'd fallen in love with was gone. Jack Talbot had killed her. Another one stood in her place. No, killing him wouldn't be enough. He must suffer. Jack Talbot was going to watch the people he cared about the most die.

Breyer moved closer as the engine fired into life. Breyer watched Talbot reach across to the passenger seat and lift a plain white envelope. He opened it, removed the papers inside, scanned the pages, and replaced them, before checking his mirrors and going. As he went, Breyer stared at the number plate, searing the digits into his memory. He was going to track Jack Talbot down. And he was going to make him pay.

7

Breyer headed back to the house still unsure about how to deal with Lucy. Never in his miserable existence had he got anything like as close to someone as he was to this sweet, delicate woman. But now she'd betrayed him. He'd done everything he could to protect and care for her and she'd repaid him with treachery. And yet, after everything, he still loved her. An image of her with the detective flashed into his mind. He squeezed is eyes and shook his head, trying to banish the sickening picture. How long had this been going on? Did she have visitors every time he was away? His stomach fell into an abyss, the sickly taste of jealousy climbed the back of his throat. His thick eyebrows knit into a deep frown as he lay a strong hand on the front door and pushed.

It didn't budge. He frowned. He pushed again. It was locked. The hairs on the back of his neck rose and a cold chill ran over him. He banged his fists on the door.

'Let me in, Lucy!'

His life with Lucy flashed through his mind as he beat the door. The individual hits became rhythmic, harder as he recalled the moment their eyes had met on one of his few trips to York almost five years ago. The risky return visits he paid until she told him she wanted to move in. Now he was standing outside, pounding the door. The door was solid, but it rattled and groaned with each blow. The whirlwind romance and marriage and blissful peace of the early days. Pounding turned to punching. The hardened skin on his knuckles was growing redder with each strike. Redder and redder until the skin gave way and tore, leaving bloody marks on the door.

'Lucy!'

The shouting was ferocious now. Even if there was somebody at home, the threatening tone would be enough to convince them to stay exactly where they were. He took a step back and raised a foot at the door. With a yell, all the force he could muster was levelled at the lock. It was no match for his fury. The thick wood splintered around the lock as the door flew in.

'Lucy!'

The scream echoed off the bare stonework, loud enough to fill ten houses. No reply. His brow wrinkled deeper as he stormed into the kitchen. 'Where are you?'

The kitchen was empty. He burst into the front room. The fire spat and crackled to itself. He turned, clenching his bloody fists into hardened knots. His heavy steps thudded up the stairs. He didn't know what he'd do now if he found her. How could she lock him out of his own house?

'Lucy?'

The voice now deeper still, and more threatening. He burst into the bedroom. Empty. Nothing moved. Nothing gone. Then his eyes fell to the corner of the room. To the small wooden door. He remembered telling Lucy that if ever anything happened and she felt she couldn't get out of the house, that she should hide there. He edged over to the corner and reached out a hand. The heavy door swung open and he stared into the cramped, dark space behind. It was empty.

She'd fled with only the clothes on her back. Breyer screamed in primal agony. She'd gone. Gone to be with the detective? She'd chosen the detective over him, and they were both going to pay.

It was only when he looked down into his knotted, ragged fist that he noticed there was something inside. Damp with sweat and discoloured by blood at its torn fringes. His aching fingers peeled back and revealed Jack Talbot's crumpled business card. He sank onto the bed and unfolded the card, pressing it flat over his knee. He stared at the name until the colour faded from the room around him. Only the white card with red-frayed edges remained. His amber eyes zoomed on two words which sizzled and popped. Jack Talbot.

He had to get out of here. He quickly pulled off the clothes he'd stolen from the charity bags and changed into his own clothes. He took the small brown duffel bag from the bottom of the wardrobe, packing it with a few days of provisions. He marched downstairs and took one last look around the cottage that had been in his family for longer than he could remember. With a deep breath and feeling of resignation he lifted his waterproof jacket from the peg, pulled the battered front door closed, and left the old place behind, fully aware that he may never see it again. In half an hour he'd be at the cabin.

He hiked south through the dense trees that made up Carr Wood, wiping the fine autumn drizzle from the end of his nose as he trudged the lonely route to the cabin as he had every month, for longer than he cared to remember. He didn't need to look; his feet knew exactly where to go. He liked to take a slightly different route each time, so as not to leave a worn path. Usually. Now he didn't care. This would probably be his last trip to the cabin, too.

The life he'd come to know, maybe even like, was over. His parents had been right about marrying a girl *different* to him. Then again, they'd been right about a lot of things. He felt he had little choice in the matter. It was her or loneliness. He'd never allowed himself to love before her. With Lucy, he couldn't fight it. "The life", as his parents called it, was harder than they'd tried to prepare him for, but it was all he had, and he'd had to make the most of it. He was growing tired though, much the same as his parents had, but now he had renewed energy. A focus. The detective was his prey now.

After miles of trudging wet autumn forest the trees began to thin out. He was near the clearing. The clearing was about sixty feet across, circled by tall trees which meant only in the summer did the place get any real light. This was to be home for the night, as it had been three nights every month or so, for longer than he cared to remember.

It was about four o'clock and the grey skies were already a shade darker, preparing for sunset. He pulled the key from his pocket and slid it into the soap bar sized padlock crudely screwed onto the door. Light flooded the dingy room as he pushed the door open. He gazed at the sparsely furnished quarters and, with a sigh, entered. This cold, dank place was now all he had.

He closed the door behind him and surveyed the all too familiar surroundings. He walked around the low table and dropped his bag on the floor. As hard as he tried, he couldn't ignore the other door in the opposite corner, the bigger of two elephants in this cramped room. He lowered himself to the damp, cold, single mattress which rested on wooden pallets and used the bag as a pillow. He faced the front door and kept the other at his feet, out of sight. As he lay and tried to formulate a plan in his tired mind, his eyes fell upon the other, smaller, elephant, propped in the corner behind the front door. The weapon with which he had killed his parents. He stared at it and cried himself into a haunted sleep.

8

The next morning Breyer awoke cold and early. The wheels of fate that would lead to Jenny's death were grinding into motion. He'd decided to head for the coast. If the detective was looking for him, others would be too. At this time of year the coast would be quiet. It was the only place he knew. He'd just have to hope that Lucy didn't tell Jack that. From the coast he could use the information on the card to track down Jack Talbot, and carry out his revenge.

He headed for the nearest town, and from there he hitch-hiked, to the closest with a bus service. Within four hours he was on a bus headed for the coast. From beneath the ragged peak of the baseball cap Laszlo Breyer stared at the passing countryside, plotting his next move. The half empty bus he was riding was due to land in Scarborough just before noon. It felt good to be in his own clothes again. The last few days in stolen charity donations had made it difficult to blend. He shuffled back into the seat wishing it was more comfortable and pulled the dark blue baseball cap over his tired eyes. He went over his plan once again.

Concentration was difficult. He'd barely slept in the last few days and while the previous evening's sleep was longer, the night had been cold. Stiffness locked his neck and shoulders though it wasn't that that was disturbing him. From the seat across came the constant ruffling of newspaper pages and incessant tinny beat of music played at an ungodly volume through cheap earphones. He frowned at the thoughtlessness. He felt glad that he lived away from "civilisation". Then he remembered that for him, the life he knew was gone. He'd have to start afresh. But still, it would be away from that kind of behaviour. He lifted the peak of his cap and shot a glance at the passenger hidden behind the pages of the tabloid. Then he saw it.

He instinctively shrank back against the window and pulled the worn peak of the baseball cap down over those giveaway eyes. His stomach lurched. Cold sweat washed over the back of his head in a chilling wave. He looked again at the front page of the newspaper, and saw himself. It was the photo from the garage forecourt in Stevenage. His mind raced at the headline; "The face of death?"

He cursed his luck. He'd been so careful. Staying away from situations that may lead him to this confounded, inevitable point. He knew five days ago, when his car skidded off the road and into a tree, that the results would be appalling. He did everything he could to protect his head. Not out of the natural instinct for self-preservation, for he knew that it mattered little. He was desperately trying to avoid exactly what followed. Unconsciousness.

Luckily, he'd been travelling quiet roads as he raced to get back north. To the cabin. Self-hatred took over as he berated himself for taking such foolish chances, but the fact was that his deteriorating marriage to the most beautiful woman he'd ever laid eyes on was on the brink of collapse, and that was all he'd had to keep him from ending his life. "The life". Risk-taking made it interesting. Now his risk taking had led to the deaths of six people over two nights.

Guilt sank its sickly teeth into his stomach and ate away. He hadn't killed anyone since... the little girl, remember? Now six were dead. And he wanted to kill more? It was wrong. He couldn't. He would go back to the cabin. Go back and stay there. Nobody would find him. The thought of suicide flashed in and out of his mind. No, go back to the cabin. Nobody knows about the cabin. Not even Lucy.

The thought cast images of her in his mind. Her and the detective. In his bed. The movement. Wild. Animal. He looked down at the crumpled ticket in his fist. He relaxed his set jaw, and his eyes refocused. His chest rose and fell quickly. One thought dominated his mind; Jack Talbot must pay. He pulled the cap back down and faced the window.

The young man reading the newspaper was more interested in the back pages than the front, so when the time came to alight, he never gave Laszlo Breyer a second glance. Breyer fidgeted with his bag pretending to do god knew what until he was the last to leave. He stepped into the fresh sea air and clung onto the peak of the cap, as the wind threatened to rip it off his head and expose him for the devil he was.

He wasted no time in heading to the sea front. He stood on the top of the cliff near the Grand Hotel and gazed as tumultuous brown sea spat foam onto the expanse of beach below. He took the winding steps down to the sea front and wandered past the rising and falling bells and alarms of endless amusement arcades. The few visitors who had braved the weather turned their collars and smiled as the wind threatened to turn their candyfloss into luminous pink tumbleweed.

His eyes turned to the sandwich board chained outside a newsagents. "Full Moon Killer Heads North" read the headline. Another surge of guilt came. *They are dead because of you.* You and your foolish risk-taking. They did nothing wrong. Not like the detective. *Talbot must suffer.* The wind seemed to agree; the sandwich board collapsed, headline down, to the damp pavement in a strong gust. Then he spied it. Down a side-street, a few yards away. Fat-Kat's (spelt F@_K@'s) Internet Café.

It was on his forays into Scarborough with Lucy, while she sold her paintings, that he'd discovered the Internet. On his parents' advice, he'd never applied for telephone, Internet, or any utilities. He didn't have a bank account. No contracts, no contacts. He was, to all intents and purposes, non-existent. But one afternoon around five years before, he'd stumbled in and discovered the wonderful World Wide Web. He knew his way around an Internet search engine. He pulled the ragged business card from his pocket and searched. Within minutes he knew that Jack Talbot was from

Welwyn Garden City, Hertfordshire, and that that was the home of Hertfordshire Police HQ.

9

Laszlo Breyer stood across from the plain and unattractive Welwyn Garden City police HQ and waited. The three-storey police building wasn't the focus; it was the green Rover parked outside. He was in the viper's nest and he didn't care. Even if he was spotted and caught, he'd still get to Talbot. He knew that at the same moment, Jack Talbot was inside, trying to bring about his own downfall. Sending somebody to the house to keep watch and tightening the net around him.

The stiff breeze picked up and he retreated to the red Honda Civic hatchback he'd stolen in Driffield. A car he knew would get good mileage so he wouldn't have to risk too many fuel stops. He'd driven down quiet country roads, sticking to the speed limit all the way. Now all he had to do was wait.

He stared at the doors for an eternity, waiting for that moment when his stomach tightened and his heart beat that little bit faster. The first idea had been to get Talbot alone. Get him alone and torture him. Overpowering him wouldn't be a problem. He could take him somewhere private and take his time with him. But that wouldn't be right. It wouldn't *feel* right. That wasn't an eye for an eye. Talbot hadn't killed him. He'd taken the one thing in the world he loved and destroyed it. No, Breyer would follow Talbot and wait and see who he met. Who he cared about. Then he'd kill *them*. *That* would be fair. He'd leave a note so Talbot knew it was his fault. Let the guilt eat away at him. Let guilt kill him slowly.

Talbot emerged from the station, gripping a white envelope. As he did the weather seemed to change. The autumnal chill lifted and the clouds parted, revealed a warm, bright sun. Talbot's face was peaceful and serene. Satisfaction written all over it. That wouldn't last. He crossed the small distance to his car and got in.

What Breyer couldn't know is that usually Jack would be heading from the station to the loneliness of his small cottage in Lemsford. Usually. Today, Jack was going elsewhere. To Finchley. To Jenny.

Breyer followed a car distance behind Jack all the way. As they approached Jack's street, Breyer saw that it was a cul-de-sac and parked up. He quickly stepped from the car, surprised at how the weather had changed. Warm. As if to give a sign that this was *right*. He skulked low behind parked cars until Talbot himself parked. He watched him get out and cross to the front door, still clutching the envelope. He knocked and waited. It wasn't long before somebody answered.

A woman. Small, delicate, pretty. Like Lucy. They smiled at one another. There was something between them. He handed her the envelope and smiled. He said something which moved the woman. They hugged. The embrace was too long just for friendship. This was it. Jack loved this woman. She loved him.

And that was all it took. Within twenty minutes, Jenny Talbot would be dead.

10

Jack had just set foot back in the station when he got a shout. Tommy was on the phone for him. Bad news travels fast. He kept all talk of his divorce from Jenny to himself. He didn't want to worry anybody else with it. It wasn't their business. Even Tommy's, best friend or not. Since his father's death Tom had got a transfer back to Finchley – to be closer to Jenny. He was spending most of his time hanging around with Bryan, his old friend and new partner in Finchley. If Jenny brought up the subject of divorce to her brother, then fine, but if not, then Jack wasn't about to. He crossed to the waiting phone imagining the hurt in Tommy's voice at not being told.

He snatched up the receiver, 'Hello?'

'Jack?'

Tommy's voice sounded different than he imagined. Jesus he was taking this hard.

'Jack, can you come to Finchley?'

'Tom, I've just got back from Finchley.'

'Jack, it's serious.'

He wanted to talk it out face to face. Typical Tom, he never liked talking on the phone. But there was no way he was going to talk him and Jenny out of the divorce. He was about to tell him that when Tommy spoke again.

'It's Breyer. And Jenny.'

Breyer. Jack had revealed the name told to him in the phone call, just to get the investigative ball rolling. But he wanted to keep the knowledge of the cabin to himself. Just for a couple of days. Let the cottage be the object of the search, if that turned up nothing, he'd tell them about the cabin. It was stupid and he knew it, but he was secretly hoping that Breyer could be captured without involving Lucy. It was a huge mistake. This was what ran through his mind as he drove to Finchley.

Jack Talbot's head swam as he pulled the car to a stop at the police tape in the street he'd left less than an hour before. Through the fogginess of his thoughts he realised how strangely alert he was, as if his mind were recording this moment for posterity. The bright low sun highlighting the veins of golden leaves that blew, paper dry, in a slow dance around his feet as he stepped from the car. He felt the sympathetic gazes of his former neighbours burning into the side of his face. Bryan reached out a quivering hand and led Jack away from the throng of investigating officers. Bryan peered at Jack with questioning eyes which looked animated buried inside his ashen face. Jack saw the flecks of blood covering Bryan's shirt and wondered if they belonged to Jenny.

'We need to talk,' he said, checking over his shoulder.

'What happened, Bryan?'

Bryan reached a trembling hand into his pocket and pulled out a slip of paper.

'I found this on the bedside table,' he said as he handed the note to Jack.

Jack unfolded the paper and read the scrawled message:

This is what happens, Jack, when you fuck somebody else's wife. You took her away from me. Now I'm going to take her away from you.

Jack reeled. The feeling of guilt like a punch to the gut. He was to blame. Jenny was dead and it was his fault. He rubbed his brow with his hand, a vain attempt to hide the flow of tears. He swallowed a sob which climbed his throat, then got a hold of his senses, 'Has Tommy seen this?'

Bryan shook his head, 'No,' his eyes flashed for a split second, accusatory. He turned away and peered up at the window.

'What happened?' Jack changed the subject.

When he looked back the accusatory stare was replaced with fear, 'I've been looking into the case, and I was coming over to see if you'd heard about... Well, it's not important now,' he looked around, forensics were filing into the house. He hushed his voice, 'I heard screams. I went in and he was... he had a knife, Jack.'

Jack's stomach lurched as if trying to jolt his brain into life and out of shock. 'Oh Jesus.'

'I had the crowbar with me from the car. He didn't hear me coming, he was like a wild animal,' he broke off, in tears of his own now, his voice a tremor. 'I'm in fucking big trouble, Jack.'

'What do you mean?'

He quietened further, 'I hit him, Jack. Round the back of the head. He was out cold. I ran to Jenny, checked her... she was gone, Jack. And then he started to come to,' he paused, moving his head closer. 'I hit him again. And again.' His teeth clenched as he relived the moment, 'I lost it. I don't know how many times I hit the bastard. There's no way I can pass it off as one hit. Forensics will know,' his voice raised slightly, 'and I'm finished.'

Jack led him further away, 'Don't worry. We'll deal with it.'

Bryan stared into nothingness. Jack saw Bryan's inner conflict raging in his dull eyes. The anger. The judgement. Jack looked up at the house. The world around seemed to fade away.

CHAPTER SIX

Jack stared out of the window at the white blanketed countryside, thinking how impossible it was that the countless flakes now falling could all be unique. Cross was silent at the retelling of the story. Jack breathed a deep, trembling, breath.

'That's the first time I've told anybody that,' Jack said, eyes coming back into focus. 'You, Bryan, and Tommy. Nobody else knows. About the affair I mean. The thing with Bryan was swept under the carpet. He got a medal for killing Breyer.' He barked a joyless laugh.

'But you think Bryan held it against you. Jenny's death, I mean?' Cross asked.

'He had a problem with me from the start. He always liked Jenny. Tommy went apeshit when he found out about me and Lucy Breyer. Barely said two words to me since.'

Cross frowned, 'Do you really think they would hold enough of a grudge to have you killed? It seems a bit much.'

Jack turned back to the window, the snowflakes coming bigger and faster now, 'I don't know.'

Jack's story had taken up most of the journey and it was not long before they arrived back at Cross's place. Jack looked over both shoulders before entering the house. Somebody was out there. He could feel the hands of fate moving to right his wrongs. He was staring at Cross's book collection when Cross entered with two cans of Stella Artois and extended an arm in Jack's direction.

'Whoa, what's this?' Jack asked, indignantly. 'I quit last night, remember?'

Cross lowered his arm, 'When was the last time you didn't have a beer?'

Jack shrugged, 'Don't know.'

Cross thrust the beer back under Jack's nose, 'Then take this. Cold turkey will kill you quicker than Wild Turkey.'

Jack took the can but didn't open it. 'You're having one?'

'A straightener. Just to put my nerves right. It's been a hell of a morning.'

Jack's mind cast back to the interview with old man Sweeney. He was convinced he seen a wolf. His words rang in Jack's mind: "It changed." Jack went cold at the thought.

'Come on,' Cross said, opening his can, 'bottoms up.'

Jack reluctantly opened the can and thought to himself when he did quit drinking, how much he'd miss that wonderful sound.

Cross snapped Jack from his thoughts, 'So what happens now?'

Jack didn't reply. He sat and enjoyed the silence. Telling Cross about the truth – most of the truth – about him and Jenny had been a huge relief. He'd never talked about it before. He'd never really thought about it. Just drunk himself into a stupor and blamed himself; blamed himself for not being able to protect Jenny. Now he'd cleared a skeleton from the closet and exorcised a ghost from the past, it gave him free reign on the future, and that felt great.

He finally replied, 'Perhaps being here isn't such a good idea. If I'm right, our copycat knows I'm here. That means it's not safe,' he locked eyes with Cross, 'for either of us. Come on,' he drained his can and rose unsteadily from his chair, 'I'll buy you a coffee.' He felt an uncomfortable flush of warmth.

Cross must have noticed his expression change, 'What?'

Jack frisked himself with a sense of urgency, 'Shit.'

'What?' Cross asked, intrigued, but knowing deep down it could only be phone or wallet, and he'd probably realised that he hadn't seen a phone on Jack since he'd arrived.

'My wallet.'

Cross tried to hide his pleasure at his own bit of detective work.

'I've left it at the B&B. I'll have to go... shit.' This expletive harsher than the one moments before. He remembered that the last occupant of the room wasn't himself, but a homeless man. A homeless man short on money. It was now almost noon, young homeless Danny would be long gone, but even so, it felt wrong not to rush to the B&B.

'I'll drive,' said Cross as he rose to his feet, much more steadily than Jack.

They raced to the Minster B&B, Jack's faith in humanity now resting on whether or not a homeless man short on cash had found and stolen his wallet, or any of the useless maxed-out cards contained within.

Jack stood outside the B&B, not shivering as much as he should have been, thanks to the fuzzy warmth of hangover. Jack rang the doorbell and shrugged back at Cross, who watched from the shelter of the car. He waited barely a second before causing the shrill doorbell to once again cut the silence. Through the frosted glass he saw movement inside. The outline of the landlady grew until the door sprung open. She was none too impressed to see Jack. He prayed that Danny hadn't trashed the place or caused a disturbance, he'd just had a good feeling about the kid and his feelings were rarely wrong. The landlady reached into her pocket and produced Jack's wallet.

'Oh, thank you.'

'You're welcome,' she sounded unhappy. She produced a note – *a note* – and handed it to Jack. It was written on the pad he'd seen in the room, his name scrawled in pencil on the outside. He unfolded it. 'I don't appreciate you letting random people into here you know.'

Jack read the note:

Jack! Thanks for letting me use your room, best nights sleep I've had in ages! Found your wallet on the floor, didn't know what to do with it so I stuck it in the drawer. Thanks again.

Cheers, Danny.

Jack looked up at the woman, 'You're right, I was just... I'm sorry. I'm sorry, if there was any damage...'

The woman shook her head and finally broke into a little smile, 'No harm done. It was a nice thing to do. But you should have let me know.'

Jack nodded like a mischievous schoolboy. He recalled the time he and Bobby Taylor got caught peeking into the girls' changing room when they were eleven. The girls were eleven too, so there really wasn't much to see. The headmaster told them off, but looking back Jack got the feeling he wasn't really that angry. He just threatened to tell their parents if it happened again and that was the end of that. This felt the same.

'Goodbye, Mr Talbot.' She closed the door.

Twenty minutes later, Jack and Cross sat in a small café drinking much needed coffee. They'd avoided the bigger chains because they were too pricey for Jack's wallet. It turned out that Jack didn't even have enough for this greasy spoon: he'd blown almost all of his cash, so there wasn't much for the poor homeless kid to steal even if he'd wanted to, so Cross ended up paying anyway. Jack was embarrassed, but Cross was good humoured about it.

'Okay Jack, I'll put it this way,' Cross had hushed his voice, but it was almost theatrical. Anyone in earshot, not that there were many in the place, could hear everything he said, 'maybe there are no such things as werewolves,'

Jack raised a solitary eyebrow. *Maybe?*

Cross continued, 'fine, but these killers all look the same. If they are from one family, it follows that they could all have the same disorder. It doesn't mean that anyone's betrayed you.'

Cross had a point. There was a connection between all three killers. A family connection had occurred to Jack more than once, though between drinking sessions he was finding it difficult to keep track of his thoughts. *Need to start writing things down, Jack.* The last time, with Breyer, there had been this movement north. Perhaps it was a coincidence that the killer was now in York. The movement north was the thing that had alerted his senses back in Carlton, where Freddie the Labrador was disembowelled. Last time there was this movement north and then the killings stopped after two nights. Maybe he was trying to get somewhere.

Shit.

Jack quickly stood, scaring Cross into almost spilling his coffee. 'I know where he's going.'

They raced back to the car, Cross throwing a ten-pound note on the table on his way out and not waiting for the change.

As they reached the car Jack asked, 'Can I borrow this?'

'What?' Cross looked completely nonplussed as they opened the doors in unison and climbed in. Jack repeated the question as Cross fired the engine into life.

'I heard you,' Cross replied, 'but I don't understand. You want to borrow my car?'

'I need it to get to Breyer's cottage.'

'*I? I* need it?'

They were already moving through the narrow streets of York heading back to Cross's place. Jack felt his brow furrow. 'What?'

'Well, I'm coming with you.' Cross said in a matter-of-fact way.

'No. Sorry, Daniel. It's too dangerous.'

'I can handle it.'

Jack didn't look at Cross who was glancing at him, trying to gauge a reaction. He gauged.

'What, you don't think I can?'

'It's just that,' he broke off, 'Jenny is dead. Because of me.'

'I don't need protecting, Jack. I'm not you're responsibility.'

'That's not what I meant.'

'Listen, my car is going to Carr Wood, with me in it, or it's not going at all.'

Jack stared out of the window; he didn't want to see Cross's self-satisfied post-negotiation face. Cross was right though. About two things. The killer was not after Jack, not yet at least. And he was a Breyer. All Jack could do now was to pray that Lucy was not at the cottage.

2

Bad luck comes in threes. That's what her mum had always said. She said it with such conviction that to her it might have been science. Now at this moment, Lucy Breyer wondered what the other two moments had been.

She had waved her parents off on their way to the hospital and dashed upstairs, changed, grabbed her car keys, and left the carefully written note which would (falsely) explain her whereabouts to her parents on the dining room table.

She hated lying to her parents, but they had worried enough over the past year for a lifetime, and over that period she had watched her mother grow old almost before her eyes. They supported her without question, and respected her wishes not to see a therapist, allowing her to work things through in her own time.

The past year had been spent working through the stages of recovery, her working things out for herself taking long walks in the park and by the river, sometimes alone, sometimes with her parents, and other times with her parents a comforting hundred yards behind, but never, ever, after dark. After dark she was always safely in the house, and at least one of her parents had always been there (usually mum). They had passed time, playing cards (the two of them had become mean gin rummy players over time), board games – Scrabble mostly, sometimes Monopoly, and if dad was there, Cluedo – and in the last few months she had even picked up her paint brush – though the results had been dark or dissatisfying. A lot of the time she slept. She slept during the day, because at night was when the dreams came.

Strange dreams, which threatened at any moment to become inescapable nightmares. One recurring dream took place in a dark room, foreign to her, but somehow familiar. Claustrophobic. In the dream it was night, but the cramped space was so small that it would have been dark even during the day. The only light filtered through a small window, and though she couldn't see the source she knew it was the moon. A full moon. She was alone in this place, but someone was outside. She couldn't see who, but she knew it was Laszlo. He wanted to get in. He wanted to get in and if he did, he would hurt her. Maybe even kill her. Every now and then the dark would be split by a terrifying howl. It was only now, in this awful moment that she remembered the howling. Loud and close. She had heard it before, but from a distance. In the dream it threatened to overtake her. Her mind flashed forward to that morning.

She recalled setting straight off for the estate agent (ignoring the frantic waves of her neighbour as he passed clutching the morning paper). The estate agent would give her the keys to the cottage. She would get to the cottage, which was waiting for the new owners to move in sometime next week, go upstairs to the master bedroom, collect the painting, and get the fuck out of Dodge and back home before sundown.

She recalled turning the radio in the car off. The words from the newscaster came back now with startling clarity. But it was his tone which told her she didn't want to hear what he said.

"Our top story, five people have been killed and another..."

She didn't want to hear bad news. She switched instantly to the CD player and now as the countryside passed by in what would be a blur, if time wasn't stretched out into an immeasurable crawl, David Bowie's voice was singing in a barely recognisable drone about turning and facing the strain. Her mind again went to Laszlo.

She was embarrassed at not having spotted Laszlo's odd behaviour, though he'd done his utmost to hide it. The clues were so obvious to her now. He knew exactly what he was capable of. Every month or so (now it was clear he was driven by the lunar cycle) he'd go away to "work". He had no real friends to speak of. He never liked to talk about his parents. Lucy suspected abuse of some sort, but never forced the issue. Even the place in the corner of their bedroom he'd told her to hide if ever *somebody* came to the house didn't give it away. It was clear now. He was afraid of himself and what he was capable of. Another flash forward.

She'd considered asking her father to drive her to the cottage, but she needed to take this step by herself. It was bad enough that she hadn't been able to support herself during the last twelve months. No; she'd go alone. It would be fine. And it *had* been fine until the weather turned and slowed her and doubled the journey time. Something had been growing inside her. As she neared the cottage an intangible fear had taken seed and sprouted, then bloomed until it overwhelmed her. The feeling that Laszlo was somehow close. The feeling that invisible hands were moving against her. Plotting. Yes, everything had been fine. Until she hit a patch of black ice.

Now her car was in mid-air flying towards the ditch beside the road. Yes, she thought as she watched the acorn-shaped air-freshener defy gravity and horizontally suspend itself in the void, fine grains in the wood catching the red light of the sinking winter sun, maybe she had ignored the warning signs. Perhaps the neighbour wanted to tell her not to go anywhere, to stay at home. To tell her that it wasn't safe out there. For all she knew the news report wanted to tell her not of some bad traffic accident, but a brutal mass murderer on the streets of York, it was after all a local broadcast. Then severe weather warnings that would have been on the radio telling her not to go to the cottage today, to wait a few more days. Mum was right. Mum was always right. Bad luck did come in threes.

3

Jack reached across and honked the horn outside Cross's place. Cross left the house tucking something into his inside pocket and waved an apology. He locked the front door and jogged up the path. He was out of breath when he got in the car. Snow flew in through the open door.

'What were you doing?'

'Had to use the toilet. Do you know where we're going?' he asked, changing the subject.

'It's pretty much one road once you hit the moors. I had GPS last time.' Then, bringing him back on topic, 'There was a toilet at the coffee shop.'

Cross ignored the speak of toilets and glanced in the mirrors before pulling out. Without looking at Jack he said, 'We'll get a printout.'

'A printout?'

'A map. From Google.'

'Haven't you got the Internet?'

Cross shook his head. 'No Internet. No mobile. No microwave.'

'Really?'

'Do you know what the studies on the dangers of microwaved food revealed?' Cross was deadly serious.

'No,' Jack replied, not really caring.

'No. Because there aren't any.' Jack expected Cross to look pleased with himself. He did not. 'Never had a microwave. Had the Internet and a mobile a while back. Too much snooping going on now. You haven't got a mobile anyway, have you?'

'It's at home. I left in a hurry. Nobody really contacts me. Anyway,' Jack felt he was being walked around something important, 'we haven't got time to mess around with Google.'

'It'll take two minutes. We don't want to get lost.'

Logical. As always. Jack had no argument. They went to an Internet Café.

Jack paced as Cross studied the map on screen. 'Why do you think the copycat is going to Breyer's cottage?'

'I don't know. Maybe it's like some sort of spiritual home or something.' He paced quickly, 'Come on, Danny, what are you doing?'

Cross had his eyes glued to the screen. It was Google earth zoomed in on the North Yorkshire Moors.

'Carr Wood, wasn't it?'

'Yeah just print it, let's go.' Jack shivered as another customer entered the deserted café, bringing a blast of bitter air with him. The hunched brute rubbed warmth into his raw, red hands and grunted a greeting at the clerk, who returned the noise. This new customer and extra work were much to the clerk's disappointment. Jack felt the cold coming off the man as he shuffled past. *Hurry up, Cross.*

Lucy was in danger. It was more than protecting a person's life that was at stake. Lucy meant something to him. Just as she had to Laszlo Breyer. *Laszlo? Whoever.* The note had said that Lucy was in danger. The copycat was closing in on her, not him. He thought about the note. He'd destroyed it soon after, but he remembered every line. He always found something unusual about the note. The wording maybe. Now it made sense:

"This is what happens, Jack, when you fuck somebody else's wife. You took her away from me. Now I'm going to take her away from you."

You took her away from me. By the time Jack received the note, Jenny would already be dead. The note must have been referring to Lucy. He'd never thought about it properly: with the killer dead, there was no threat; now the copycat had turned up, it changed everything. The copycat wasn't going north to get to Breyer's home. He was going for Lucy. Now Jack had to stop the copycat.

Only two people knew about that note. Him, and Bryan Dempsey. He *had* been betrayed. Cold sweat poured over him.

Nausea rose. How could he have been so blind? *The drink. The damned drink.*

All through the copycat case Jack had felt a resonance – maybe that's what the resonance was. At first, he thought that it was his body's recognition of the patterns of the case. Signalling how he could catch the killer this time around where he'd failed before. But it wasn't that. It was something else. Or at least now it felt that way. He recognised it now as the idea that he knew somewhere in his bones that this was about Lucy. He knew that there was nothing on earth that could bring Jenny back. Nothing in life is more final than death. But he knew that if he could save a life at the hands of this maniac – prevent a death – that it would represent something greater than the saved life itself, if that were possible. This would be a chance at some sort of redemption. And that would bring closure.

'Have you seen this?' Cross had his nose inches from the screen.

'Seen what?' asked Jack, approaching, 'Let's go.'

'Look,' Cross pointed at the screen. 'This is Carr Wood,' Jack impatiently agreed as Cross moved his finger to another part of the screen, 'so this must be the cottage.'

Right again. 'So?'

Cross pointed to a third part, 'So what is that?'

It was a clearing, about sixty feet across. In the centre sat a small building.

'It's a cabin. It was Laszlo Breyer's. Print that too and let's go.'

He did, and they left.

The print-out said the trip would take an hour and a half. It hadn't factored in the snow. The small, winding roads would add another hour to the journey in these worsening conditions. If the weather had been as bad on the moors, the roads may even be closed. All of this and the sun was due to set in little over an hour. That would play into the hands of the copycat.

He thought everything over. He still was uncomfortable about this family connection of the Breyer's. In the back of his mind, something didn't add up. Was the incident in the seventies the father? And Jenny's killer and the copycat sons?

'Got a pen?' he asked Cross.

It was only now that Jack noticed Cross leaned forward in his seat peering through the blizzard. Whooshing waves of snowflakes endlessly blew at the car.

'Glovebox,' came the only reply.

Jack rummaged for a second and retrieved an orange Bic ballpoint, the red lid pocked with teeth marks.

'Paper?'

'If there's none in there, then there's none.'

There wasn't. Jack reached into his pocket and pulled out the note from Danny. He smiled to himself, thinking that Danny must be well on his way to Doncaster by now, out of the elements, with his friends, and warm. He turned the note over. The back was blank, save for his name. Without thinking he circled his name that Danny had scribbled on the back to isolate it from his thoughts. He wrote down the key words of the case, an old technique he'd used in the past, hoping the words would fire some previously unthought-of connection.

Carr Wood.

Finchley.

Carlton – Homeless Mike.

Colin's Café.

Kenny McKenzie – Lorry.

Old man Sweeney.

Wolf?

Lycanthropy.

Full moon.

Empty grave - Body snatching.
Footprints - Only leading AWAY from grave?
Cell regeneration.

He stopped. The red ink seemingly jumping from the page.
'Fuck me.'
Cross glanced over, 'What?'
'It can't be.' His voice sounded distant, not like his own.
'What?' Cross's voice rose, impatient at being kept out of a one-man loop.
'What if it's real?' Jack said.
'That's what I've been trying to tell you!'
'No, listen.' Jack ran through the idea once more before verbalising it. 'What did the book say...?'
'Which book?'
'The Hungarian one.'
'Magyar's book?'
'The werewolf one, yeah.' Jack turned and looked at Cross's profile as he squinted through the driving snow, 'What did it say would happen, if somebody shot and killed a werewolf, a real werewolf, but didn't use silver bullets?'
Cross turned to Jack. He opened his mouth to speak, but no words came. For a second. He thought Cross might actually pass out.

4

At 2:37PM, just as Jack Talbot and Daniel Cross were negotiating the use of Cross's car, in an intensive care unit in the York Hospital, Kenny Mackenzie was clinging to the final moments of his life.
He was conscious of his life flashing before his eyes. And surprised. He had been convinced the idea was rubbish. The

images were fleeting. From the earliest memories of fights at school, first kiss (Melanie Jackson), first screw (her big sister). That sunny fortnight in Marbella whizzed by too, including posing for his favourite photograph with Karen and the kids while the skinny, sunburnt Welsh guy struggled with the camera. Then, suddenly, the thoughts were no longer fleeting. A chill descended and he was thrown back into the cab of his lorry with the hitcher. And this moment was painfully slow.

On the outskirts of Doncaster, Kenny switched the A1 for the single lane of the A19. The first stars dotted the deep blue sky outside as Kenny glanced over at his passenger. The man who called himself Larry was sound asleep. He turned the radio down, but the thought of Larry so desperate to stay awake haunted him. He decided to rouse his passenger.

'Larry.'

The man with the amber eyes didn't move a muscle. He questioned if he should leave him. Larry said he'd wanted to get to York before dark. Night was falling as the remaining few minutes of daylight slipped into memory. Even if he woke Larry, or whatever his name was, there was no way on earth he'd get to York any quicker. He'd already said that he was exhausted. Wasn't it better for him to get an extra fifteen minutes of shuteye? Perhaps he was meeting someone and didn't want to be groggy for the meeting. It was a possibility. He decided he'd have one more go at waking him, that way he could convincingly tell Larry he'd tried. He turned the radio back up. The opening bars of Martha and the Vandellas chimed as they belted out *Nowhere to Run.*

He cleared his throat.

As he did the dying embers of the sun disappeared below the skyline.

'Larry!'

Larry sat bolt upright. His hands gripped the dashboard. Kenny jumped, hands losing control of the wheel for a second. He dragged the lorry back into the lane, but over-corrected. Larry's rigid body pressed back into the seat. Teeth clenched. Veins bulging in his neck. His head spun to face Kenny. Kenny saw the whites of those amber eyes were red and ringed with tears. The pleading sorrowful look was one that Kenny knew would haunt him, if he made it from whatever was going on alive. Through the clenched teeth the passenger let out a primal, guttural scream. Kenny was sure it was some kind of seizure.

'Jesus Larry, you OK?'

Kenny fought to prevent the lorry crossing the lanes to a blazing cacophony of car horns. He tried to keep one eye on Larry who convulsed violently – lurching forward to the windscreen, then smashing back into the seat, fingers pressed into the dashboard all the while. Finally, his head came to rest on the dashboard, between his rigid hands. The cars passed freely, but still blared horns sounded. Kenny finally brought the lorry to rest in the hard shoulder.

He clicked his seatbelt free and leaned across, putting a large comforting hand on Larry's shoulder. At the touch of his hand, Larry's head jerked back around and a scream more animal than man threw Kenny against the dash, knocking the radio off. Stiff with fear, he pushed himself against the driver's side door. A loud creaking emitted from within the hitcher. He screamed as he somehow grew in his seat, bracing against the seatbelt.

Blood appeared at his fingertips. Kenny couldn't comprehend what he was seeing. He thought the fingers were pressing too hard into the dash. Then it appeared the fingernails were growing, until they finally fell to the floor of the cab, forced from behind by sharp, pointed nails much denser than those of any man. Larry's hands were somehow much bigger than before, though until this point Kenny hadn't noticed, such was his disbelief at what was unfolding. Thick black hair sprouted from the back of the hands, which beat the dash more intensely when the loud creaking stopped, only to be replaced by a high-pitched whine.

The new sound threw Larry into agony as he thrashed against the seatbelt. His head tilted back, veins throbbing, his lips parted revealing a bloody mouth. Kenny realised what the whine was. The hitcher's canine teeth stretched downward, growing inexplicably until they were more than an inch in length. As they were growing a loud crack sounded.

The hitcher's face changed shape as if the bones had broken from within. The human screaming had long since stopped, the savage scream that replaced it somewhere between a large dog's growl and a lion's roar. The hitcher's nose and jaw began to elongate and force themselves away from the rear of the skull, stretching the lips into a tight snarl.

Whatever was sitting before Kenny now bore no resemblance to the man he'd been facing moments before. The lean and athletic man was gone. The creature before him now was huge. Long hair had sprouted not only on the hands, but covered the whole of the body. The ears had contorted to a long point. The creature turned and snarled at the petrified driver. Kenny's stomach rippled and fluttered. The skin on his testicles crawled and shrank tightly. Every muscle in his body tensed. He'd seen enough. He scrambled for the door handle as the creature ripped at its seatbelt, shredding the remains of the clothes which hadn't already ripped at the seams.

Blind panic took over. Kenny fumbled the door open and ran into the A19, leaving everything behind in the cab. Brakes screeched. Horns sounded. Headlights swung left and right. Kenny ran in front of the stopped cars. Between the rising crescendo of horns, the savage roar pervaded.

He glanced over his shoulder to see the cab shaking as the beast trapped inside thrashed against its glass and metal prison. Then, amid the chaos, Kenny heard a loud smash of glass. Without looking he knew that the creature had flung itself through the windscreen. He ran into the road; cars missing by inches and did not stop until he'd reached the outskirts of civilisation. He couldn't know, but he was leading the creature towards that same civilisation. Towards York.

In a bright flash of memory he was in the darkness of the Colin's Café, flanked by Colin and Alison. Then he was alone. Trapped beneath the shutter of the café's front door, watching Alison sprinting, shrinking into the darkness of the alley across from the entrance. Colin was behind him, dead. The beast was behind him, too. Then the beast was on him. He felt the weight of the great wolf as it tore at his lower limbs.

Through the terror he thought he heard the sounds of the hospital room and the voices of those trying to save him. He heard their voices and felt the creature ripping at his flesh. Then he felt nothing. The only sound was the fragile beat of his heart. It slowed, each beat fainter than the last, till it beat no more.

5

The first thing Laszlo Breyer had become aware of was the singing of birds. Cold wind breathed against his naked skin. His eyes snapped open. Where was he? He sat up in the back seat of a car, the smell of wet decaying metal hanging in the air. He turned to see the rusting bodies of the car's comrades: more cars, washing machines, fridges lit by pale morning sun. A graveyard for white goods. All victim to progress and planned obsolescence. He wracked his memory, looking for the reason he was here. It came all too quickly.

Every time was the same. He'd had to go through the same routine. The surprise at waking up naked, in a foreign, unknown place. Though the transformation back from beast to man was much easier than the reverse. The first thing was there was no pain. He usually slept through it. The wild exertion was tiring, so sleep was difficult to fight. The second thing was, "coming back" the beast knew it was going to happen, through some ancient instinct that might be available to man, if he weren't so out of touch with his surroundings. He thought of it as an animal knowing its number is up and it wandering off to die alone. So every time he'd wake up lost and alone. And naked. But that wasn't the worst part.

His eyes shot down to his hands. He flipped palm, back, palm again. *No. Not again.* Blood. It wasn't the sight of blood that was the worst part, he had grown used to that. It was the not knowing. Being covered in blood and not knowing if it was the blood of one, or six (or even twelve, as it had been once, many moons ago). Not knowing if it was the blood of some menace to society, the wolf had an instinct for sniffing out threats to its Alpha status, or an innocent child. *Remember the little girl? God, how she screamed.*

A surge of guilt washed through him and he leapt from the car, bending double beside it and vomiting. Bright red vomit steamed in the bright white snow. The copper smell of blood rose and large thick chunks made him gag again. The chunks were flesh. He had killed. He turned away, not wanting to know, but his eyes caught sight of a partial tattoo. *At least it was an adult.* Another stream of vomit came. Again red. This was bad. His mind made a leap. He didn't have time for this. He had to go. *To Carr Wood. To find Lucy.*

The final part of his routine was getting ready for society again. Getting cleaned and clothed. Winter was good for getting cleaned. He found a drift of fresh snow that had piled up against a dead tumble dryer. He grabbed handfuls of snow, using the icy powder to clean his hands and face. He left a pile of pink snow behind and went in search of clothes.

Getting clothed had become easier these days; all of the major supermarkets had clothes banks outside. The flipside to this was that most of them had security cameras. He always disappeared after raiding the bin, so nothing had ever come of his bizarre CCTV appearances. All of the reasons above were why he preferred the controlled surroundings of the cabin. His next destination.

He headed for the road and tried to thumb a lift, to no avail. There was no shelter from the snow flurries on the roadside, and even less sympathy from passing drivers. There was a killer on the loose. Hitch-hiking in modern Britain was hard enough, but when your reputation precedes you (even if nobody knows it's *your* reputation) it becomes nigh-on impossible. The walk was a long one. Ten hours. Probably more, thanks to the snow. The cold north-easterly wind was like the Bora back in Hungary when he was a child. He didn't mind the winter. He enjoyed the freshness of the crisp air. He wanted a hat, not to keep his head warm but to hide his features. "Always have a hat", his father had told him, in a thick Hungarian accent. Breaking that particular commandment was the least of his sins. By the time the faint winter sun sank below the horizon he'd only be half way to the cottage. He'd make the rest of the journey on instinct, as the beast, but that wasn't what he wanted.

He wanted Jack Talbot to suffer. He wanted Lucy Breyer dead and he wanted Jack Talbot to know it was because of him, just like Jenny had been.

Killing Lucy would be a problem. Logistics aside, he knew that Lucy loved the cottage and just had to hope she'd moved back in, now she thought it was safe. If she wasn't there, he'd try her parents. No, the problem wasn't logistics. It was feelings. *Human* feelings. He had great affection for Lucy. The wolf had none. The wolf knew nothing of affection. Just primal instincts. To fight. To eat. He'd have to lock himself up with Lucy and when the sun set, the wolf would take care of the rest. She was tainted now detective Talbot had defiled her, what did he care? Talbot would find out; he'd make sure of that. He'd leave another note. Then he'd wait. Hide and wait. When Talbot's blood coursed with the sickly feeling of guilt at what he'd done, when he was least expecting it, he'd meet the same fate as Lucy. Breyer just had to reach the cottage before sundown.

6

Heavy silence hung in Cross's car. Jack turned the note over in his hands, not really reading it. He thought of the famous Sherlock

Holmes quote about eliminating the impossible. It was the only theory that fit. He couldn't believe he'd missed it. He'd closed his mind to the possibility, thinking it was only folklore, and then remembered another saying about the presence of smoke and the absence of fire. He turned the note again, this time his eyes falling on the one word not written in his scrawling red handwriting.

His name – printed – in blue.

He stopped. He stared at his name printed carefully on the back of the note.

'Phone,' Jack said urgently. 'I need a phone.'

Cross was still navigating the blizzard, 'What's wrong?' He sensed the seriousness from Jack's tone.

'I need a phone. Now.'

'We'll pull over at the next services.'

The next service station was ten minutes away. Jack never said another word until they got there and Cross never asked what was going on. At the services Jack marched from the car to the bank of payphones. One payphone out of the three there wasn't out of order. A woman was using it. If you'd asked him later, he wouldn't remember if she was young or old, attractive or otherwise.

Cross handed Jack some change and headed for the coffee shop. 'Back in a minute.'

Jack nodded, not really listening. The woman on the payphone was saying how much she missed whoever she was talking to and that she'd be able to charge her phone at the hotel and that she'd be arriving at the hotel soon and that she'd be back in a few days.

Jack cleared his throat.

The woman turned with a frown but didn't argue. Jack was a friendly guy, but he could look a mean bastard when he wanted to. He'd played his share of bad cop roles in his time and was now glaring from beneath a furrowed brow. The woman hung up and stormed off. Jack leapt at the phone and dialled. He paced as far back and forth as the cord would allow for what felt like an eternity to the metallic buzz of the ringing tone. Finally, somebody answered.

'Hello?'
'Bryan? It's Jack.'

7

Tommy sat at his cluttered desk in Finchley police station and read the forensics report again. This case was a weird one. Wolf fur. Not just any old wolf fur. Something closely *resembling* wolf fur. Fucking Jack Talbot. It couldn't be a *normal* wolf. It had to be a *new* kind of wolf. Then there was Homeless Mike's sketch, identical to the man seen on the petrol station CCTV last year. The man that killed Jenny. *Jenny*. Jack Talbot. Fucking rat. If he could keep his dick in his pants, Jenny would still be alive. He leaned round the bulky computer monitor, no expense spared at Finchley station, and said, 'Bryan...'

That was as far as he got. Bryan's phone rang. Bryan was a good friend. He'd been as upset as Tommy when Jenny died, and Tommy didn't think it was just because he'd seen it all. Bryan was also just as pissed off at Jack as he was. He'd found it odd that Bryan wanted to discuss the Breyer case with Jack rather than him on the day that Jenny was killed, but shit happens. It was always good to get fresh eyes on a case, a case which Jack knew better than anyone. And if Bryan hadn't gone to see Jack that day, he wouldn't have found Breyer. He would have slipped through the cracks again. Of course, as it turned out the info, he had on Breyer wasn't needed, and in its own way did lead to the capture of the killer.

Bryan lifted the receiver to his ears and clicked his fingers at Tommy, 'Hello, Jack. Where are you?'

Bryan's brow slid down over his eyes as he listened to Jack. He turned away from Tommy slightly. Tommy noticed his friend's cheeks slowly turn a deep shade of crimson. Bryan rubbed the back of his neck, 'Okay, Jack. I'll tell him.'

He slowly put the phone down. He swivelled his chair back round to face Tommy, 'Jack's in trouble.'

'And?' Tommy sneered, almost laughing.

'No, it's serious. It's the copycat. He's going to need our help.' Bryan looked serious.

He'd had his disagreements with Jack too in the past. That's why Tommy didn't like it. Something wasn't right.

'How come you give a fuck all of a sudden?'

'The case...'

'No, no. This isn't the case,' his eyes burned into Bryan. He'd been dicked around once too often on this case. It stopped now. 'There's something else... What?'

Bryan looked around, 'Let's go outside.'

Tommy didn't need to see the flurries of flakes blowing wave after wave through the snowstorm outside.

'It's fucking freezing...' Tommy was smiling.

Bryan was not. 'Tom. Seriously.'

Tommy stopped smiling and stood. 'Okay, let's go.'

They stood in the doorway and eyeballed the lonely smoker until he was intimidated back indoors. 'Sad bastard,' Tommy muttered shaking his head at the thought of voluntarily standing outside in this shitty weather.

'What have you dragged me out here for, Bryan? And why are you so keen on helping Jack Talbot out? What's going on between you two?'

'He's in trouble and he needs us, Tom.'

'I'll repeat,' Tommy said, with a stern look that told of his dislike of having his time wasted, 'why do you give a fuck?'

'Because it's not his fault.'

Bryan stared at Tommy, now testing his own resolve. Tommy had known Bryan long enough to recognise a glimmer of fear in that steely gaze.

Tommy thought through the possibilities of what that could mean, settling on the most obvious, and least satisfactory option, knowing full well what the repercussions of such acknowledgement were. It was always in the back of his mind, nagging, nibbling, but ignoring it hadn't made it go away. Now it was front and centre. Tommy caught a glimpse of his reflection in the window and almost felt sorry for Bryan. Almost.

'You'd better start talking.'

CHAPTER SEVEN

Bryan Dempsey eased his car around the housing estates of Finchley. His car knew the route by itself now. The sun was bright in the blue sky as he stepped into the crisp November air and looked at the house. A gentle breeze blew crisp golden leaves down the path. The autumnal colours in contrast to that bluest of skies. It was picture perfect. Almost.

Something's wrong.

He wasn't sure what it was. Just the jitters. He knew that Jack had been around moments earlier, but his car was gone now.

He had no way of knowing, but the disquiet was brought on by the sudden and violent movement that his subconscious glimpsed in the upstairs window. He eyed the house as he walked around the car and raised the boot open. He reached for the bunch of petrol station forecourt flowers. That's when he heard the screaming.

He snapped his head round to the house. On the face of it, all seemed normal. Looking back into the boot, he dropped the flowers and snatched up the cold metal of the crowbar. He stalked across the lawn, crowbar raised, not stopping to close the boot. As he crunched carefully up the gravel drive to the back of the house, the next-door neighbour peered through a crack in her door, her suspicious gaze glaring out and taking in all that surrounded her. She shrank back on seeing Bryan brandishing the heavy metal bar. He raised a finger to his lips to quiet her and then made his hand in the shape of a phone.

'Call the police,' he whispered, moving all the while.

The old woman quickly vanished behind her closing door without signalling. He'd just have to hope that the sight of him stalking with a crowbar was enough to spark the old lady into action. He edged to the rear of the house and rounded the corner to the back. The hair on the back of his neck stood on end. The floor was littered with splintered wood; the back door ajar with a gaping wound where the lock should be. As he entered the kitchen, the previous three and a half months flashed before his eyes.

He hadn't seen Jenny for over ten years, *twelve and a half,* when she walked into the corner shop that day. She was as beautiful and graceful as she had been the day she left, she'd aged really well, but there was a sadness in her eyes. *Problems with Jack? Was that why she was home?* Her eyes brightened a little on seeing Bryan.

'Jenny?' His voice cracked a little. He wiped his clammy hand on the back of his trousers. He needn't have bothered as Jenny bypassed the outstretched hand and gave him an enthusiastic hug.

'Oh my God, Bryan! Hi!' a dazzling array of white teeth displayed.

'How are you, Jen? You look great.'

Her cheeks reddened a little, 'I'm fine,' she said, putting a dash of emphasis on the '*I'm*'. 'It's dad. He's not doing so well, I'm afraid.'

'Oh,' Bryan's smile dropped, 'I am sorry to hear that,' he said, giving his *am* the same weight as Jenny's *I'm*.

'He's been unwell for a while as you know.'

As you know. Bryan saw Jenny's dad from time to time around the village (you have little choice in the matter when you live anywhere with a population of under five hundred), but they always chatted about the weather and how well, or badly, the Lions were doing. Or how England were mad to fire Peterson and they'd never have another batsman like him. And Bryan always asked about Jenny. Her dad said he'd pass on the message, but you never really knew in that situation. Now he did.

'I haven't seen him for a while,' Bryan uttered, thinking aloud more than in conversation. He pulled his thoughts together and offered, 'That is a pity. I always liked your dad.'

Jenny's face brightened, 'Yes,' she was unsure of where to put her eyes, but they finally settled on Bryan's, 'he always liked you.'

It hung in the air for a little too long. Bryan wanted it to last longer but didn't want things to become awkward. He blurted, 'Well, I have to go, but...'

He paused weighing up whether or not to say what he was thinking. It only lasted for a heartbeat, but he felt Jenny must have noticed.

'There's a nice little coffee shop opened on the high street, maybe we could catch up sometime?'

Jenny seemed relieved that the split-second silence was gone, 'Sure,' she offered a smile, 'it's a date.'

The silence was back.

'Well,' Bryan smiled trying to ignore it, 'great then, so, I'll see you...' And cue... nothing. *Very smooth, dickhead.* 'I'll see you.' He confirmed with a nod. *You're blurting again.*

He left before the whole thing became a disaster, feeling a gentle glow of embarrassment rising in his cheeks, but deep down he felt good. He honestly felt somewhere in the back of his mind that they had a chance of rekindling whatever you could call what they had going on before Jenny left for the city.

And that's how it went. Meetings at the coffee shop became more frequent, then moved to Bryan's house. Nothing happened, physically. Not at first. Jenny would hint at her deteriorating marriage to Jack, then offer: "I shouldn't be talking to you about this" before becoming embarrassed or upset. Despite this they very quickly became close again. Tommy wasn't to find out, even though he and Bryan were good friends – Tommy liked Jack a lot, they were partners after all, and he wouldn't take any extra marital activity lightly.

Bryan snapped back to reality on entering the kitchen. The waft of cooking filled the air as a pot of potatoes bubbled away to itself on the stove. Bryan reached over and turned off the gas. Wielding the crowbar he stalked into the downstairs hall. He peered upstairs as he approached the living room. He placed his hand flat on the door, his mind working overtime to separate the past and the present. He fought away a montage of thoughts of him and Jenny, in this house and his.

He was whip-cracked back to reality by the sound of struggling from upstairs. The hollow sound of a vase teetering, then falling, from a wooden table and landing with a dull thud on thick carpeting. The bedroom. He sprang into action, taking the stairs swiftly but quietly, two at a time, the noise of struggling enough to mask his footfall.

He rounded the corner to the bedroom to see a man huddled over Jenny's body. The vase glugged water into the carpet as her feet became still. He rushed the man, who half turned from his crouch just as Bryan swung the crowbar. The face was instantly recognisable as Laszlo Breyer, the Full Moon Killer. The crowbar made contact and the shockwave of the violent blow shuddered up the metal with a dulled whack off Breyer's jaw. It sent him sprawling, face down and out cold.

Bryan knew just looking at Jenny that she was already gone. He rushed to her side, crouched at Breyer's feet and leaned over Jenny's face to check for breathing. There was none. The rest of their past together whooshed at him like flakes in a snowstorm.

One day, when Jenny was lamenting Jack's commitment to their marriage, it happened. They'd gone from the coffee shop, to Bryan's house, to sharing the same settee, and before they realised what was happening, they were kissing. After a few seconds it stopped, and Jenny got up and left, despite Bryan's protestations. They tried to talk it over when they next met. And that was when they kissed for the second time. This time it didn't end abruptly. It was passionate and warm and it took Bryan back to those halcyon high school days. When it did end, there was a *What happens now?* discussion, in which Jenny highlighted her feelings for Jack, much to Bryan's befuddlement.

It occurred to Bryan that Jenny didn't want this to happen. That deep down she still had feelings for Jack, but their relationship had become so cold and distant, that it felt nice to be wanted again. That's what Bryan was to her. She felt she was the centre of somebody's attention.

Bryan recalled Jenny telling him his mum's first opinion when they were in high school. "A real catch" her mum had said, after their first meeting. She'd agreed. It was nice to be the centre of his attention. That week, the week of the second kiss, was the same week the Jenny's dad died.

It had been on the cards for a while and in the end, it was a release. Jenny said she used to wonder how somebody's death could be described as a blessing. Now she understood. Bryan sensed there was a part of her that wanted this to be a catalyst for her and Jack to get things back on track. It was true.

Fate decided to give Jack a break in the long, drawn-out case he and Tommy had been working. They couldn't both be at the funeral. It was her husband or her brother. Somebody had to stay and work. Of course, that had to be Jack. That night Jenny asked Bryan to stay with her. No funny business, she just didn't want to be alone. She stayed at Bryan's place. Later that same week Bryan slept with Jenny for the first time in twelve years. It was every bit as passionate as he remembered.

He pressed her to go through with the idea she'd been toying with for such a long time. Divorce Jack. The marriage was on life support. When Jack missed the funeral, Bryan sensed a shift in her attitude. Jack's visits were increasingly infrequent. When he did visit, he was put up in the spare room. They hadn't shared a bed in months. Yes, the marriage was on life-support, and when Jack missed the funeral, that was the day she turned off the machine. Two months later, on the very day Jack was supposed to visit the wife of the killer he was tracking on his new case, he'd received the divorce papers. It was a difficult, but necessary step, which she couldn't have taken – wouldn't have taken – without Bryan's support.

Now Jenny was dead. Now she would have her own funeral. Everything had come crashing down. His one chance at true happiness. First Jack had taken her, now Breyer. How had he found her?

Another noise in the room brought reality back to Bryan. A groan emanated from within the deathly silence of the four walls. The room where just last night, Bryan and Jenny had made love.

Was it Jenny? Had he been wrong? He looked at her. She looked so still. So beautiful. So peaceful. As if she were asleep. Red spots bloomed on her white blouse from where the knife had inflicted its damage. She wasn't asleep. She was dead.

He was entertaining the idea that the groan was his when, from his left, came another. And movement. Breyer. He'd started to raise himself up. Bryan filled with a surge of adrenalin the likes of which he'd never felt. Without realising it, he was standing over Breyer. Feet planted astride him, his knuckles whitening on the now warm metal of the crowbar. A low growl rumbled in his throat. He raised the bar deliberately with a trembling hand. The speed with which Breyer was moving surprised him. He tensed his arm and brought down the metal with such speed to slice through the air. The blow vibrated up the iron on contact with the back of Breyer's skull. It dropped him flat on his face. He groaned and made to get up again.

Bryan raised the bar quicker than Breyer could raise his now fractured skull. Once again he brought it down upon the same spot. This time Breyer didn't groan. He collapsed flat to the floor, his body convulsing in sickening violent jolts. Bryan raised the crowbar again. He brought it down hard. Again and again until the convulsions became a twitching of the feet, then the fingers. Each blow vibrated less and less as the bar sank repeatedly into the same area of raw meat and shattered bone. The copper smell rose, and each blow sprayed a fine mist of warm blood onto his shirt and face.

He could never remember how many times he hit Breyer. It was more than eight after the man was dead. The skull was a pulp at the back and chunks of bone had disappeared into brain tissue. Bryan panted for air. The dullness of rage had now come into crystal clarity. His grip weakened on the dripping crowbar and it fell from his grasp. He turned to leave; the police would be here any minute.

He stopped as he passed the bedside table. There was a slip of folded paper. It hadn't been there last night. Was it for him from Jenny? He picked it up and unfolded it. But the note wasn't for him. It was for Jack. He read the note to the end and started again from the beginning. Jack and Breyer's wife? Breyer did this because of Jack Talbot?

As he staggered from the kitchen, his breath still short from his frenzied attack on Breyer, he spotted the plain white envelope on the table. The divorce papers. He lurched outside and back down the gravel driveway and sat on the front lawn of the house, knees drawn up to his chest. The rising wail of sirens floated from the ether. The police were coming. Soon Jack would be here. He'd have to tell him something.

2

As Tommy Wainwright stood in the snow swept car park listening to Bryan's tale, anger rose within him. Before either man knew it, one of his ham fists had settled on Bryan's face. As big as Bryan was, the blow came as a surprise and knocked him sprawling into the snow.

Bryan held up his hands, 'Wait!' but there was little chance of that.

Momentum alone was enough to carry him onto Bryan, they rolled in the snow exchanging blows, Bryan trying to soothe Tommy all the time. He managed to get a grip of his emotions. He dragged Bryan to his feet.

'All this fucking time. You let me blame Jack for what happened to Jenny.' He panted, plumes of breath rising into the dusk.

'It wasn't something we planned.'

'He slept with Lucy Breyer because of the divorce.'

'I know,' Bryan puffed clouds of breath into the air. 'It got out of hand. I didn't know how to tell you.'

Tommy half turned away; face contorted in a mask of disgust. Bryan knew not to speak, unless he fancied rolling around in the snow again.

'At least Jack had the balls to tell me about him and Lucy,' Tommy said.

Bryan's head dropped in shame.

'He didn't use the divorce as an excuse, either. But you,' the same disgust washed over him, 'fuck me, Bryan. It was because of you. That's why Jack fucked Lucy Breyer. That's why Jenny's dead.'

'Don't you think I fucking know that?' Bryan screamed. 'I loved her, Tom. I always loved her. That's why I don't sleep at night. That's why I have to see a fucking therapist. Not because of what I saw. Because of what I've done. Not to Breyer, that piece of shit deserves to be dug up and dragged around wherever he is. What I did to Jenny.' Bryan was a big guy and it made Tommy awkward to see the thin traces of tears freeze to his red cheeks, 'I killed her.'

Tommy's turn to stare at the floor, 'Come on, don't say that. It wasn't your fault. Shit just happens.'

'Does it?' Bryan's voice was loud and faltering.

'You just wanted her to be happy.' His hands had stopped shaking and his chest rose and fell slowly now. 'I get that, but why didn't you say something?'

'You were so angry, Tom. Have you ever seen yourself angry? It's fucking terrifying.'

Tommy knew it was true. Bryan was a big guy, but Tommy had a look that could cut a man in two. Everyone told him that. Jack Talbot had been on the receiving end far too many times.

'So what happens now?' Tommy asked.

'Jack's on his way to North Yorkshire. He thinks the killer will go after Lucy now.'

'How does he know she's there?' Tommy asked.

'He doesn't. But it's all we've got.'

Tommy stood hands on hips and thought for a second, 'How long will it take us to get there?'

Bryan raised his eyes to the snow filled skies, 'This weather? We can be there maybe ten o'clock.'

Tommy nodded. 'We'd best get a wriggle on then.'

3

Jack Talbot trudged from the payphone and got back into Daniel Cross's car. He felt the snow tumbling down the back of his collar, but he was numb to the cold. To everything. Cross appeared, slid into the driver's side clutching two coffees-to-go.

'I put sugar in, I wasn't... Are you OK?'

Jack turned to cross and collected the coffee. He looked up at Cross, 'Jenny was having an affair.'

Cross slumped, like the news was a body blow, 'Jesus, Jack... I don't know what to say.'

'Not a lot you can say.'

'Are you sure? About the affair I mean.'

Jack nodded. 'It dawned on me when I saw young Danny's note. He'd printed my name on it. The note from Breyer. It didn't have a name on it.'

Cross seemed lost. Jack went on, 'The only way Bryan would have known that the note was for me was...'

'If he'd been at the house before,' Cross finished his sentence. 'But that doesn't mean they were...' he tailed off, not wanting to complete the dirty little thought.

'There was always something. I couldn't put my finger on it. I was too absorbed in my work, then shocked at her death, then numb from the drink. Today was the first real time I've thought about it. That might sound strange.'

Cross shrugged, perhaps not wanting to imagine what the last year and a bit had been like for Jack.

'I was too busy feeling sorry for myself. Blaming myself. Maybe that's what Bryan wanted. For the note to distract me,'

Cross puffed a breath of disbelief into the car.

'I don't blame him. This should make me feel better, but it doesn't. It's still my fault. If I'd paid more attention to her, she'd still be here.'

'Don't do this Jack.'

'It's OK,' Jack said, voice toneless, shocked. 'I pushed her away. I can't blame Bryan Dempsey for being attracted to her. She was beautiful. Really. We just... drifted, I suppose. Everything else was more important. I took her for granted. No wonder she looked elsewhere.'

Cross sat silently for a second. Jack was just starting to wish he'd speak when he did.

'What happens now?'

Jack turned to Cross, his eyes focussed, 'We go to the cottage and if Lucy Breyer is there, we hope we get to her before Laszlo does.'

Cross nodded. Without saying a word he fired the car into life.

Jack held on to his stomach in a pointless bid to stop the feeling of being on rough seas. Everything was shifting and he felt that the situation was getting further and further from his control. He glanced at the clock and knew immediately that there was no way of reaching the cottage before dark. They had wasted twenty-five minutes at the services. *How is that possible?* He couldn't fight the image of himself and Cross bursting into the kitchen and to find Lucy being devoured by the wolf. The fragile flame of hope flickered, and Jack knew the slightest hold up now could spell tragedy.

As Cross sped for the barren, desolate North Yorkshire Moors, the car was silent. There was no way that they could have known, but had they stayed on the road for another five minutes, instead of turning off to use the phone, they would have passed a lonely hitchhiker. Now that hitchhiker was half an hour ahead of them – in the back of a truck, with a dozen frightened sheep for company – and heading for the cottage.

4

Breyer sat in the back of the truck, bitter North Yorkshire wind screaming through the wooden slats. Despite the pure white blanket of snow, the sense of desolation was inescapable. The livestock squeezed into the corner as far as possible from him. They observed him with suspicious eyes, bleating wildly when they were forced closer to him by the camber of the road. The road perched on the crest of a hill which swept down on either side into vast shallow depressions that carried to the horizon. The snow had slowed now but its white blanket stretched as far as the eye could see. The truck rumbled then stopped.

He stood to a crescendo of bleating, the sheep jockeying for farthest position from the unwelcome guest. The hitcher peered over the cabin and saw a fork in the road. He hopped over the side and edged to the driver's window. Its squeak barely audible over the howling gale as it lowered.

The rugged old farmer shouted over the wind, 'That's as close as I can get you.'

Breyer nodded a thank you. The farmer rolled up his window and gave a thumbs up before pulling away. Alone, Breyer turned and weighed up his options. There was little point taking the road from here. The snow meant there was little difference between the roads and the moors between the cottage anyway. He opted for the moors.

He trudged into the six inches of snow which had fallen in the last twenty-four hours. The cruel wind pummelled him as he beat a path for the cottage, knowing that by the time he reached it, he would be something else. Inhuman. And that the creature would fulfil the prophecy in the note left for Jack Talbot. He thought that he might actually be able to kill Lucy, if he found her. It felt more and more like he was losing control, and that the beast was taking it. The beast had been stirred and something was driving it forward with more purpose than Breyer could himself muster. And it was more than he could fight. The taste for blood, perhaps.

He trekked through the snow towards the setting sun, dreading the inevitable. When the sun set and the only light available was that reflected from the silver lunar surface, he would become something unspeakable.

The pain which the transformation brought was like some kind of death and rebirth, three times a month, for as far back as he could remember. The part he dreaded most, though, wasn't the physical pain; it was the memories. The memories that tumbled from a sad, traumatic and haunted past. The trauma something that perhaps fuelled the creature's rage. When the sun set, it would all fall into place. The pain. First his, then Lucy's and, by proxy, Jack Talbot's. Yes, soon the sun would set, and that would be that.

5

In the darkness, Lucy Breyer was faintly aware of David Bowie, still urging her to turn and face the strain. That and a faint hissing. She was more aware of a dull pain in her shoulder, and an even duller pain in her head. And in a flash, it all came to her. The trip to the cottage to collect her painting, deceiving her parents to do so, and that patch of black ice. Leaving the road. David Bowie was still singing the same song. Her eyes sprung open. She glanced at the clock. Almost 3PM. The CD must have gone around in a loop. Twice.

The car had come to rest in the shallow ditch beside the road, somehow the right way up. The airbag had deployed covering her in a fine white powder. She had still hit her head, perhaps against the window, and her shoulder hurt from where the seat belt had locked and probably saved her life. The hissing came from under the crumpled bonnet of the car, accompanied by a gentle rising of steam and a faint whiff of petrol fumes. She frisked herself checking for other injuries and found none. That was a piece of good fortune to balance the rotten luck which had forced her from the road.

She surveyed her surroundings. There was a tinge of recognition of the area, even after a year. She must be close to the cottage. Maybe that had been luck, too. She looked back at the clock. Her parents would be back from the hospital and frantic by now. They'd have read the note, called the friend whose name was mentioned, and realised the whole thing was a lie. Now she was stuck here, with no mobile phone signal, close to the cottage. And close to sundown. She had no idea if she could be at the cottage before dark. And she hadn't been out after dark since... she beat the steering wheel and horn in a flurry of frustration, anger and foul language.

The feeling of calm and control that had been with her this morning was gone, replaced with something that felt like fate toying with her. These bleak surroundings were not finished with her just yet. An inch or two over the horizon, thin tendrils of clouds draped across a deep orange sun. Soon the sun would set and the already dark skies would turn black. She did not want to be outside for that. She turned off the engine with a hand that felt like a lead weight. Flinging the door open, Lucy Breyer stepped into the cold, and set off in the direction she hoped would lead her to the cottage.

6

As the blood red sun was sinking below the bleak horizon, Jack and Cross struggled through the countryside on a long road which crested the rise between two undulating depressions. The path had been partially cleared by the dual wheels of a truck, otherwise the journey would have been impossible. Cross stopped the car when they reached a fork in the road.

'Looks like the truck went the other way,' he said peering down at the printed map.

'We'll have to go on foot from here.' Jack said, opening his door to a blast of bitter wind.

His stomach rolled. The conditions were worsening by the minute. It would take them even longer to reach the cottage through this and that was time neither Jack Talbot nor Lucy Breyer had. The sour taste in his mouth made him want to vomit. He'd been finding it more and more difficult to swallow it down in the car, now he spat it out and moved around to the boot and took the two torches from inside. In his mind's eye that fragile flame of hope flickered. He peered through the open hatch back and into the front of the car and saw Cross frisk himself and pat his shirt pocket with some relief.

'Are you ready?' Jack shouted, over the howling gale.

Cross nodded and left the car and stepped into the deep blue twilight. The remaining moments of daylight that reflected from the white winter blanket reminded Jack somehow of the cemetery. He shuddered at the memory of that deep wound of exploded dirt gaping in the perfect white surroundings.

'Jack, look at this.' Cross shouted over the icy wind.

Jack strode to the driver's side and found Cross staring down. Jack turned on a torch, its silver beam twinkled in the snow surrounding the footprint. He handed the other flashlight to Cross as he manoeuvred the shaft of light along the trail.

'That must be him, right?' said Cross.

Jack followed the trail with his torch until it disappeared over a rise in the distance. He nodded, 'Cottage is that way. Let's go.'

The two men followed in the hitcher's footsteps into the night, fully aware that at any moment, he would be a man no longer.

7

The hills rose ahead of Laszlo Breyer as the final sliver of red glowing sun disappeared below the horizon. His heart seemed sluggish in his heavy chest. It was coming at any moment. He braced himself for the searing agony of metamorphosis. The death and rebirth of his mutation from man to beast. His breathing became rapid; shallower. He stared at the ground as he trod through the pure white snow, bitter wind biting his face. It was the expectation that killed him. Knowing that as he became less man and more beast, that images of the past he'd rather forget would flood back. And now it was time.

He felt his heart quicken, the pulse throbbed deep and powerful. He could hear his heartbeat and the blood coursing through his veins, then – nothing. It all stopped. But there was no relief. He knew it was temporary. He knew what was coming. He stopped dead and braced himself. Every muscle in his body tensed. He fell to his knees as sweat trickled between his shoulder blades. He felt the temperature rise. His clothes seemed to tighten, further constricting the chokehold on his heart. He ripped off his coat and jumper and threw them to the ground. He was ready for the pain.

An atomic explosion of agony detonated, its epicentre deep inside those darkest recesses of his brain. He screamed a guttural roar and his muscles seized as the first of many images flashed through his mind.

Bright moonlight glistening off the narrow, wet, cobbled streets of York. The old couple staring at the map. Arguing. The sticky warmth of blood. The look of fear in her eyes. Fear mixed with anger in his. A whip-crack of noise and pain dragged the killer kicking and screaming back to the present.

His muscles tensed. Burning from within. The fiery furnace expanding the flesh above. His athletic build swelling – growing muscular. His screaming bones ached. Bang. Another set of memories and images exploded into his mind's eye.

The dark dirt country lane. Cold hard ground underfoot. The unconscious body. Two more dismembered at his feet. A third screaming. Not fear. Anger. White skin-tight T-shirt torn. Soaked in blood. Screaming, "Fucking eat him." Another surge of fiery pain.

He stretched his arms out in front of him ploughing channels into the snow. Thick, dark hair sprouted from the backs of his hands. They convulsed, fixing themselves into a claw. Searing heat emanated from the core of the bone as the metacarpals slowly, agonisingly elongated before his eyes. A pop preceded more images. More memories. They came faster now.

Foul stench of soiled clothing. An alley between two tall brick buildings. Light crunch of crimson snow. Unwashed man hollering abuse. "You fucking don't belong here. Go back to where you come from." The snapping of brittle bones. Silence. Pain.

The burning heat started in his mind and surged in waves through to the extremities of his shifting body. The waves extended to the tips of his fingers. Each one pushed his fingernails. Extending outward until they fell away. Thicker, denser nails behind them. Shark-teeth replacements which extended beyond the reach of their predecessors.

Another wave of pain brought the next set of impressions of that wild creature he was moments from becoming.

Dog barking. Hiding in trees. Hunger. Hunger. Blinking red eye. Dog scared. Silent. Blood. Pain.

From somewhere inside his skull he heard a high-pitched whistle. He felt it. This didn't come with burning. This was ice cold, and infinitely more painful. His teeth. The canines screamed as they extended downward in exquisite agony. His facial bones resonated and trembled. Then, with a loud crack, they separated. It felt as if his face had caved in on itself before he felt it push out again, bones searing until they formed a snarling muzzle. For the briefest of moments he felt he couldn't breathe and he was back in the nightmare box of memories.

Darkness. Paralysed. No; restricted. Awareness. Convulsion. Trapped. A coffin. No air. Can't breathe. Can't...

Dense hair had grown on his hands and arms. The growth of his muscles had torn away the trousers. His feet had changed as his hands had, ripping the stitching from the shoes, until they too fell away. The man was almost dead. The beast almost risen. More flashbacks came faster now.

River. Warm air. Wind whispering through grass. Little girl. Screaming. Screaming. Blood. Silent. Man. Gun. Pain. Darkness.

Suddenly the memories changed. No longer those of a man remembering the beast. Those of a beast remembering a man. Memories of a man who loved. Who dreamed. Who spoke and heard words that the creature could not understand.

A man. Older. Love. Sadness. "I'm sorry, son". A woman. Her pity. Their pity. Tears. "My Laszlo. It has to be this way". Regret. A weapon. In my hands. The man's hands. A short weapon. Rough wooden handle. Silver blade. Tears. Pain. Death. Relief. Release.

Yes, the man was gone. The beast let out an ungodly howl. The kind that Lucy Breyer sometimes heard when her husband was away, if the wind was blowing the right direction. The images came faster, as if to confirm the transformation from man to beast.

A doctor's office. A kind man. "You understand, Mr Breyer, that this operation is irreversible". A voice. My voice. The man's *voice. "I don't want to reverse it. I don't want them to have to live with what I have had to". The doctor nods, trying to hide his pity.*

A boat. An old boat. Wooden. Creaking. The seas rough. The man and woman. Younger now. Speaking, but not in English. Hungarian. "Don't worry, little one, soon we will be there, in England".

Angry people. The Countryside now. Warm summer's night. Carrying torches of fire. Shouting. Hungarian. "Monsters! Get out! Go!"

The man was now gone. His memories blinked from existence. Laszlo Breyer had become the wolf. He rose from all fours onto his hind legs and let out a screaming howl of pure rage. The silent silver moon smiled down upon its creation. Soon the beast would be at the cottage. Soon the beast would be with Lucy Breyer.

CHAPTER EIGHT

The shadows rose and fell in the footprints as the thin silver beams of torchlight shone and twinkled on the surface of the snow. The footprints had a fuzziness about them as fresh snow blurred the sharp edges. If the snowfall continued at its current rate, they would soon lose the trail completely, and in his mind's eye, Jack Talbot saw the flame flicker.

He and Daniel Cross trudged in the lonely darkness towards the cottage, torches trained on the trail beaten by Laszlo Breyer, shoulders hunched to keep out the cold. The biting wind no longer a constant gale, now coming in bitter, savage gusts. The ominous dark of Carr Wood flanked them to their left, the cold quickness of death threatening to leap out at any moment. Their breaths formed in clouds before them which the wind snatched away in violent bursts, the ferocious gusts rushing through the falling snow in speeding currents. They struggled up the latest in a series of rises, which would be followed by the inevitable downward swoop, but this one was different.

As the snow-covered moors swept away before them, something became visible in the distance: a dark mound in the trail of footprints. Jack stopped, grabbing Cross's arm. Cross looked up at Jack, who pointed at the dark shape in the distance. Both men trained their torches on it, squinting into the strange blue darkness. The men stalked along the line of footprints. As they got closer to the huddled shape they slowed. Jack reached a hand back to stop Cross.

'Clothes?' said Cross.

The single trail of footprints led to a large winter coat and jumper bundled together. A pair of ripped trousers and boots lay in a hollowed flat shallow in the snow a yard or so across. But that wasn't the reason the two men had stopped. There had been some sort of wild commotion. It was smattered with blood. Jack walked along the edge. The grisly crimson mess glistened in the torchlight.

'Fresh.'

He leaned closer, Cross at his shoulder. Just off the main area were two channels, with small bloody squares peppering the edges.

'What is that?' asked Cross, leaning in closer. 'What are…? Shit. Fingernails.'

Jack leaned in himself. Five each at the end of two bloody canyons. Cross vomited.

'Cross. Look at this,' Jack barely recognised his own voice. It sounded hollow, distant.

Cross turned his gaze to Jack's torch beam. At the far side of the bloody hollow the trail of footprints continued. Only they were different. Cross got closer. As he did it was clear to see that the second trail of prints was bigger, and not those of a man. Cross patted his breast pocket through his coat.

'Jesus.' Cross stared down as he followed the prints, 'Looks like two legs up to here,' he pointed his torch at the neater set of prints, 'then four legs onwards,' to where the prints became clustered.

It confirmed everything. What had been theory an hour ago, was now chilling reality. Cross inspected the prints. The violent gusts they were shouting over stopped, as if sensing the magnitude of the moment. Huge snowflakes gently drifted to the moors. Suddenly, from the darkness, came a deep, ungodly howl.

Both men stood bolt upright. Neither moved. The hairs on the back of Jack's neck rose in a chill. The wind kicked up again, shaking both men to life.

'That wasn't a man.' Cross said, casting furtive glances in all directions.

'No, it wasn't.' Jack's voice full of doubt. The words fell unconsciously into the night as his keen eyes scanned the woods.

'Lucy.' Jack snapped back to reality. He prayed that she wasn't in the cottage. It seemed Cross had the same thoughts.

'How far is it to the cottage?'

Jack checked his watch. 5PM. Thoughts flashed into his mind. It would be dark for another fifteen hours. Tommy and Bryan, if they were coming, wouldn't be here for maybe another three. He and Cross had been walking for just over half an hour, which meant they wouldn't reach the cottage for, 'Thirty minutes. Twenty-five if we get a move on.'

The thought dawned on him that if Lucy wasn't at the cottage, and that the killer had the same idea, that he and Cross were walking into a death-trap. He glanced at Cross, who looked less excited and more nervous with each step. He felt sorry that Cross was involved, but if Lucy was in danger, he'd need Cross's help. He'd spent the last year trying to keep people from getting hurt, like Jenny had. Now, here he was, leading Cross into a life or death situation to save Lucy. How could he have been so stupid? He'd learned nothing.

He stopped. He grabbed Cross. Cross tried to walk on, 'Come on, there's no time.'

'Wait Danny,' Jack shouted over the rising wind.

Cross halted. It was the first time Jack had called him Danny since they were drunk. He stared over his shoulder at Jack.

'If you want to go back...'

Cross shook his head.

Jack desperately tried to convince his friend. 'It's OK. This is my thing, I don't want...'

'No Jack,' Cross interrupted. 'Ever since this started I've had a feeling that there was more to it. This is the kind of thing somebody like me waits their whole lives for. There's no way I can stop now, especially if the woman's in danger.'

Jack nodded.

Cross's eyes twinkled. 'Besides,' he said, reaching inside his coat and into his shirt pocket, 'you need me.'

Jack smiled when he saw what Cross was holding. They set off again, and hoped that Lucy Breyer wasn't home.

2

Lucy Breyer was stuck in the one place she didn't want to be. Until dawn. She stared into the fire, thankful she'd asked the estate agent to ensure there would be logs ready and waiting for the new owners. But that was the single comfort here. Everywhere she looked, she was reminded of Laszlo. Her mind drifted to the good times early on. Then to the monthly absences. The angry accusations. Outside, the wind howled. The thought of taking the gun down from the display plinth over the kitchen fireplace had crossed her mind, but even now, after all the time seeing it every day she'd lived here, she couldn't be sure if the damned thing even fired.

The night outside wailed and howled. The kind of night she was happy to have a roof over her head. She jumped as the gently crackling logs let out a loud pop. Her eyes were instinctively drawn to the window. From the corner of her eye she caught a movement. A shadow passing through the bushes. The fire cracked again. She put a hand to her chest to stop the escape of her pounding heart. She'd always felt so safe here, now she was frightened and tired. The idea of sleeping in that bed sickened her. There was a fire here and its warmth did provide some comfort and sense of home. Downstairs also had the added bonus of being close to escape.

Icy wind whistled through the frames of the sash windows and her body trembled in a violent shiver. If she was to sleep downstairs, she'd have to collect another blanket. From upstairs. She'd have to leave the safety of the settee and the comfort of the blanket already wrapped around her, then go to the hallway in the dark. The idea was not appealing. *Stop being such a wimp.* She kicked the blanket off her legs and headed for the door. The wind died to a whisper and she was now aware of other sounds. The house creaking which at one time would have had no effect on her whatsoever. But in this new silence every noise was amplified. She peaked around the corner of the door frame into the darkness. Moonlight shone off the endless white outside and cast a strange blue glow into the kitchen. She'd forgotten the shadows and shapes of the place. It had never struck her before, but now the cottage gave her the creeps. It felt as if she were being watched; her every move scrutinised by unseen eyes.

And that shadow outside.

The idea of leaving the cottage altogether and spending the night in the car was an option. It had left the road but landed right side up. It could be warm with enough blankets. At least she wouldn't have to spend the night in this creepy old house. An acute sadness touched her as she remembered how much she'd once loved it here. The idea of leaving suddenly seemed strange. It was a house. Just a house. Stone and brick. It couldn't hurt her. She'd spend the night in the living room by the fire and at first light, walk towards the nearest village until the point along the way where there was a mobile signal. Then she could call dad.

That was tomorrow; now she needed blankets.

She edged out into the blue glow. She reached a hand around the corner and hit the switch. No fumbling, her hand still knew where to go after a year. The upstairs landing light came on throwing a shaft of technicolour into the hallway. She hurried upstairs as if the devil himself were chasing her.

She was almost right.

It was as her foot touched the top step; she heard the kitchen window explode. Splintering glass tinkled to the stone kitchen floor. Glass and something else.

Something alive.

Something huge.

Her mind raced to answer the question of what it was, and filled the gaps in her knowledge with all manner of horrors. Any one of them would have been better than the reality. She let out a scream. If whatever it was needed any help locating her, it just got it.

Her mind plucked out one of the plethora of memories flashing before her eyes. It was Laszlo. He stared at her, those amber eyes focussed with an intensity she'd never seen.

'Don't be silly, Laszlo,' she smiled. Standing hunched in the cubby hole in the corner of their bedroom.

For once her smile wasn't reflected in his chiselled eastern European features, 'I'm serious, Lucy.' She stopped smiling. 'If anyone comes into the house this is where you hide. I want you to promise.'

His eyes pleaded more than his words ever could.

The small doorway in the corner of their bedroom led to an equally small room, barely big enough to fit a man, the wooden door to which had been reinforced with steel bars. A tiny cell door, she thought.

The cell was where she was heading now. She heard the scurrying of claws displace glass on the stone floor. The sound of snarling grew as the thing left the kitchen. Then she heard the heavy feet thud on the stairs. She had never set foot in the tiny room in the corner of their bedroom but promised to use it in an emergency. This qualified. She burst into the bedroom, the presence behind her already upstairs. Whatever it was, it was unnaturally fast. The snarling grew louder as it gained on her. She set her eyes on the tiny door and slid for it. The heavy door's hinges groaned and slowly, with all her effort focussed, the door moved. The thing was already in the room with her as she crawled into the space.

She turned and saw the huge predator through the ever-decreasing gap as the heavy door thudded closed. A huge wolf with snarling jaws was bearing down on the other side. She fumbled for the bolt in the darkness. The creature slammed the outside of the door forcing it open a crack, a thin shaft of light bursting into the hiding cell, the creature's wild eyes coming into view for a horrific moment. But the blow wasn't enough to force the door wide. It had done that for which it had been designed. Straining every sinew she slammed it shut and in the heavy blackness, slid the dead bolt into the hollowed stone. Laszlo really didn't want anyone in here.

For a terrifying second, she realised that this was like her dream. The thick, cold metal bars, and the rough wood of the door. Laszlo trying to get in, to hurt her. This room was smaller, much smaller than in her dream, but... Another thought followed – no, a realisation, more terrifying than the first: she had been having the dream since she was a child. It all fell into horrifying place. She wasn't here because of circumstance; she was here because of fate.

That wasn't the thing she found most frightening.

All she could think of, sitting here alone, the cold stone floor chilling her as sticky cobwebs pulled at her clothes, tugged at her hair, in this tiny black dungeon, all she could think of were those eyes. Those amber eyes. The creature's eyes – *Laszlo's* eyes. They were wild now, full of rage, but they were undoubtedly his. She would never be able to explain it rationally – after all, Laszlo was a man; Laszlo was dead – but she was certain. The door rattled as blow after savage blow rained on the other side. She could make out the level of frenzy by the shadows moving in the thin crack of light that poured beneath the door. The light burst into stars through her tears, and the wolf growled louder than her screams. She squeezed the cold metal bolt in both hands, fixing it in place, and prayed for help to arrive.

3

Jack Talbot and Daniel Cross strode purposefully up another rise in the landscape. Jack was tiring. It became harder to lift his leaden legs from the weighty grip of the snow. He couldn't have imagined how difficult this would have been just twenty-four hours ago, with his body steeped in alcohol. It was still in him, but with Cross's regulation and management he was in much better shape. Drinking at regular intervals to keep the shakes at bay meant the rolling fog in his mind was now a manageable mist. He lugged a heavy foot close to the top of the rise. As he planted it the cottage came into view. He felt a surge of renewed energy.

'Look!' cried Cross, 'It's here!'

Jack felt relief at the sight of the cottage two hundred yards ahead, but it soon faded when he saw the glow of fire in the downstairs window. Somebody was home.

'Shit,' Jack said to himself as much as Cross, 'the window. Look!'

Cross's eyes followed Jack's finger, which pointed not at the gently glowing window of the living room, but at the hole where a window should be at the opposite end of the house.

They hurried, both men seeming to draw a fresh sense of urgency from the sight before them. Gusts of howling wind covered any noise from inside, but as they neared the old building the sounds of wild growling rose and drifted until plucked from the night by the gale. They ran the final few yards to the house. Cross reached the front door first.

'Locked!' he shouted against the wind.

'The window!' Jack replied.

Jack scrabbled through into the half light of the kitchen, landing uneasily, shattered glass crunching underfoot. The attack upstairs was frenzied, but the only noise was the wolf. Sickness washed over him in a wave. They were too late. Cross landed behind him with a crunch. His face whitened when he heard the beast upstairs. He pointed over the fireplace.

'Get that.'

Jack turned to see the old Winchester. He reached up, grabbing it from the wall and thrust it at Cross. Cross shoved his hand into his shirt pocket and removed the object carefully carried from his living room in York. A shining silver bullet.

He grabbed the bolt handle. It screeched in objection at Cross's manhandling as he tried to slide the bolt aside to load the bullet.

'Come on.' Jack urged.

'It's stuck.'

Cross's faced trembled with strain as the bolt handle finally gave way. He loaded the solitary bullet into the gun and with the same stress slid the bolt back into place. He removed the safety guards. It was ready. He nodded at Jack.

A scream came from upstairs. Lucy. Jack exhaled a breath of relief – she was alive. The relief and thought both vanished before the scream ended. Without pause for thought, Jack bound upstairs, the full moon watching through the landing window, the armed Cross locked and loaded at his heels. The world seemed to fade out as time slowed. He noticed the smallest details. The floral design in the wallpaper on the staircase. How the tall table in the recess on the upstairs landing was a little too small and spindly not to look out of place where it was. Then he was upstairs.

Jack turned to the source of the horrendous noise. In the bedroom, the hulking monster was clawing wildly at the corner. Was he too late? Another scream. Lucy was alive. Beyond the wolf, Jack saw a small wooden door, deep claw marks gouged into it. He'd remembered seeing the door a year ago, but never paid it any mind. Now he couldn't tear his eyes away from it. The wolf had made a hole revealing thick metal bars inside. Jack peered through the bars; straight into Lucy's eyes.

'Jack!'

Frenzied attack became stony silence. The beast turned. Its hulking figure blocking out the sight of Lucy's terrified eyes. It was only now Jack got a real sense of how big the wolf was. Its amber eyes settled on Jack, and its brow drew into a deep scowl. The bed the only thing standing between him, and this monster. Jack took a tentative step back. He held out a hand to Cross on the stairs beside him, 'Get ready.'

Cross already had the gun raised, but his position on the staircase meant he only had a narrow view of a few feet of landing. Jack edged backwards until he was out of sight.

The wolf glared, a low growl coming from deep within his throat. It lowered its head, eyes burning into Jack. It lasted less than a second, but to Cross and Jack it felt like minutes. The wolf and Jack stared, each finally coming face to face with his nemesis. Breyer growled, then, without warning, charged.

Lucy screamed as it bound over the bed with freakish speed.

'Now!' Jack shouted.

It happened in moments. For a split second the wolf came down in the centre of the landing, and he hoped, the centre of the sights, preparing to leap at Jack. The silence was shattered by gunshot. The wolf, ready to pounce, cried out and was thrown with barbarous force. It smashed the spindly table in the recess below the window to splinters and hit the wall, leaving a splatter of blood. It lay motionless, smoke rising from the bullet wound in its leg. Jack rushed past the monster to Lucy. She scrambled from the hiding hole and hugged Jack. His legs almost buckled. Lucy was safe. They had done it.

'Oh, thank God you're OK.' A trembling laugh followed.

'Jack, what are you doing here?'

'The killer. He's back.' Jack felt no shame at stating something so obvious. He cupped her face in his hands, 'It's...'

'Laszlo. I know.'

Her eyes were ringed with tears. He hugged her again and squeezed tighter now. Not through any sense of love, nor anything sexual, it was pure relief. A weight had lifted. He became aware of Cross talking behind him.

'Jack?'

Jack turned. Cross, deadly pale, stared at the wolf.

'Jack...' his voice trembling uncontrollably, 'it's still breathing.'

It wasn't possible. Jack grabbed Lucy's hand and led her to the top of the stairs. Lucy edged around the corner and Cross took her hand. Jack edged around too, watching the chest of the huge creature rise and fall in shallow breaths.

Jack turned to Cross, 'Please tell me you've brought more than one bullet.'

Cross was lost in the moment, his gaze fixed on the gentle rise of the beast's chest.

'Danny!'

He snapped out of his trance and nodded. He reached back into the inside pocket of his coat. As he fumbled around his face took on a newer shade of pale. A huge sigh came as he made a grabbing motion in the pocket. He pulled the trembling hand free and clutched a second bullet. The wolf stirred.

'Hurry up, Danny.'

Cross struggled with the bolt handle. It ground back with a scream as he slid the bolt. The bullet slipped from his grasp and bounced downstairs. Jack led Lucy down for the bullet.

'I've got another,' Cross shouted.

The wolf shifted its weight. Cross reached in for the bullet, swiftly pulling it from the pocket and sliding it into the rifle. He tried to load the bullet; the action was stuck.

'It won't move.'

From the foot of the stairs Jack looked up at Danny. Cross's voice had an odd quality to it. Jack realised that he was about to cry.

'Just leave it. Come on!'

The rifle clattered to the floor as Cross stumbled downstairs. He had got about halfway down. Then the growling came. Cross burst past and took Lucy into the kitchen. Jack followed, and broke around the corner into the kitchen himself. The wolf tumbled downstairs and smashed into the wall. Cross helped Lucy through the window. Cross followed, watching the wounded wolf struggle to its feet. Jack raced for the shattered window. He half turned to see the wolf limping towards him from the corner of his eye. He and the wolf jumped in unison: Jack for outside, the wolf for Jack. The wolf reached for him claws outstretched. Jack just cleared the window. The wolf had missed. It landed onto the shattered glass of the kitchen floor and howled in pain.

'The cabin!' Jack pointed into Carr Wood.

They ran, unsure of exactly where to go to find the cabin, but sure in the knowledge that the dreadful, wounded monster that was once Laszlo Breyer was close behind them. They sprinted for the dark of the forest. He thought they'd done it. That they'd succeeded. That they'd escape and all would be fine. The reality was that they didn't know where exactly it was they were heading, that it was far away, and that the wolf was faster. And in his mind's eye, Jack watched as the faint flame of hope flickered, then blew out.

4

Tommy's Toyota snaked along the country roads with slushed snow spewing behind it. Inside, Tommy and Bryan sat in total silence. Tommy glanced at the dashboard clock, then angled his watch to his eyes for confirmation, hands still glued to the wheel. What Jack had told Bryan on the phone made no sense. It couldn't be Breyer. Breyer had been buried in the same cemetery as Jenny. (What an insult *that* was.) No, it couldn't be him, Jack must have been mistaken. It had to be a copycat. Probably a family member. He knew that if this copycat was anything like Laszlo Breyer, he was a fierce adversary. The treacherous snow filled roads were worsening by the minute. He cursed the conditions.

The journey had been totally silent. He hoped for Bryan's sake it stayed that way. The last thing Bryan needed was to give him an excuse. All this time Bryan had let him blame Jack for Jenny's death, and never said a word. He sensed that Bryan was as eager to help Jack as he was, and understood now the reluctance he had shown in not rushing to point the finger at Jack in the aftermath of the whole Breyer affair. Yes, he was angry, but that wasn't the driving emotion. If anything happened to Jack now, he'd never forgive himself. Or Bryan.

In his peripheral vision he saw Bryan grip the grab handle with all he had as the car swung to and fro. He knew he was driving too fast, but if Bryan dared tell him to slow down...

The car rose over an incline which dipped away wildly. Tommy jabbed the brakes with his foot. The car fishtailed as he fought to regain control. The car spun wildly and the men were thrown like rag dolls until the car settled in the middle of the road facing the way it had just come.

Bryan clicked the seatbelt off and jumped from the car into the freezing night.

'Fuck's sake Tom are you trying to get us both killed?'

The words drowned by strong gusts of biting wind. Tommy jumped from the car, 'You fucking got us into this. I'm trying to get us out.'

Bryan glanced along the road. He did a double take, 'Look!'

Tommy stared along the road to Cross's abandoned Volkswagen. Without another word both men jumped back into their own car and crawled onward. The headlights swung until the two cones of light settled upon Cross's forsaken Polo. Tommy edged the two hundred yards distance, then stopped. They grabbed their torches, flicking them on in unison, and jumped out into the darkness.

'This way,' Tommy shouted, head down staring at the tracks of footprints left by their quarry.

After thirty minutes of hiking they came across a pile of bloody clothes. The cottage was thirty more minutes away.

5

Jack's torch beam danced through the trees of Carr Wood. Cross and Lucy ran just ahead of him, trying to stay on their feet in the perilous conditions. Jack didn't dare look back. He didn't need to. Every few yards he'd hear an anguished snarl from behind. It was far too close for comfort – pained, but very much alive.

'Why isn't it dead, Cross?' Jack shouted breathlessly.

Cross didn't look back, but Jack heard him quite clearly, 'I only hit its leg.'

It was at that moment, as he jumped over fallen trees and ducked low branches, after watching Lucy and Cross do the same ahead of him, the whole picture of Laszlo Breyer's sorry life flashed through Jack's mind.

A silver bullet alone wouldn't kill the wolf. It had to be a lethal shot. When wounded with silver, it would stay wounded, but if the injury was just a flesh wound, it wouldn't kill. Cell regeneration wouldn't happen. Couldn't happen. Likewise if the fatal blow wasn't handed out with silver, then it wouldn't stay fatal. The cells would regenerate, every full moon. Until there was life. Laszlo Breyer had recovered from the gunshot wound from Eddie Sweeney. He'd recovered bit by bit and woken up as a wolf. Woken up trapped in a coffin barely big enough to hold him. He'd have tried to escape, minutes at a time, until the oxygen ran out, every full moon for months. He'd done it in 1978, and again two nights ago. Breyer's smashed skull reformed, and as it did, his body experienced the reverse effects of his violent death. His skull would rebuild back to the condition where his fingers twitched. Then his feet. Then, as the skull and soft mess of brain within were almost fully formed, the whole body would be taken over with violent convulsions. He shuddered. Now, the same Laszlo Breyer that lay dead a few nights ago was chasing them through the woods. Badly injured, but very much alive.

As they ran Jack swept the torch left and right, hoping to catch something in the search beam. The snarls still came from behind, but now they seemed further away.

'We're losing him,' Jack shouted to the others.

Beams of light cut through the darkness until, almost as one, they settled on something through the thinning trees in the distance.

'Here!' shouted Jack.

All three sped towards the structure hoping it could provide shelter until help arrived. They ducked and leapt over the uneven terrain in single file as they approached the relative sanctuary of the cabin. Twigs snapped underfoot as they swept low branches aside. Another growl came, this one further still.

A thick log marked the edge of the clearing. Cross jumped. He planted his leg at the other side. The ground gave way underneath and there was a loud crack. Cross let out an agonised scream. Lucy almost landed on Cross as she bound over the log. Jack came down at the other side eyes fixed on Daniel Cross.

'Shit,' he said through gritted teeth. His voice trembled. Not fear or pain. Shock, 'The ankle. It's broken.'

Jack looked down. Cross's foot was at a right-angle to the shinbone. Jack looked back up at Cross's pale face, his eyes were lost in disbelief. To get so close to safety and have it so cruelly snatched by fate. Another growl, this one closer.

Cross looked up at Jack. 'Go. Go without me.'

There was so little time. The wolf would be upon them any minute. Cross looked resigned to his fate. And what an awful fate it would be. Eaten alive. Savaged by a wild animal. Jack handed Cross's torch to Lucy, 'Get in the cabin.' He reached down and dragged Cross to his feet. Lucy stared in shock at Cross's horrific injury.

Jack turned to Lucy, 'Lucy. GO!'

She jolted to reality and raced for the cabin. Jack and Cross close behind. From the darkness of the woods came another snarl. So close now it made Jack's skin crawl.

'Leave me, Jack. We won't make it.'

Jack gritted his teeth. To get so close. He tensed and felt himself double in strength. Lucy reached the cabin door as the growling grew louder. An ungodly howl echoed through the woods lit by that deep blue lunar luminescence.

'Oh God.'

Lucy began kicking the door. She glanced over their shoulders back into the woods. Her eyes wide, she turned back to the door and kicked with more force and urgency. Jack and Cross hobbled closer, followed by the sense that this thing could leap after them at any second. With a loud crack the door gave way, padlock clanging to the ground.

Jack glanced back before entering. He lugged Cross into the cramped space of the cabin. Three little pigs in the wooden house. He pointed at the door in the opposite corner.

'There!'

Lucy ran to the door and Jack gently nudged Cross to follow her. Jack toyed with the idea of barricading the door. The image of the wolf bursting through it like paper entered his mind and he ran after the others.

Lucy screamed, 'Jack, hurry!'

He entered that small, strange place in the rear of the cabin to find Cross and Lucy huddled in the back of the cage. Jack entered and grabbed the heavy chain coiled on the floor. He wound the chain around the bars at the door before scurrying beside the others.

'Turn off the torches.'

A twin click of switches and the cage room was plunged into darkness.

'What is this place?' Lucy whispered. But she knew. She'd seen it in her nightmares. Now she was wide awake.

Jack gave a gentle shush. Outside a floorboard squeaked. The wolf had arrived. Cross gritted his teeth, clearly in agony. There came another sound from outside. Light footsteps. Jack eyed the chain which bound the cage door and prayed it was enough to keep the wolf at bay.

Then, in the pitch darkness of the cabin they heard the front door creak. The wolf was inside.

6

Jack watched through the crack in the door leading into the main room, his chest still heaving from the exertion of the sprint through the woods. Behind him he could hear Lucy trying to control her breathing and Cross gasping for air through pained, shallow gulps. They'd travelling the thirty-minute walk in less than twenty. Jack was amazed that he'd been able to run at all, considering that he'd been swimming in wine the previous morning. Way back when he was thinking of killing himself. Ending it all was far from his mind now. Quite the opposite. Funny what the fear of God will do to you.

All the narrow angle of sight would allow Jack into the next room was a view of the back wall painted with moonlight from the small window. More dim light flowed into the darkness as the front door was edged open. Jack's breath tumbled in silent clouds from his gaping mouth. He froze. The floorboards groaned. Lucy breathed heavily from her nose over the hand clasped to her mouth. Jack moved back alongside her and squeezed her other hand, either to calm her or quiet her; even he wasn't sure which. On the far wall a large shadow grew to an impossible size. Then, it stopped.

There was silence. Jack, Lucy and Cross held their breaths, all eyes glued to the door to the cage room.

It exploded into splinters. The wolf landed in front of them, face bloodied, eyes wild. Jack leapt back to the rear of the cage and pulled the chain tight around the door. The torch in Lucy's hand flicked on and the wolf limped through the circle of light, snarling. Jack sensed that what the wolf really wanted was Lucy – though it wouldn't care who it hurt to get to her. Jack felt the breeze from an extended claw which swung through the bars at the imprisoned. It was too far for the wolf to reach.

'Laszlo, no,' Lucy pleaded. The wolf ignored her. Whatever trace of Laszlo had been, was gone.

The wolf reached into the cage, its massive arm barely fitting through the bars. Jack glanced at the gap alongside the cage, too narrow for the wolf. The wall was scarred with deep scratches and Jack realised that this was where Laszlo Breyer had been coming, every full moon, for the last God knows how long. He'd locked himself in here, so he wouldn't do what he had done to the poor souls in York, Carlton and the others.

The wolf swung again and again it missed, realising that it wasn't going to reach them from the end of the cage. It snarled again. Lucy screamed.

'The torch, turn off the torch,' Cross urged with a barked whisper.

Lucy turned off the torch and once again the room descended into that haunted moon glow. The huge monster eyed them before turning and limping back into the main room. Its huge shadow eclipsed the window, plunging the cabin into silent, terrifying darkness. Lucy's sweaty hand squeezed Jack's with the trembling reserved for those trapped in mortal fear. From the next room a light squeak followed by the light knock of wood on wood.

'The shutters. It's closing the shutters,' Jack whispered through the dark.

The darkness remained, but from the next room the gentle weight pressure brought a groan from the floorboards.

'Turn the torch back on,' Jack urged, pressing everybody back into the corner.

The torch came on and lit up a bright set of scowling amber eyes. Lucy screamed. The wolf growled and once again reached into the cage. Whether it was the wolf or the panic that caused it, Jack didn't know, but the torch fell to the floor and rolled a semi-circular beam of light across the wall. A cacophony of growls and screams filled the old wooden cabin. The torch beam rocked back and forth and in it the reaching claws of the wolf appeared and disappeared. Jack reached a hand for the torch, knowing that one powerful swing from the wolf meant he'd lose the whole thing. His fingers touched the cold metal and rolled the light beam around and away from the wolf. The growls rose and Jack grabbed the torch. The wolf snarled and limped into the other room.

Jack shone the torch at the floor outside the cage where a pool of bright red blood had formed. 'He's hurt, Cross. You've hurt him.'

Cross answered weakly, 'He's not the only one who's hurt.'

Jack turned and Cross's pale face came into view. He glanced down at Cross's ankle. The skin around the wound where the bone had pierced the skin had taken on a weird yellowish hue. 'Lucy, take care of Daniel's leg for him.'

The air was gripped by an odd silence. There was no heavy breathing, no snarling. The wind had even dropped to nothing. For the briefest moments Jack thought that the wolf had given up. That they were safe. He'd realised that the distance through the bars to the back of the cage was too great. Maybe he'd slunk off into the woods to die.

The relief was short-lived. The wall separating the two rooms shuddered with a huge *BANG*! Everybody spun to face the direction of the noise. They scurried back to the opposite wall, Cross remaining hunched in the farthest corner. There was silence again. Then...

BANG!

This one louder than the last. The wall bowed in the middle before springing back to its original form.

It dawned on Jack what was happening. 'Shit. He's giving himself another way in.'

If the wall gave way, the wolf would have two sides from which to attack. They might fight him off for so long, but with Cross being so badly hurt, it was only a matter of time before the wolf got to him. Or all of them.

7

'Fuck me,' Tommy stared at the trail of blood leading to the wood from the kitchen window.

Bryan stared down at the wolf's footprints. 'It's him. The prints lead away from the house,' he replied, voice hushed as low as the wind would allow. He turned his eyes the shattered window. 'We going in?'

Tommy nodded and climbed through the window, grinding glass into the floor as he landed inside. Bryan followed.

'Watch your step,' Tommy said, pointing at the rifle before Bryan could land on it.

Tommy knew there was nobody here. That the hunt had moved on. 'Jack?' he shouted, hoping he was wrong, his voice reverberating round the house.

Total silence.

He glanced into the hallway and at the foot of the stairs he saw the light catch something. He got closer and saw it was a silver bullet casing. He reached down to pick it up and noticed the blood spatter on the wall. He turned and quickly climbed the stairs. That same full moon watched him ascend, as it had Jack a short while earlier.

'More of the same up here,' Tommy announced when he saw the shattered table and another Rorschach test splodge of blood on the landing wall. Bryan muttered from behind.

'What is going on here?'

Tommy turned to see Bryan standing in the bedroom staring into the corner. A small thick wooden door which had been rendered matchwood sat forlorn, deep gouges ploughed into it.

'Somebody wasn't supposed to get in or out of here,' Bryan said, inspecting the damage.

'Looks like our man.'

Bryan nodded. Tommy was lost in thought for a split second.

'What now, Tom?' Bryan asked.

Tommy's eyes hardened, 'We'd better get to that cabin.'

8

BANG!

The wall heaved and creaked.

'The wall won't hold,' said Cross.

The wolf threw itself against the wall again and a plank of wood cracked, the noise so similar to the sickening snap of Cross's ankle. The fractured plank fell revealing the room on the other side. The wolf limped a few steps back and once again launched its full weight into the failing wall.

BANG!

Again it bowed and cracked, more planks falling now. The wolf backed away, one more hit and he would have a hole big enough to reach through.

As the wolf took off for his final assault on the weakened wall, through the gap where the planks once were, a glint of light caught Jack's eye.

It was a short-handled tool. A silver spearhead stuck onto a short wooden handle rested in the corner behind the door, light bouncing from its silver surface.

BANG!

The wolf crashed into the wall again, and again another plank failed. This time Breyer didn't back away. He reached through for Jack and the others. They spread themselves along the longest edge of the cage, backing as far as they could from the reach of the beast. It clawed back and forth reaching for something, anything to get a purchase on. Jack kicked out trying to force him back. Jack saw the wound on the creature and wondered how long it could last losing so much blood. Backed across the longest edge, Lucy joined in the kicking at the desperate reach of the snarling wolf. Suddenly, it stopped and withdrew. The front door swung open letting in a blast of biting wind. The wolf left, dragging its wounded leg in its wake.

'He's giving up. Is he giving up?' Lucy said.

Jack wasn't listening. He turned to Cross. Cross lay motionless in the corner.

'Jesus,' Jack uttered.

Lucy turned and saw Daniel Cross, pale, clammy, perfectly still in the corner of the cage, and screamed.

'Oh God, is he dead?'

Jack reached for a pulse on Danny's neck.

BANG!

The far wall on the longest edge shook. The wolf was trying to expose the cage from outside. From *all* sides. It was in a race with the rising sun. A race it would surely win.

Jack slapped Cross's face, 'Come on, Danny boy.'

The whole cabin was shaking with the blows. Jack slapped Cross again. He adjusted his fingers trying to find any semblance of a pulse. Was this how it ended? For all of them? He switched neck for wrist and dug his fingers in deep.

'Come on Danny, fight,' he whispered.

BANG!

'Danny, wake up!'

Lucy was crying beside him, the wolf trying to break in and Cross dying in front of her proving too much.

Then, something. Faint, but there. A pulse.

'Wake up, Danny.'

Jack glanced into the other room. He saw the silver spear.

Jack turned to Lucy grabbed her and stared straight into those brown saucer eyes, 'Lucy, Danny's alive, but if we don't wake him up, he won't be for long. In the next room is a weapon. It looks like silver. If I get it...'

'No Jack!' she shouted, 'No.'

BANG!

The long planks of wood in the wall were tough, but with each blow they groaned and creaked a little more than the last.

'Lucy, I have to. If I don't Danny's going to die,' Jack said earnestly, 'and I can't let that happen.' He stared into her eyes, 'I have to get that spear. I'll be right back. While I'm gone, you try and wake him up, OK?'

BANG!

She jumped at the noise and it brought her distant eyes into sharp focus. She nodded.

'As soon as I'm out, lock the door behind me.'

Lucy nodded again, her face streaked with tears. Jack turned and unscrewed the bolt on the chain, before slowly pulling the heavy cage door open. He took a deep breath and stepped out into the darkness.

9

Tommy and Bryan bound through the undergrowth with their torches trained on the bloody trail that had led them from the cottage deep into the frosty darkness of Carr Wood. The gusting wind seemed to be less frequent now, or perhaps it was just that he didn't notice.

Breathless, Tommy led, driven onward by the lingering feeling of guilt. If anything happened to Jack now, he couldn't bear the thought of living with himself; moments of wonder at what the last year had been like for Jack dashed through his conscience. Taking the blame for Jenny's death without saying a word. Maybe because he did blame himself. Life was seldom so simple.

He knew one thing for sure. He had to make it to that cabin.

Through the crunch of snow and snapping of twigs, between the deep gasping breaths he and Bryan were taking, came an unsettling noise. Faint, but unmistakable. A wild animal in a frenzied attack. Snarling in anger, the creature sounded a long way off; without a word, he and Bryan sped up.

They pushed on, using every bit of their days playing rugby together to leap, duck and brush aside branches. The faint noises grew steadily louder as they neared: growling and rhythmic beating of wood. Tommy drew a deep breath and his determined eyes narrowed, as he ran, his grip tightening on the cold metal of the now loaded Winchester.

10

BANG!

Jack jumped as the wolf continued its assault on the outer wall of the cabin. The panels were cracking and groaning with each blow. The circle of light from the torch scanned the cabin as Jack scurried from the cage room. The silver spear glinted in the torchlight and Jack hurried towards...

BANG!

The wolf's rhythmic attack had finally borne fruit. A gust of wind shot into the cabin through the hole in outer wall of the cage room.

'Jack!' Lucy screamed.

He wasn't sure if the scream was fear alone. There was a hint of something more. Of pain. Was she scratched? Or worse, bitten.

He span round and through the hole saw the wolf in the moonlight outside. He could only see the top half of Lucy's fragile frame, but it was clear she was struggling with the dead weight of Cross's unconscious body, dragging him away from the danger outside.

He quickly crossed the cramped room, the silver spear his target. Jack reached down and grabbed it; its splintered handle rough to the touch.

Something's wrong.

He couldn't say exactly what it was, but it was there, as sure as the biting wind that whistled in from the darkness. The banging. It was in a perfect rhythm. Between each bang was just enough time for the wolf to retreat and launch itself back at that fragile wall. Now, the banging had stopped. He span and stared through the gap. The wolf was gone.

'Jack, please hurry,' Lucy begged.

Jack turned the torch off. It seemed the wind outside had stopped. For a second it felt that time itself had stopped. The cabin was filled with pin-dropping silence. At that moment the door creaked. Jack held his breath and took a step back against the wall. His breath streamed from his nostrils in two steady plumes as the door swung open. He pressed his back to the wall. In the darkness, the wolf's heavy breathing cut through the silence as it limped into the room. The door was pressed against Jack's ear, his feet fanned sideways to avoid contact.

A sound from the other side of the door stopped Jack's heart. The wolf was sniffing. He had seconds before it found him. A low threatening growl emanated from the darkness. Jack's grip on the spear tightened. The door slowly peeled away from Jack's ear.

'Laszlo! Stop!' Lucy shouted, her voice quivering, though Jack wasn't sure if it was fear or anger.

Jack's grip tightened on the weapon and his hand trembled, ready to strike. The door started to slowly swing closed. He awaited the vision of the beast. He would be nose to nose with it. It would strike, and it would strike hard. But it wouldn't be able to stop Jack striking too. He was sure to die, but at least he'd kill the wolf. Save Cross. Save Lucy. He braced himself, ready to plunge the spear as far as he could into the monster.

The door swung shut.

But the wolf was walking away. Towards Lucy.

'Please, Laszlo,' Lucy sobbed, her delicate face pressed against the bars.

The hulking beast crossed the short space, now walking on two legs, its ears touching the low ceiling.

'I'm sorry, Laszlo. I didn't mean to hurt you.'

The wolf stopped. As if Laszlo was still inside and had been awoken. Maybe he'd been there all along, driven by rage and revenge. The beast seemed soothed and its huge shoulders rose and fell as the wounded creature took in air. Lucy looked as if she were about to speak when the wolf snarled. Lucy screamed and Jack saw the muscles in the wolf's back flex as it prepared to launch itself at the cage.

It was now or never. If he didn't take this chance the wolf wouldn't be content killing Lucy; it would almost certainly kill both him and Cross. Tommy and Bryan weren't coming, or if they were, they'd be too late. Just in time to find three bodies. Maybe walk into certain death themselves. He had to act. He pushed himself off the wall and crossed the space to the wolf, spear ready to strike.

As he neared, Breyer half turned, looming over him. The half turn presented the left side of the wolf to Jack. Before the giant creature could react, Jack's right hand, and the spear, were set for deadly impact. He thrust the blade upwards hard into the beast's side. He felt the tip grind past the ribs on its collision course with the one part of the monster that perhaps was human: the heart. The great creature let out a haunting howl; purging over a hundred years of hell. Pain. Guilt. Shame. Love. Relief. Release. The wind held its breath. The heavy atmosphere in the cabin lifted. There was a stillness in the air like never before.

The wolf swung a huge fist sending Jack flying into the wall opposite the window. Jack crashed into the wall and crumpled to the bed. He strained to get up. Move or die. His brain sent signals to his limbs, but without response. He braced for the inevitable. He peeled his heavy eyelids open. The wolf cried out, sinking first to one knee, and then slumping to the ground.

Jack expected to feel relief. He didn't. He simply watched as the wind kicked up and swung the shutters open. Over the tops of the trees the perfect pale disc of the moon smiled down into the cabin. Jack felt the sticky warmth of blood trickling down the back of his head as he battled with his heavy eyelids to stay conscious.

He glanced at the wolf. It lay motionless, its amber eyes staring at Jack. The eyes had no anger in them now. Jack recognised something else in them. Perhaps a flicker of remorse. Maybe even gratitude. It slowly lowered its eyelids and raised them again. Laszlo Breyer's final breath was a long, low, moaning howl. And then he was gone.

Jack closed his eyes again. The sound of rattling chains was far away. The sound of voices. Like the echoes in a large hall. Jack peeled his eyes half open to see Tommy and Bryan staring at the body of a wolf that was shifting, transforming into that of a man. That of Laszlo Breyer.

His body was overcome with exhaustion. His eyelids became too heavy as sleep overtook him, the last thing he saw was huge snowflakes floating past the window. He took one long last look at the full moon, so peaceful, so beautiful, before he closed his eyes and drifted into a long, haunted sleep.

AFTERMATH

Was this what it felt like to be dead? The bright light radiated red through his tired eyelids. There was still the sense of another in this place with him. Somebody close, in distance and in feeling. There was a warmth, finally a warmth after the endless winter. Thoughts flashed of people past. Of Jenny. Of Tommy. And Bryan. And a young homeless man named Danny. And a beautiful artist. And an old man who shot his daughter's killer. Laszlo Breyer. And Daniel Cross. The man who lived in a museum of the macabre. Jack smiled to himself.

He heard talking. Distant echoing voices. He tried hard to centre. To tune the dial so that the voices would come into focus. Then they stopped. He peeled an eye open. He was staring at a magnolia ceiling. A magnolia ceiling in a hospital room. A hospital room into which warm sunlight cascaded. Maybe this is what it felt like to be alive. He glanced to his left. His blurred vision waved in and out of focus before the two images finally settled into one.

'Welcome back, Jack,' smiled Daniel Cross.

His left foot was in plaster, his pale toes poking from the end. His pallid face smiling at Jack. It was good to see him. Comforting.

'How long have we been here?' croaked Jack.

'A week. Long enough for me to get this on,' he raised his leg and wiggled his toes, 'and for you to get your noggin bandaged.'

'Oh,' Jack reached up and touched the stiff gauze of his bandaging, 'right.'

So it wasn't a weird dream.

'No, it wasn't,' Cross answered, surprising Jack.

'Where are we?'

'We're in York Hospital,' Cross replied. 'We'll be well looked after here.'

'When can we go? I think I've had enough of Yorkshire.'

'Wash your mouth out,' Cross snapped, smiling.

'How's the ankle?'

'I'll never play the piano again.' He smiled. 'It's going to be fine. Might not even have a limp the doctor reckons. I was lucky. I think Lucy must have reset the bone.'

He turned and stared out of the window, admiring the conditions outside. He turned back.

'Tommy visited. Bryan's not doing so well. The sight of Breyer, you know, changing, took a lot out of him. He's in therapy. Tommy said...'

There was a knock at the door.

'Can I come in?'

Jack saw Cross nod his regards before he turned to see the figure silhouetted in the doorway.

'Tommy,' Jack said.

He strode into the room and thrust a brown paper bag towards Jack.

'Grapes,' he said as he stood at the end of Jack's bed.

Cross motioned to stand, 'I'll leave you two to...'

'No, it's fine,' Tommy interrupted, gesturing for Cross to stay, 'I shan't stay long,' he cleared his throat as if about to enter into a well-rehearsed speech. 'I owe you an apology.'

Jack shook his head, 'You were right to suspect me. I would've questioned me as well, if I were investigating.'

Tommy was shaking his head. 'Not for that. For everything. I had no idea the problems you and my sis... Jen, were... anyway, what I'm saying,' he corrected himself, 'trying to say is, what happened, happened. Rightly or wrongly. You had your reasons. And I suppose...' he tailed off again. 'Well, if ever you need anything.' He outstretched a hand, 'Well, you know.'

Jack looked at Tommy's large outstretched hand and remembered the friendship they had shared before Jenny's death.

He reached up and, as firmly as he could, shook the hand. 'I know.'

Tommy nodded and turned to leave.

'Tom,' Jack shouted after him. 'Bryan. How's he doing?'

'He'll be OK,' Tommy lied. Bryan hadn't uttered a single word in the days since the incident and wouldn't utter another for two months, 'I'll tell him you said hello.'

Jack nodded, 'Thanks, Tom.'

Tommy left and Jack stared at the wall. It was good of him to say what he'd said, but deep down, Jack felt, there would always be sadness at the way things worked out. Jack Talbot and Daniel Cross sat and shared the silence bathed in the warm glow of that low winter sun. Outside, the only snow visible was in grey hardened piles or thin icy patches with green blades of grass growing through. Soon it would be spring. Life goes on.

Jack smiled. He wondered about Lucy. He thought about the idea of them becoming a couple but quashed it quickly. He needed to get his life together. The last thing they both needed was a constant reminder of this sorry affair. He toyed with the idea of what might have been for less than a second before Cross spoke, as if once again reading his thoughts.

'I forgot to tell you, Lucy left a card for you,' he said, pointing at the envelope on Jack's bedside table.

Jack turned to look at the envelope. Hand-made, yellow and decorated with delicate hand-drawn butterflies. His eyes ached. He would read it later. Now didn't seem like the time.

'Looking forward to going back to work?' Jack asked, eyes still focussed outside.

Cross barked out a laugh. 'I think I'll be needing a holiday before that happens. Somewhere warm. Anywhere warm,' he glanced across smiling. 'You?'

Jack smiled too. 'Maybe I'll go back to work.'

'The police?' Cross tried his best not to sound surprised.

Jack shook his head, 'No, not the police. I always wanted to start my own detective agency. Go private.'

'You should,' Cross this time sounding earnest.

'Maybe I will,' he stared at the unending cycle of life outside. 'Maybe I will.'

The sun had set. Jack and Cross both sat silently in the dark of the hospital room, a shaft of cold light pouring from the hallway, a television echoing a gameshow from a nearby room. Jack turned to look at the yellow envelope Lucy had left. He admired the hand-drawn butterflies before turning it over and opening it. It was a simple note in looping handwriting, with no date, no address. He read.

As he read he smiled, though the note was matter of fact, it seemed that Lucy was OK in herself, and that comforted him. Then he felt a frown darken his face.

He turned to Cross, who was lost in his own little world. 'When did she visit?'

'What?'

'Lucy. When did she visit?'

'She didn't visit. She came in with us. She was admitted.'

'Admitted?'

'Shock, I think...' he tailed off. 'Oh Jesus.'

Jack got to his feet, pain radiating through his whole body. He tottered unsteadily for the door. He heard Cross follow.

'I'm sure it was routine, Jack.'

Jack marched along the sterile hallway, breathing that hospital smell, sure that Cross was limping behind him. A tired nurse along the corridor frowned as she caught sight of them and started towards them.

'Erm, where do you two think you're going?'

'Lucy. Lucy Breyer,' Jack said as they closed the distance between them. 'Where is she?'

'What's going on, Jack?' Cross said.

'The nurse replied, 'I don't know. She didn't leave an address.'

'What about contacts?'

'We didn't take any, she didn't stay overnight. She didn't want to give any details. She checked herself out.'

Cross asked, 'What is it, Jack?'

Jack handed Cross the note.

Dear Jack,

It's hard to know what to say to somebody at a time like this. I had planned to say everything I wanted to your face. They were asking too many questions at the hospital and I think it's quite important now that I have my privacy.

Can you believe the press were calling and asking for interviews? All I want to do is to put the whole affair behind me.

I wonder if you thought (or think) about me. About me and you. The idea did cross my mind about 'us'. We seemed to be a good match (at least, I thought so). We clicked from the beginning and I want you to know that what happened between us, whilst happening very suddenly, is not something that I'd do with just anybody. But I suppose (hope?) you already know that.

It's so difficult to organise my thoughts. This is just an outpouring. Forgive the lack of cohesion.

I said I wanted to forget everything, but I can't. As much pain and suffering he caused both of us, I know that deep down, Laszlo was a good man. That the other side to him, the one that led him to you, whilst being part of him was not who he really was. It sounds strange, awful even, but I hope somewhere in your heart you can find it within yourself to forgive him.

And I won't forget you, Jack. Maybe when things blow over, I'll look you up, but for now I'm afraid it would all be too much.

For now, I will just disappear. Where nobody can find me. The physical scars will always be a reminder of *what happened to me. To us. I just hope time is a little more forgiving on my soul.*

Take care, Detective Jack Talbot. ;-)

Yours, Lucy.

Patients shuffled to the doorways in ill-fitting gowns as Cross read the note. Such excitement on the wards was frowned upon by administration, but welcomed by the bored who convalesced. Jack grabbed the nurse.

'She talked about scars. What scars? What does she mean?' Jack shouted.

The nurse's eyes widened with fear. Behind the nurse Jack saw an orderly turn and rush towards the commotion. Jack grabbed the letter from a dumbstruck Cross, who now looked as pale as the night of his injury. He hung on the words of the nurse as Jack waved the letter in her face. Jack felt sickness rising in his gut.

'In this letter, she mentioned physical scars. What scars did Lucy have?'

'Mr Talbot, you're hurting me.'

The nurse struggled until Jack let go. They stared at each other, both short of breath. A tall orderly joined, standing between them, facing Jack. Now every door along the sterile hallway was filled with patients.

'Please, tell me. What happened?' He pleaded with the nurse.

Cross hung at his shoulder, awaiting the response of the nurse. The nurse regarded Jack. She opened her mouth and the words almost tumbled from it in slow-motion. Cross's mouth fell slack. Jack's knees turned to rubber under him. He stared as she uttered those words which would haunt him forever.

'She was bitten, Mr Talbot. Lucy Breyer was bitten.'

You've made it this far, congratulations! Almost done...

To stay abreast of the latest developments with future book releases, and my blog of all things unexplained, I can be found at the following:

My website: www.marcwshako.com

My Facebook page:
https://www.facebook.com/marcwshako/

Follow me on Twitter at...
https://twitter.com/MarcWShako

Just one more thing...

Reviews are gold for authors!
If you liked *The Death of Laszlo Breyer*, please consider rating and reviewing at Amazon.com!

Thanks for reading!

MARC W SHAKO'S forthcoming novel

GHOSTS OF SEPTEMBER

Lovers of speculative fiction, welcome to the strange world of Marc W. Shako.

Ray Madison is trapped in a nightmare.

Slave to the grip of alcoholism, Ray is stuck in the past, reliving the same week over and over - the week where his life fell apart. But all that is about to change...

Ray goes to bed on a normal Wednesday evening, but the next morning what awaits him is far from routine. Thrown back in time with no explanation, horrified Ray discovers the date: September 6th, 2001.

Faced with the worst week of his life all over again and scrambling for answers, with only the mysterious stranger Charlie for help, Ray is trapped in a race against time, with terror fast approaching.

The clock is ticking...

"Quantum Leap meets 9/11."

GHOSTS OF SEPTEMBER
is set for release autumn 2020

For more information visit:
http://www.marcwshako.com/ghostsofseptember.html

MARC W SHAKO

presents

<u>INFINITY</u>

When a morally ambiguous hacker awakens in a dank warehouse chained to a table, you'd expect him to be horrified. At least *surprised*. Not our guy: he knew this moment was coming. All because of his birthmark. As it happens, the exact same birthmark as his captors.

It's not that he's a bad guy, just that some of the jobs he took got his previously white hat... dirty. He was running from responsibility, now it has caught up with him. The job his new friends have for him is dangerous. Dangerous enough to get him killed.

The most vulnerable people in the city have been vanishing...

They need his help to get them back.

Infinity is a dark tale of a group of unlikely heroes taking on the dregs of the city – scumbags who are hiding the darkest of secrets.

Read on for an excerpt...

I'd known this day was coming for a long time. God knows I'd prepared for it, and now it had finally arrived. Prepared for it emotionally, I mean. Before I even opened my eyes I knew what was going on. And I knew why it was going on.

The last thing I could remember was the party. It had been a good one, for the most part. Sad, poignant (like all Last Parties were), but the music was pumping, the drinks were in rich supply, and even though it was his party, Remy was in great form. Only 26 years old, turning 27, but drinking like a Viking and joking around like he always did. His wife, Chrissy, sure she was emotional. I mean, she's the guy's wife, and it's his Last Party. The reasons she was sad were pretty much the same for every spouse at one of these things.

Firstly, and this one I shouldn't really have to explain, it's his Last Party (emphasis on the word *Last*), they're always emotionally charged. Come on, it's the final meeting with everyone you know and love. If somebody invites you to an LP, you go. You go, and you take as much food and drink as you can carry, and if there's any left over (and this is a fucking huge *if*), the guest of honour gets to keep that shit for however long he's got. The Second Reason Chrissy was upset about her husband's LP is why everyone gets upset at their significant other's LP (it's selfish, but my inkling is it's the *main* reason); it's a glimpse into your own future. Your own very near future.

Chrissy's birthmark was the same as Remy's. In the same place as everyone else's (obviously). On both of their wrists was the number 27. That was the thing with the birthmarks. Everybody could pick someone with a number close to their own. Unless you're too high or too low. (That's one of the reasons I'd always been single, but that's another story.) Chrissy was a few months younger than Remy, and by the time her LP came around, it was anybody's guess if *he'd* still be around, at least the kid would be born, and who knew, maybe the kid would be luckier. Just because his folks were both 27s, didn't mean he'd be a 27. If he was lower they'd be too dead to reap any benefit from it.

If you're like a 40 or a 50 or even an 80, basically long enough to benefit from it, you have a kid and that poor little scrap of life comes out in single figures, you get to retire, well, for five years. Four before, one after. (Or one before and four after, if that's all the maths allows.) All on the government's bill. Your old job waiting for your return.

And the birthmarks were the reason I always wore long sleeves. The birthmarks don't develop until you're two years old (unless you're a 1), so there was no official record of anyone's number. It was illegal to request the information too, like at a job interview. It could be used to discriminate. Unless you were a cop or a soldier or something like that, the government never knew. So yeah, my folks always told me to cover up, and they were serious as shit when they did. So I covered up. And stayed single. Girls always wanted to know your number. Christ it was worse than the discussion of how many women you'd slept with. No, I'm not a virgin, before you ask. Yes, prostitutes. No, I don't feel bad.

So when the day finally arrived, I had been expecting it. I peeled my eyes open, the strange taste of my last drink at Remy's Last Party still in my mouth, and saw the birthmark. But the birthmark wasn't the unusual thing. An infinity sign birthmark *is* an unusual thing, don't get me wrong, but I couldn't see all of it. Because of the shackles. Cold, heavy, iron shackles. I mean, seriously? I'm going to live for ever but I'm not the Hulk.

"And which assface spiked my fucking tequila sunrise?"

Yes, I drink tequila sunrise as my beverage of choice. Little judgemental, aren't we?

I could see one of them. He looked about Remy's age, but skinny, and white, dressed like Iggy Pop if you ever saw him wearing clothes. I addressed the room, though, because I heard another voice, deep lots of bass. Probably a black dude.

Oh, I'm racist now? Do you think it belongs to a little old Chinese lady? No, so let's move the fuck along.

When the third voice answers, I get a surprise.

"I did."

A chick.

It's just when I'm dealing with this minor surprise (yes, I'm aware that women can do nefarious shit, I just wasn't sure it included drugging people and shackling them to old wooden doors) that I see it. On Iggy Pop's wrist. His birthmark is like *my* birthmark. Now it's not too much of a stretch for even my groggy mind to imagine what the others' birthmarks look like.

"You got it," Iggy says, presenting his wrist, "we're like you."

"I have never drugged anyone and shackled them to a shitty old splintering door in a cold and frankly unwelcoming warehouse." I answer, because even though I'm groggy still, and my head feels like it's got three potatoes rattling around where my brain used to be, being next to impossible to kill brings out the cocky in most people.

The black guy appears from around the back of me at the head end, "Sorry bout that, we're kinda new at this."

He talks like Samuel L. Jackson, but he looks like somebody stuck Scottie Pippen's head on Usain Bolt's body, oh and I fucking *told* you he was black. Then the girl appears and she looks so much like that speedster chick off that TV show *Heroes* that I swear to God, it might be her.

"Can you take these off? They're pretty uncomfortable." My head's clearing now and I manage to raise one of the shackles.

"Answer this question first, then we'll talk," she says.

And I know what's coming before Iggy Pop opens his skinny mouth and I know, I know I'm supposed to be all Joseph Campbell's Hero's Journey and refuse the call, but I'm tired of fucking prostitutes and I can already imagine watching society making the same fucking mistakes over and over and me not forming any real relationships and any I do stumble into end with me having to watch people I actually give a fuck about die so when he says, "We're getting a group together. It's serious shit. Serious enough to get you *killed,*" I look him square in the eyes and smile.

Iggy stares back at me expressionless, "You look like you're gonna say 'yes', and you don't know what it is yet."

That's true. "Well, I trust you guys know who I am. So I don't think you're gonna ask me to kill somebody."

They just look at each other.

"Are you going to ask me to kill somebody?"

The Chick answers, "No, we're not. But when you find out about who we're dealing with, you might want to."

Short story *Infinity* is available NOW on Amazon Kindle!

https://www.amazon.co.uk/dp/B074VZ3LR8/ref=sr_1_6?s=digital-text&ie=UTF8&qid=1502968791&sr=1-6&keywords=infinity

ABOUT THE AUTHOR

MARC W. SHAKO is a novelist of speculative fiction, screenwriter, and aficionado of all things paranormal, from Yorkshire, England. When not reading or writing about the undead, hauntings, modern-day wolf-men and UFOs, Marc can be found watching football, playing the guitar with various degrees of success, or engrossed in his latest addiction – binge-listening to podcasts.

Printed in Great Britain
by Amazon

42344636R00145